# Untouchable

## A P Bateman

Untouchable

By

A P Bateman

# Also by A P Bateman

## The Alex King Series

The Contract Man

Lies and Retribution

Shadows of Good Friday

The Five

Reaper

Stormbound

Breakout

From the Shadows

Rogue

The Asset

Last Man Standing

Hunter Killer

The Congo Contract

Dead Man Walking

Sovereign State

Kingmaker

Untouchable

## The Rob Stone Series

The Ares Virus

The Town

The Island

Stone Cold

**DI Grant**

Vice

Taken

**Standalone Novel**

Never Go Back

**Short Stories**

The Perfect Murder?

Atonement

Further details of these titles can be found at:

www.apbateman.com

*For Clair*

# Chapter One

Casablanca, Morocco

King sipped the hot and fragrant sweet tea and watched the Mercedes pull to the curb. The Range Rover followed. Ahmadi got out of the rear of the Mercedes, cutting a fine figure in a dark blue Tom Ford suit with a crisp white shirt open at the neck. Two buttons down, but not spread too far. King imagined the shirt cost more than his own entire outfit, but that didn't take much. The bodyguards got out. Three in all. He wondered if they had kissed their loved ones goodbye this morning. He checked his watch. The bodyguards only had a few minutes to live. Tough, but those were the breaks. The greater good. The big picture. At least he wouldn't be pulling the trigger. He could have done with more bodyguards joining him, but those were the breaks.

The boy got out of the same door as Ahmadi. Like father like son, the boy too wore an expensive suit. King knew the boy to be eleven years old. What kind of man took his eleven-year-old son to business meetings? But King already knew the answer. The kind of man who trained his kin young, indoctrinated them, even. In twenty years, the boy would be doing his own deals with terrorists and another agent would be standing in King's place. King checked his watch again. It was a cheap, yet durable military style watch. A plain face, a screw-down crown and a NATO strap. Durable as hell. It went better with his cover than his own vintage Rolex, and it was the watch his 'legend' had worn into prison after sentencing. Details mattered. He carried no phone, no credit cards either. Just a single debit card to access ten-thousand pounds in savings under an assumed name. The only form of ID he carried was a well-thumbed and heavily stamped passport. It looked good. An older photo to go with the assumed name and plenty of visa stamps to match his legend. King sipped some more of his tea and watched as the bodyguards split into different directions. The lead bodyguard led Ahmadi and his son into the restaurant, followed by another. The third waited outside while the Mercedes and Range Rover drove away to find some parking. With that, a second Range Rover thundered past, the bodyguards intending to wait for their charge down the road.

King was seated at a table outside a café across the street. Throngs of people walked past, some tourists but many Moroccans just going about their day. The warm air was heady with the aroma of spices and strong coffee and delicious breads and baclava, but crucially interspersed with the stench of cigarette smoke, drains and vehicle fumes. The sounds of vehicle horns, whining engines and worn exhaust pipes, people bartering and shouting, and construction machinery filled the air, an assault on the senses. He checked his watch again. Less than a minute to go.

King watched the old Volkswagen Transporter drive past and pull into the curb fifty metres further down the road. The vehicle was dented and scuffed and looked fit for the scrapyard, but then again, so did most of the vehicles in Casablanca. Either that, or the extremes of new BMWs, Range Rovers or Mercedes, visual proof if it were ever needed that the divide between rich and poor was never further apart, and truly a global trait. Another old VW Transporter pulled up short of the restaurant. King finished his tea and checked his watch a final time, before removing the Ray Ban Aviators he had bought eight months ago in the duty-free at Gatwick and slipping them into the thigh pocket of his cargoes. He dried the palm of his hands on his knees, then pushed out his chair almost a foot, his eyes on the motorcycle further down the road, its rider stretching his legs and drinking from a bottle of water. The motorcycle was a Suzuki SV-1000. A powerful street bike with a comfortable riding position and savage acceleration. King looked back up the street where a truck piled high with melons had parked behind the first VW Transporter. The bodyguard standing outside the restaurant seemed to have noticed none of these things, and King wondered how alert the man would be and what his reaction would be when the time came. But he did not have to wonder for long. The VW pulled out in front of the truck and accelerated towards the restaurant and the truck loaded with melons followed, before swerving erratically, counter steering with excess and lifting onto two wheels. With a screech of tyres, it carried on lifting and tipped onto its side, its load crashing into the road. The bodyguard watched incredulously as the melons squashed and scattered and children leapt into the

3

pile stealing what they could carry, some already eating what was split and crushed. The VW Transporter stopped outside the restaurant and the bodyguard was cut down with a burst of automatic gunfire. People scattered and screamed, and men piled out of both Transporters, weapons held at the ready as they stepped over the body and filed into the restaurant and opened fire.

King crossed over the street and stood in the cool shadows as he waited. Three men pulled the boy with them to the lead vehicle. He was bundled roughly inside, his suit torn and stained with blood, but from the way he moved King could already tell that the blood belonged to other people. They clambered in after him and closed the door as the vehicle sped away. Three more men walked out confidently, one of the men changing over to a new magazine as he walked. Six men in, six men out. King stepped out and kicked the last man in the back of his knee, snatching the weapon as he fell. He could tell from the weapon's weight that the magazine was at least half full. He fired into the man's face before he hit the ground and followed up with three shots into the closest man's back. The lead man started to turn but was less than halfway around when King emptied the rest of the compact Kalashnikov AKS-74U into him. King tossed the weapon onto the ground and picked up the man's CZ-75 9mm pistol which had clattered into the street. He checked the magazine as he walked and when he got level with the confused driver of the van, he shot him once in the head and made for the motorcycle. The man saw the gun, held up his hands and King swung his leg over the machine and turned the ignition and pressed the starter button. He tucked the pistol into his waistband, selected first gear and pulled out into the road, the rear wheel spinning as he kept all his weight over the fuel tank to stop the motorcycle from lifting its front wheel. He feathered the throttle to control the rise and knocked the gears up from first through neutral, second and third and had a hundred miles per hour on the needle before the first bend and throng of people in the road.

The VW Transporter was driving on its handling limit for the streets, the driver swerving to avoid children and goats, stray dogs and motor scooters as Casablanca put on a show of diversity and blocked its path with a *Youtuber* posing for selfies in front of an orange Lamborghini. The van swerved in time but knocked over a bicycle laden eight feet high with beach toys and souvenirs on a custom-made rack. The man guiding the bicycle fell to the ground and his mobile stall toppled and spread his wares into the road. King, with nowhere left to steer stamped down on the gears twice, then twisted the throttle and squeezed a quarter pull of clutch, launching the front wheel into a wheelie. The *Youtuber* dropped his phone and dived for safety as the front wheel touched the bonnet of the supercar and the bike rode up the wedge-shaped car and launched into the air. King stood on the foot pegs; his knees slightly bent to cushion the landing some ten feet to the rear of the Lamborghini. The motorcycle landed heavily and bounced, King fighting hard to regain control, which he did with a twist of throttle to right the wobble. The VW Transporter was now only sixty metres in front of him, the driver swerving and stamping on the brakes to try and force King back.

King knew that he did not have much time. There were four men in the van ahead of him, and he could hear police sirens somewhere. They were heading downhill now, the port in sight. From there the options only favoured the kidnappers. Vehicle changes, fast speedboats, passenger ferries – all could present a place to hide, a way out of the city. There was even a heliport. With a helicopter waiting, the boy could be lost within minutes. Or at least that was the plan.

The rear doors of the van opened, and King swerved and dropped back to avoid the burst of gunfire from a Kalashnikov. There were screams and King could only imagine where the bullets had ended up with people scattering on all sides. He weaved the motorcycle across the road and bounced up the pavement, people parting ahead of him like water against the prow of a ship. The van had accelerated, and King caught sight of people being thrown into the air as it drove relentlessly through the crowds. King weaved back into the road and gained rapidly on the van. The men inside the van were being thrown about in the cargo bay, and while the man with the rifle was reloading, another was clamped around the boy to restrain him. The third man had made it to the front passenger seat and was leaning out of the window aiming a pistol at King as he swerved and dodged fleeing pedestrians. King wound the throttle on full, the front wheel almost touching the rear bumper, and in one fluid move, he released his grip on the throttle, drew the pistol and shot the man in the forehead from less than six feet away, the motorcycle dropping back all the time as it underwent engine-braking. He struggled to tuck the weapon back in his waistband, and by the time he got back on the throttle, the van had skidded out onto the main road and left the busy street behind. King accelerated hard, the powerful motorcycle whining as he used all the engine revs and gear changes, threading the machine through traffic north of one-hundred-and-thirty miles per hour. He flashed past the van and around a truck laden with bottled water, then came hard off the throttle, stamped down two gears, and was engulfed in tyre smoke as the motorcycle skidded and decelerated down to fifty miles per hour and the van caught up with the truck giving King all the cover that he needed to draw the pistol and fire. The man in the passenger seat slumped and sprawled across the gearstick and the driver struggled to control the vehicle, swerving both left then right and crashing into the truck beside him. King tried to accelerate out of trouble, but the truck caught his rear wheel, and the motorcycle defied the laws of physics by going in what felt like every direction at once. King held on as the motorcycle was launched in the air, then landed on its rear wheel. He didn't know it at the time, but he twisted the throttle and the machine accelerated and went past the point of no return. King was spat to the rear and the motorcycle twisted and spun and when the tyres caught traction on the tarmac, it twisted and turned and rolled down the road amid sparks and fuel and caught fire. King was sliding on the tarmac, and just as the tyres had done, his boots caught the road, and he was upended and thrown into a series of summersaults and rolls. The van continued down the road in front of him, and as King staggered to his feet, he could hear nothing but vehicles skidding and horns sounding behind him.

King looked around him but could not see the pistol. He watched the van now in the distance, then turned and looked at the traffic now stationary behind the truck and the burning hulk of the motorcycle. Shouts turned to chatter and from what French and Arabic he knew, he realised that he wasn't the most popular person in Casablanca right now.

An open-topped Porsche and a slick-looking man in his thirties wearing a white shirt, wrap-around sunglasses and talking on his phone using EarPods is a universal thing, and King headed towards the estate agent/salesman, reached inside and unlocked the door. He unfastened the protesting man's seatbelt and pulled him out. The man tried to fend King off, but was no match for King's strength, who twisted away from his blows and shoved him hard to the ground. King was behind the wheel and working his way through the seven speed PDK paddle-shift gearbox. With a break in the traffic flow, he had the Porsche at over a hundred miles per hour in seconds and was still climbing in speed when he caught sight of the van pulling off the road onto the slip road leading directly to the port. He eased off and rode the brakes, keeping the van in sight but maintaining distance. The driver of the van had seen King fall off the motorcycle, likely seen the burning wreckage in his mirrors. He would not have seen King take the Porsche, so there was no sense in giving away his advantage.

The van headed away from the commercial port and to the marina. King held back, but certainly the Porsche fitted in here with newer, expensive vehicles and chic cafés, restaurants and boutiques. It would have been a different story in the old fishing port. He reached over and checked the glovebox hoping he'd get lucky, but this wasn't the America, and he already knew the chances of finding a gun was slim to none. The van slowed ahead of him, and King eased back but he could already hear sirens behind him and knew that it would only be a matter of a minute or two before he would see the flashing lights as the police closed in.

The van screeched to a halt and on a raised platform on the edge of the marina and breakwater separating the calm harbour from the raging surf of the Atlantic Ocean, a helicopter's rotors were spinning. The remaining man in the rear of the van roughly pulled the boy out of the vehicle and pushed him ahead of him. The boy tried to run, but the driver grabbed him as he got out from behind the wheel and the two men sprinted for the waiting helicopter. King accelerated hard, the Porsche bellowing from its exhaust, it's tuned six-cylinder engine whining as the turbo kicked in. One of the men turned and fired and the windscreen and bonnet were peppered with bullets. King raised a hand to protect his eyes from the shattering glass and heaved the vehicle to the left to take cover behind the van. King leaped out over the passenger seat and ran to the open rear doors of the van, where he picked up one of the dead men's' weapons. He checked the magazine of the Browning 9mm pistol, knew he had at least twelve rounds remaining from the inspection holes in the rear of the magazine, and eased the breach open a fraction to see a glint of brass. Ahead of him, the helicopter lifted off, banked an impossibly steep turn and spun around heading northwards up the coast. It was probably the easiest day's work the pilot had ever had, and from the way the two men sagged as they neared the helipad, the last thing the kidnappers had expected. But forewarned was forearmed, and King stopped running and fired at one of the men, sending three 9mm bullets into the man's back. The second man turned, but he had the boy in front of him and a gun at his head. The boy was sobbing. The man looked confident. In his periphery, King was aware of vehicles pulling up, people getting out. Uniforms, suits. He dared not look, could not take his eyes off the man's in front of him. Twenty metres. It could well have been twenty miles for all the good it would do him. Again, in his periphery, weapons were being aimed and someone seemed to be taking charge, holding people back.

"Give it up," said King. "Put the gun down and let the boy go." His finger tightened on the trigger.

The man smiled. "Shoot me and my muscle reflex will

cause me to fire. I have a great deal of pressure on the trigger. Now, back away and..."

King fired and the boy sagged as his leg gave out. The man's weapon discharged, the bullet passing just inches above the boy's head. King's second shot hit the man in his throat and as he staggered backwards, the third shot hit him dead centre in his forehead.

King dropped the weapon to the ground and raised both of his hands above his head as he turned and faced the police officers now sprinting towards him. There were shouts and weapons aimed at him, but he knew the drill and he got down onto his knees as rough hands pushed him down and handcuffs secured his arms behind his back. He was dragged unceremoniously to his feet and marched towards the waiting police vehicles, while paramedics tended to the boy, who was writhing on the ground behind them.

Ahmadi barged his way to the front of the crowd, his blue Tom Ford suit and white shirt no longer looking so stylish now that it was ruined with someone else's blood, and much of his own. His nose had been clearly broken and his right eye socket was as black as night. He eyed King warily, snapped something at the highest-ranking police officer and ran to his son's side as he was loaded onto a gurney and wheeled without delay to the waiting ambulance. Behind him, two bodyguards looked fraught. They had lost colleagues and would most likely be losing their jobs before long. Ahmadi returned and spoke to the police officer again as the ambulance drove through the parting crowd with blues and twos. King watched Ahmadi dominate the police officer. He was clearly a man of influence, and a man used to getting what he wanted. He pointed at King, spoke sternly with the police officer, and the man dutifully walked over, stood his men down and ordered the handcuffs to be taken off. King rubbed his wrists, looked Ahmadi in the eyes.

"You saved my son..." he said humbly, his accent almost neutral English, the slightest hint of Middle Eastern only detectable on the word saved, which he pronounced as *saved*. "I will be forever grateful," he said, stepping forwards and kissing King on both cheeks. King, familiar with such customs, composed himself in time. "You are my guest," he added. "I will reward you greatly. Please, come with me. I will have my driver take you to my home while I visit my son at the hospital."

"I don't need a reward," King replied.

*Always resist, never suggest...*

Ahmadi shook his head. "Please, indulge me. I must be with my son in hospital, but I wish to talk to you, show you the extent of my gratitude." He spread his hands compassionately, hopefully. "It is in my faith. You have saved my son, and in turn, my life. For if I lost my son, then my life would have been no longer worth living. I must repay the debt you have put me in."

King studied the man before him. He was a man used to his position of power, but King could see a chink in his armour. His vulnerability. "Alright," he replied. "But I have travel plans and won't be able to stay long..."

Ahmadi smiled. "I will be more than willing to have you flown anywhere in the world, if you spare me a little of your time."

King considered this for a moment, glanced back at the black Mercedes and the two bodyguards standing beside it, then looked at the Iranian and nodded. "Let's go, then."

\* \* \*

11

The drone had been holding a steady hover two hundred feet above the marina and three hundred feet to the west over the ocean. Its gyroscopic stabilised HD camera had recorded the pursuit from the restaurant and the entire encounter with Ahmadi below. Directional parabolic recording capabilities had captured the conversation in detail.

Across the marina, seated in the rear seat of a new Land Rover Discovery with blacked-out windows, Caroline Darby studied the feed on her laptop screen, watching the man she loved get into the Mercedes with the target. "All call-signs," she said into her radio as she watched the vehicle pull swiftly away. "The fox is in the henhouse..."

# Chapter Two

S ardinia
**Three months earlier**

The knife had been honed to a razor's edge and it sliced through the flesh easily, running cleanly along the spine until it pulled clear. King used the tip of the blade to put the fillet to one side while he flipped over the red snapper and slipped the blade in behind the gills, gave a little twist and ran the blade smoothly from head to tail. He watched Caroline drifting lazily on her back, the sea glistening around her, the seabed clearly visible twenty feet below her. Her white bikini showed off her tan, as well as her well-proportioned figure. A quarter of a mile away, the strip of golden sand was busy with beachgoers, but the yacht afforded them privacy and independence. The disposable charcoal barbecue had stopped smoking and started to glow red. King had placed it on the transom, using a coil of anchor chain on top of a wet towel to protect the fibreglass underneath. Beside the barbeque, an identically shaped melt in the fibreglass was a permanent reminder of his first culinary efforts eating *al fresco*.

A bell sounded on the starboard side of the vessel and King dropped the knife, wiping his hands on a rag as he crossed the deck and slipped the fishing rod out of the holder. He had left a little drag on the reel, and as he positioned the rod in his hands, he wound down the drag, increasing the gear on the reel. The rod dipped and the line tugged, and King waited for the third and hardest tug before he struck quickly and sharply, snagging the hook into the fish's mouth. The tip of the rod bounced and played in all directions, and King gave a good pull on the rod before reeling in the slack. He repeated this half a dozen times before reeling continuously. He could see the sizeable mullet fighting the line fifteen feet below the yacht, and he released some line to tire the fish before reeling in again – not for the sport, although he was enjoying the thrill - but a tired fish was less likely to come off the hook when landing, than a fish full of fight. After five minutes, he had the mullet on board, had humanely dispatched it with the edge of his hand and was working his way through it with the blade. He watched Caroline, who was now swimming towards some submerged rocks a hundred metres distant. She was happy. They both were. Three months of cruising around the Mediterranean in a forty-foot yacht from beach to island to historical harbour, they had taken in the Balearics, the French Riviera, Italy, and Croatia, and had called off the Greek Islands due to a terrible storm in the Aegean and Eastern Mediterranean which had seen them head over to Sicily for shelter and onwards up the country's west coast to Sardinia. They had settled into a good routine of sight-seeing, lounging on deserted beaches and islands, swimming from the yacht and docking in marinas and harbours every few days to stock up on water and supplies. Bountiful village markets gave them all the fruit and vegetables they needed, while King had developed handy fishing skills and they both enjoyed diving for crabs, lobsters and molluscs. King's hair had grown out, his lean and muscled body was bronzed, and his scars showed up white. Caroline was now diving from the rock. He wanted to join her but was hungry and had drawn the short straw. King had already chopped up a simple salad of tomatoes, cucumber and onions and had twisted in pepper and salt and plenty of lemon juice. He watched Caroline start her return swim, and he laid the fillets on the grill, seasoning them with just salt and pepper and a squeeze of lemon which hissed and flamed on the hot coals. The fish was so fresh that it simply smelled of the sea, and the lemon was so fragrant that it stung his eyes as he turned the fillets and seared the flesh, the skin bubbled and charred and crisped.

"Smells amazing," she said, pulling herself up the swim ladder and perching delicately on the rail.

"I'm getting the hang of this cooking lark," he replied.

"Well, at least you no longer melt the boat or set fire to the boom sail."

"I thought we were forgetting about that," he said curtly.

"Never." She reached for her towel and dabbed her hair. Normally a mousey blonde, it had lightened in the sun and salty air. She too, was bronzed and the simple, healthy diet and daily swimming had left her fit and toned. "Beer?"

King shrugged. "There's no such thing as drunk sailing..."

She smiled and wrapped the towel around herself, went down into the cabin. When she emerged a few minutes later, King had the salad and fish dished onto plastic plates and she had slipped into a vest and shorts. She carried a cold bottle of Italian beer for King and a glass of white wine for herself. She looked past King and frowned at the boat that was approaching them. "Alex..." she said, her tone mirroring the concern in her eyes.

King moved his towel to reveal a worn and well-used Beretta 9mm pistol. She could already see that it had been made ready. Old habits died hard. "It's heading right for us," he replied, calmly squeezing more lemon onto the fish. "Just wait and see how it pans out..." Caroline bent down and unfastened the locker. Inside was a Very pistol and flares, lifejackets and survival kits and a double-barrelled shotgun. There were various laws around the world, but universally the shotgun was to be considered part of a ship's equipment. The shotgun was loaded with oo-buckshot. King had no time for unloaded weapons. The safety was enough. "Leave it," he said. "Wait out..."

"Just making it accessible."

King nodded. "On second thoughts, take it out and sink the bugger..." He paused. "Or we can lay another place for lunch, I'll leave you to decide..."

Caroline frowned, but as she watched the boat draw closer her heart fluttered and she stared back at King, her face ashen. "But..."

"You never really retire from this game," he commented flatly. "Stewart always told me that."

Caroline did not reply. She had only met King's MI6 mentor once, and too many people had been aiming guns at the time to change what opinion she had gleaned anecdotally. She watched Neil Ramsay staggering on the deck despite the mirrored surface of the sea. The cruiser's engines reversed, and the vessel eased alongside. King caught the rope thrown by a crewman and walked it up the port side and fastened it to the cleat. Another crewman reached over and secured the stern.

As usual, Ramsay wore a rather drab-looking suit costing no more than two-hundred pounds from a store that also sold food. He managed to make hard work of the marginal gap between the two vessels and the buffers. King held out a hand to aid him, then comically retracted it as the man reached out, then stumbled into the boat.

"Welcome aboard," said King. "I'll prepare the plank..."

"Not my decision," Ramsay replied curtly. "There were a great many changes after Simon Mereweather's death."

King nodded. Nobody had seen it coming. MI5 had undergone a caretaker leadership in the interim period and now a new director was in place. King had no longer been part of MI5's plans. It had been felt by many parliamentarians and civil servants that the Security Service had expanded its remit and was now being put back in its box. He looked past Ramsay at a rather severe-looking woman in her mid-forties. Attractive, but with a defensive demeanour. Her brunette hair was greying and had been pulled back in a ponytail. She was smartly dressed, but unlike Ramsay she had managed an outfit that suited the occasion. Cream trousers with a white blouse and a gossamer thin grey cashmere sweater. Her Birkenstock sandals were smart enough to go with her outfit, but suitable enough for boating. She hopped aboard without asking permission, or King noted, for assistance.

"Stella Fox," she said extending her hand to King.

King dropped his towel onto the pistol and took her hand. Firm, dry, positive. "King," he told her.

She released his hand and offered hers to Caroline, who ignored the gesture as she studied the woman measuredly.

The woman wasted no more time on Caroline, but if she felt knocked back then she didn't show it. "You may or may not know, but I am the new director general of the Security Service."

"We still get the newspapers," King replied.

"We appear to be gate-crashing your lunch," she said airily. "Would you like us to come back later?"

"Yes," Caroline replied. "Or maybe never."

The woman smiled but said nothing. She turned to King, who was dishing up the salad and piling the fish fillets on top. Caroline watched, then ducked down into the cabin and returned with more plates, glasses and wine. She had shown her feelings, but she wasn't a petulant child.

King offered Ramsay some food but knew the man would refuse. Ramsay liked his food beige and crispy. The fodder of high-functioning autistics. He handed Stella a plate and Caroline poured her some wine sparingly. "There's no dessert," said King. "So, you'd better get it out sooner rather than later."

"Neil said that you were a direct so-and-so," she smiled thinly.

"I'm sure he said more than that."

"Indeed."

King ate a mouthful of the snapper. Impossible to get any fresher. A swig of the cold beer washed it down nicely. "The interim directors signed the paperwork. We're not accountable for past actions. No crimes were committed in the pursuance of our duties in the eyes of the law." He paused, eyeing her warily. "So, if you're not here to arrest us, then you're here to recruit us."

"And there's no chance of that," Caroline said behind her glass. "Life is good."

"Nine-millimetre pistols at the ready just a few

hundred metres from a shoreline peppered with innocuous tourists, just because a boat approaches you directly, would suggest you will always be looking over your shoulders." She paused, glancing at the towel that King had used to conceal the weapon. "I feel we would have been safer arriving by pedalo."

King smiled at the thought of Ramsay in one of those yellow, pedal-powered tourist boats. "It's China, Russia and Iran," he commented flatly. "I guess we could toss in North Korea for that matter."

Stella Fox did not hide her surprise, glancing at Neil Ramsay as if he might have tipped off King beforehand. Ramsay shook his head minutely, just enough to assure her. "A new axis of evil," she replied. "It's called the Iron Fist. Five fingers, each representing an imminent threat to the West, but that when they combine into a fist, mean possible destruction."

"That's four," Caroline commented before sipping some of her chilled wine.

"Belarus," said King. "Russia's sock puppet."

Stella Fox raised an eyebrow, then turned to Ramsay.

"I told you," he said matter-of-factly.

"Indeed..."

"Told her what?" Caroline asked.

"That King is an asset," Stella replied. "You, too, for that matter."

"The entire team," Ramsay said quietly.

"But the Security Service don't want the likes of us," King commented. *Beyond our remit* was what many said. *Untouchable* was another well-touted term. Well, the interim directorship certainly listened. All you have left are flat-footed watchers and unarmed uniformed security guards."

Stella Fox nodded sagely. "All the suave Oxbridge toffs at the Secret Intelligence Service and all the ex-coppers and red brick graduates at the security service." King said nothing. He had served a dozen or more years in MI6, and he was anything but suave. But he knew the type. The men and women in the embassies, the men and women running foreign agents or assets. Peter Stewart had run the covert operations wing and the men and women there had been a different breed. People like King. "Your recent work exposed an organisation that has been doing the Prime Minister's bidding for more than a hundred years. This cannot stand. Sir Galahad Mereweather has deflected all subsequent enquiries, but I know that they will continue unabated. MI6 are all over it. They get to assert their remit and we get side-lined. Instead of the intelligence services coming together and making it a safer place for the British public, we are significantly weakened." She paused, taking a large gulp of her wine and seemingly more relaxed than when she had first arrived. "Losing Simon Mereweather was a blow. He continued in the vein of Charles Forrester, a man whom you both worked for. Possibly, Simon Mereweather did not do enough to cover your tracks, or protect you. Not knocking the man or speaking ill of the dead. It's just that I am aware of your past, King. Or what I have been able to glean. You worked in special operations and that wing was protected by the firm at all costs. I want to do the same. I want to create a department within a department, within a safe. Nobody gets to look in, nobody gets to point fingers and expect an enquiry at the drop of a hat. We cannot forge ahead and meet today's oncoming threats with one hand tied behind our backs."

King ate a few mouthfuls of fish and salad as he mused on her words. He had always liked Simon Mereweather, despite the gulf between them. Mereweather was worth hundreds of millions, possibly more when the family money was considered. King was raised in abject poverty in a council tower block and spent time in care and prison. Despite the former director's wealth and privilege, the man had understood grass roots and the political system. They had been played in their last assignment. Nobody had seen Mereweather's death coming. "And this Iron Fist. What's the situation?" he asked.

"You guessed correctly. Those five countries are our biggest threat. Singularly, they are manageable. Collectively, well, that's another matter entirely. Despots and megalomaniacs. Two of those nations are a nuclear force. Russia is planning on sneaking nukes to Belarus and Iran has been attempting nuclear capabilities for decades. North Korea have them now, although collective intelligence still shows them to be low yield with propulsions systems that still don't worry the United States. Well, Hawaii maybe."

"Maybe not a threat to the US," said Caroline. "But there are other countries out there..."

"Precisely," Stella Fox agreed. "Right next door in South Korea for one. Japan for another. And the situation between Taiwan and China is another Ukraine in the waiting. That bloody nutjob Kim Jong Un might be persuaded to send a missile into Taiwan taking the political heat off China in return for food, arms and consumables, all the while knowing that China would still stand firmly with them against retaliation."

"Like the playground bully's companion. There but for the bully." Ramsay paused. "The war in Ukraine showed the world that China has given unwavering political support for Russia, while Iran had no qualms about supplying Russia with drones and missiles. Now, with all five countries entering an accord, however unofficial it may be, each is bolstered by the other and what we fear most is a rise in confidence. Testing the boundaries, probing our defences. We've seen it for years with Russia and China's hacking programs, and every day our air force and navy head off Russian military aircraft from our airspace or hunt a nuclear submarine in our waters."

King nodded. He knew the score. Everybody working in intelligence knew it to be true. Russia had given up making a secret of it decades ago. "This is a NATO matter," he said, then added, "Why does any of this concern us?"

"Because it doesn't exist," Stella Fox replied. "There's just a few people's word for it. We know the Iron Fist is a thing, but we can't find a shred of solid evidence. Our biggest lead so far is an Iranian arms dealer and fixer for several terrorist organisations."

"And you want him dead," said King.

"No," she replied emphatically. "We want him replaced..."

# Chapter Three

**rticle in the Financial Times**

## Artificial Intelligence Could Wipe Out the World's Economy

As artificial intelligence (AI) continues to advance, experts warn that it poses a significant threat to financial security. With the ability to process vast amounts of data quickly and accurately, AI is becoming an increasingly popular tool for financial institutions. However, this same technology could also be used to perpetrate fraud, money laundering, and other financial crimes.

According to a report by the Association of Certified Fraud Examiners, 58% of fraud cases involved the use of technology, and this number is likely to increase as AI becomes more prevalent. AI-powered bots can conduct transactions at a much faster rate than humans, making it easier for criminals to move money undetected. They can also be used to analyse data and identify patterns that may indicate fraud, making it easier to cover up illegal activities.

One of the most significant concerns with AI is its potential to create what's known as a "black box" problem. This occurs when the algorithms that drive AI systems become so complex that even their creators cannot understand how they work. This lack of transparency makes it difficult to identify when an AI system is being used for nefarious purposes, allowing criminals to exploit the system undetected.

Another potential issue is the risk of data breaches. As AI systems rely on vast amounts of data to function, they are vulnerable to hacking and cyberattacks. If a criminal gains access to an AI system, they could potentially use it to access sensitive financial information or even take control of the system entirely.

To combat these threats, financial institutions must take a proactive approach to cybersecurity. This includes implementing robust security measures, such as multi-factor authentication and data encryption, and regularly monitoring their systems for unusual activity. Additionally, they must ensure that the AI systems they use are transparent and explainable, allowing for easy detection of any anomalies.

AI has the potential to revolutionise the financial industry, it also poses a significant threat to financial security. As such, it is crucial that financial institutions take the necessary steps to protect themselves from potential AI-related threats. Failure to do so could have severe consequences for both the industry and the wider economy.

# Chapter Four

L ondon

"We've created a legend from scratch. It's vague enough to feel real, detailed enough to whet their appetite. These things are extremely difficult to get right. We're confident that it will pass scrutiny." David Garfield paused. "All we need now is to add some real time experiences."

"Real time?" King asked, staring between Garfield, Ramsay and Stella Fox.

The MI5 director nodded. "We need to stage some events, create some red flags that will hold up and be easily confirmed."

"Indeed," Ramsay agreed. "We should aim for three months. Six would be better, but we don't know what the target will achieve within six months. Three gets us into the man's inner circle in time." He paused. "It's not ideal.

Ideally, we want our man inserted now, but three months will give us time to work on his cover, too."

King stood up and walked to the window overlooking the Thames. It was an anonymous office in a building full of accountants, solicitors and financial lending services. A top floor corner office taken under a three-year lease and paid for with money side lined for clandestine operations and untraceable to MI5. The name on the door was 'Moorland Associates' with no further explanation. David Garfield had made the offices his base and from here he would run MI5's new clandestine services with Neil Ramsay as his second in command. The view outside was one of his favourites. Glimpses of the London Eye, Waterloo Bridge and Big Ben with the river snaking around the South Bank. Tourists and Londoners alike walked the pavements and bridges, and taxis and red double decker buses kept the city moving. As much as he loved the coast and countryside, this part of London always made him feel comforted by its lack of isolation.

"Who is your agent?" he asked, not taking his eyes off Big Ben in the distance.

"He's a good man," Ramsay replied. "But we are not about to divulge his real name. This needs to be tight."

"None taken..."

"No offence meant," Stella Fox interjected. "All you need to know at this time is he's an exact doppelganger for Ahmadi. He's also a fellow Iranian, so he will be familiar with the culture and idiosyncrasies. He's almost the same age as well."

"What's his experience?" King asked.

"He's an agent for the task, so he's been recruited simply on his appearance," said Garfield. "He's willing to do it because his family were wiped out by the Iranian regime.

His sisters were arrested for protesting women's rights. One was killed in custody and the other disappeared. His brother, mother and father were all killed when the correction police swooped on their home, and they did not comply quickly enough. Our man was visiting an elderly relative in the north of the country and escaped to Turkey." Garfield paused. "He's fired up for revenge."

"Could be dangerous," said King. "Revenge tends to cloud judgement."

"Once he's in, he's in," Ramsay commented. "Ahmadi will be ours for interrogation and we will then feed our agent with critical information to retain his cover and move against the Iron Fist."

"Information he should have before he goes undercover," said King.

"Ideally," Fox replied. "But that's what you'll be doing before the switch. Getting everything that we need to know. We already have Ahmadi's mannerisms from surveillance video and his accent from intercepted communications."

King nodded, but he still did not look away from the postcard view of London. "You've got it all thought out," he said. "Except for the obvious, that is."

"Which is?" Ramsay asked incredulously.

King turned around and smiled. "Neil, with respect, if an identical copy of you was enough to fool Mrs Ramsay on appearances, I think she would notice a difference in the bedroom." He paused and shrugged. "And god forbid pillow talk of any nature..." Ramsay flushed red with embarrassment and returned his gaze to his laptop. "Forget the physical... What about the first *do you remember when?* anecdote?"

"I know," Stella Fox replied. "But we're not alone on this, we have the very best analysts and researchers digging into every aspect of Ahmadi's life. The agent will have to decide on what is said, how to steer the conversation and what to avoid..."

"And the bedroom?"

"The same goes for that," Garfield interjected. "Maybe a bout of abstinence will be what's called for..." He paused. "They've been married for thirteen years, maybe abstinence is already implied?" he said light-heartedly, but saw that humour wasn't welcomed and shrugged. "It could be an issue, yes..."

"Do you have a picture of Ahmadi's dick?" King shrugged. "His wife will know, trust me."

"We have everything we need," Stella Fox said unperturbed. "We even have footage of their love making in a hotel room on a business trip to Paris. Nothing sensational or out of most men's repertoire..."

King raised an eyebrow at the service's thoroughness. "Well, there's one person you're not going to fool, and that's his son." He walked over to the table and thumbed through his copy of the file. "I never had a father, so I'm no expert," he said. "But I'm pretty sure an eleven-year-old boy's hero is his old man, and I'm pretty sure he would know if a stranger was taking his hero's place." He glanced at Neil and said, "Your daughters would know if you were being impersonated, wouldn't they?"

"They barely know I exist..." he sighed.

King shrugged and looked at Stella Fox. "Are you a mother?"

"I am."

"How many?"

"One."

"Boy or girl?"

"A girl," she replied a little tersely. "She's seven."

King nodded. "And do you think that your little girl would be fooled by another woman taking your place?"

"That would depend," she replied thoughtfully. "If the person had the same incredible likeness that our agent has, had undergone the surgery..."

"You're reaching," he said. "I can see it in your eyes. You want this, and your judgement is clouded." King shook his head. "I'm talking about the way you lay beside her on her bed and read a bedtime story, or the way you bend down and kiss her goodnight, or the way you put a plaster on her knee."

"Perhaps. Perhaps not," she said with a shrug.

"Well, it's your agent's life if he doesn't fool the man's family." King paused. "Does Ahmadi's boy go to boarding school? Many children of such men do."

"He does," Ramsay informed him.

"Then it would make sense to install your agent when the boy leaves for school after the holidays. That way, if communications like Facetime can be avoided, then perhaps when the boy has spent a few months away..."

"I like it," Stella Fox nodded enthusiastically looking at both Ramsay and Garfield in turn. "Make a note of that for the analysts."

"Shit, if you're still at the *make a note of that* stage, I'm not sure I want in." King flicked through the file and paused on a page. "This list of assets Ahmadi owns... you noticed he has a helicopter, too?"

Ramsay frowned, flicking through the file. He frowned and read, "Vehicles – Jaguar XJ220, Aston Martin Vantage, Porsche GT2, Ferrari 575 Maranello, Alfa Romeo – unspecified, Mercedes S-class, Jaguar E-type, Sikorsky 109, Ducati Monster 900, BMW 1200R..."

"The last two are fast motorbikes, the Sikorsky is a helicopter." King paused. "You'd better make sure your agent can fly. It's a sure-fire way for him to be caught out."

"Just like that?" Stella Fox stared at him.

"I know a guy," King replied. "While we're at it, get the carpool guys to give him some advanced driving instruction in one of the fast BMW's. He'll need to know his way around a fast motorcycle, too. I'll take him out for that."

"You?"

"I ride bikes," King replied. "And I'll need to get to know the guy."

"Why?" Garfield asked.

"Well, if I can get into Ahmadi's organisation, it would be the perfect way to bolster the agent's cover. He'll have a friend in camp who can show him the way."

"How the hell would we get you in with Ahmadi?" Stella Fox asked incredulously.

King tossed his copy of the file onto the table and said, "It's in there. Staring you all in the face." He paused. "His son..."

# Chapter Five

**D**onbas, Ukraine

The general nodded as he was guided around the site by the lieutenant-colonel and his own 2-I/C, a young major who looked battle-hardened and fit. He had earlier inspected the armoured division three miles outside the city, and now he inspected the missile carriers that were parked in a semi-circle, their deadly arsenal aimed at the civilian targets of Kharkiv. The two battalions of BM-21 Grad mobile rocket systems totalling thirty-six vehicles could send one-thou-sand-four-hundred and forty rockets in a single volley, each vehicle capable of sending forty rockets in twenty seconds. Each nine-foot-five-inch rocket had a range of twenty kilo-metres and carried a payload of forty-four kilos of high explosive. Compared to the British Starstreak, Sky Sabre and M270B1 GMLRS systems, the BM-21 Grad was low-technology and outdated by its NATO counterparts, but

Russia had the numbers and the people of Ukraine had been bombed into poverty and desperation. The visiting Russian general was about to get a demonstration in merciless firepower.

Just over one thousand metres away, lying prone and having done so for three days, Rashid made a minute adjustment to the Schmidt and Bender scope atop the Accuracy International .338 Lapua Magnum rifle. Two hundred metres behind him the Land Rover 110 was parked facing away from him with his escort of three battle-hardened Ukrainian soldiers waiting patiently, if not nervously under the cover of trees and bushes they had cut and used to cover the vehicle. He just hoped they would hold their nerve, because what he was about to do went against everything in the sniper's manual and they would need to drive like the Devil himself to evade reprisal.

The general seemed pleased with the arrangement and the lieutenant-colonel was using the event to further his career, adopting a sycophantic demeanour, smiling and nodding enthusiastically when the general spoke. With his second in command standing to one side - answering questions when asked but keeping it minimal for his commander to shine – Rashid saw his chance, and in doing so, he could limit the damage to the mission. Two shots were the maximum a sniper could get away with in the same position and happenstance and fate had aligned and as he centred the crosshairs on the back of the lieutenant-colonel's head, he had lost all sight of the general's face. Taking up the slack on the two-stage trigger, he readjusted his aim, expelled a deep breath and squeezed when all the air was out of his lungs. The rifle hammered against his shoulder, and he worked the bolt ejecting the spent case and sliding another .338 soft-nosed bullet into the chamber. Both men fell with the same shot and Rashid had the crosshairs centred on the major before the man had realised what had happened. The gunshot thundered across the valley and Rashid had time to take the recoil and locate his target again in the reticule before the bullet struck the young major in the forehead. Two shots, three men down. Rashid folded the weapon's bipod, rolled over and gathered up his mat and the small bag of sand he had used to keep his elbow steady. He scrambled to his feet and ran in a crouch to the drainage culvert and knew that he was already out of sight from the bemused Russian soldiers in the village. There was gunfire behind him, but he wasn't concerned because he did not hear the whizz of bullets near him and he was well out of range from shoulder-fired AK-74's and the AK-12's that the Russians were equipped with, and by the time the soldiers opened with a salvo of 66mm mortars on likely sniper positions, Rashid was inside the Land Rover. The three Ukrainians were caught unaware, and boots were being fastened, coffee tipped out of enamel cups, cigarettes extinguished, and weapons made ready. Rashid wasted no time. He got behind the wheel and fired up the engine, a salvo of mortars landing nearby – so close that he felt the concussive blast in his chest and the roof, bonnet and windscreen of the Land Rover was littered with soil, stones and debris. He had the vehicle in gear and was flooring the accelerator with the last of the men scrabbling to throw himself in through the rear door. Mortars landed in front of them and behind, and the copse in which the Ukrainians had holed up over the past three days took a direct hit, birch trees were swiftly felled and burst into flames behind them. Rashid had the Land Rover up to sixty-miles-per-hour, bouncing and weaving across the field towards the road beyond. A quarter of the world's richest soil is to be found in Ukraine alone, and the fields in this area were rich chernozem deposits, in some places two metres deep compared to the UK's average of just five centimetres. Naturally, with such good soil and agriculture once the lifeblood of the country – the entire world for that matter – the field was vast and reminded Rashid of Salisbury Plain where he had trained many times in the army and with the SAS. He estimated the field to be over a thousand acres, and it straight up bordered another four that were no smaller. Eventually, the mortars were behind them, and they were moving too quickly and too erratically for the rockets to have any effect. Rashid allowed himself to relax behind the wheel, but it was short lived as the soil less than ten feet to his right tore up, sparks flying and starburst ricocheting high into the air could only mean one thing – heavy calibre bullets with staggered phosphorus tracer rounds. And from the point of impact, it could only mean that a helicopter was in pursuit. Rashid veered to the left, the bullets following them before he lurched again to the right and zig-zagged the Land Rover across the field. They could hear the engine and rotors closing in on them, and the panic in the other men's faces told Rashid all he needed to know about fear. One of the men opened the door and bailed out into the mud, rolling and bouncing on the ground as he slowed. Rashid glanced in his wing mirror, just into time to see the man obliterated by a burst of fire. Mud, stones, blood and body parts churned into the air.

"Return fire!" Rashid yelled at the other two men. "Now!" It was only intermediate 5.45x39mm ammunition, but the men fired their AK-74 rifles out of the windows, and the helicopter reared into the air and banked hard around them. When the nose lowered, its gatling gun rattled and a stream of 12.7mm bullets cut through the bonnet of the Land Rover and the engine died in a fog of steam and smoke. Rashid barely had to touch the brakes to slow on the rutted, clagging surface. "Out!" he shouted, and he picked up the AK-74 beside him and made it ready as his boots hit the dirt. He watched the helicopter bank away and aimed the rifle, emptying the entire magazine down the side of the fuselage. He changed magazines and looked around for somewhere to run. There was simply too much ground to cover to get to the trees to his right, and both men had taken off across the field with twenty metres or so between them. Rashid knew that he had to split the pilot's task, and he sprinted in the opposite direction. The Kamov KA-52 'Alligator' attack helicopter carried multiple missiles and weapon systems and as it completed its turn, it unleashed two 88mm unguided rockets and the Land Rover went up in flames, spewing torn panels and pieces of tyre over a twenty-metre radius. The gatling gun rattled for a few seconds and a track of bullets ploughed the field between the two men. Rashid knew that he was out of options. If he had snatched the sniper rifle from the cab, then maybe the .338 bullets could have damaged the rotor, but he knew that the AK-74 lacked either the power or accuracy to cause the pilots to worry. All they had to do now was back off, climb in altitude and pick them off with the aircraft's guns, but the pilot seemed hell-bent on terrorising them, and flew a low overpass intersecting them which sent Rashid and the other two men sprawling onto their stomachs as the downdraft from the rotors tore up the dirt and pressed the men briefly into the soft earth.

Rashid lost sight of the helicopter, but he could hear it just behind him, feel the reverberation of the mighty engines in his chest. He glanced backwards and immediately wished he hadn't. The pilot pulled the aircraft into a low hover, the gunner bringing the gatling gun on target.

That was it. His time had run. He slowed, turned around, damned if he was going to take it in the back. A burst of 12.7mm would turn him into chopped meat, so he knew that it would thankfully be a swift death. It is widely believed that you never hear the bullet that kills you, so hearing the whoosh and thud made Rashid jolt, but as he remained on his feet, the helicopter split in half and the rotors spun away as the two pieces of aircraft fell to the ground and were engulfed in flames. Rashid glanced back towards the road, then the vapour trail from the missile dispersing in the air like sea mist before a warm summer's dawn.

Rashid turned and watched the two Ukrainians heading back across the field towards him. The look on their faces said it all. Relief. And then confusion, as they watched the burning hulk of the cockpit and fuselage, and the ruptured tail section twenty feet away. The pilot and gunner were screaming, but Rashid was drawn to the dark grey Toyota pick-up truck bouncing towards them across the field. Often referred to as a 'technical' the vehicle now seemed to be the freedom-fighter's go-to piece of equipment right after the Kalashnikov.

King put down the FIM-92 Stinger man-portable surface to air missile system and leapt out of the bed of the pick-up truck. He was wearing olive cargo pants and a grey T-shirt and looked to have borrowed a camouflage jacket a couple of sizes too big for him. He nodded to the burning hulk and the screaming men trapped inside. "Going to take some prisoners?" he asked nobody in particular.

"Let them burn..." replied one of the Ukrainians.

"Yes!" the other Ukrainian added enthusiastically.

King walked over to the cockpit. He had seen something all too similar in the Congo twenty-years previous. He drew a pistol and extended the men the same mercy his mentor had back then and fired twice through the plexiglass silencing the screams. It was his mess; and he alone would sort it out.

"What the hell are you doing here?" Rashid asked, still dumfounded by the fact King was standing beside him.

King nodded to the truck and said, "Later. I'll explain on the way."

"Where to?"

"Out of range of those Russian missiles for one," he replied getting up into the bed of the pick-up.

"And for the other?"

King shrugged. "We're putting the band back together..."

# Chapter Six

rticle in The Times

## Could Russia Use A.I. to Destroy NATO?

Artificial intelligence (AI) has become increasingly prevalent in various sectors, including security and defence. NATO, the North Atlantic Treaty Organization, is an inter-governmental military alliance comprising 30 countries in Europe and North America. NATO's security systems are designed to protect its members from various threats, including cyberattacks, terrorism, and military aggression. However, the use of AI in these systems also presents certain risks that need to be addressed.

One of the main risks of using AI in NATO's security systems is the potential for these systems to be compromised or hacked. As AI systems become more sophisticated, they also become more vulnerable to attacks by enemy states who may attempt to manipulate or control them for their own purposes. This could include using AI to bypass or disable security measures, steal sensitive information, or launch cyberattacks against NATO member countries.

Another risk is that AI systems could be used to exploit vulnerabilities in NATO's security infrastructure. For example, an adversary could use AI to analyse patterns of NATO military operations or communications and identify weaknesses or areas of vulnerability. This could allow them to launch targeted attacks or gain access to sensitive information, compromising the security of NATO's member states. Moreover, AI systems could also be used to create disinformation campaigns aimed at undermining NATO's security and cohesion. By creating convincing 'fake news' stories or propaganda, AI could be used to spread false information and manipulate public opinion. This could lead to increased tension between NATO members and erode trust and cooperation, making it easier for adversaries to exploit divisions and weaknesses within the alliance.

Another potential risk is that the use of AI in NATO's security systems could lead to unintended consequences or errors. For example, if an AI system were to misinterpret data or make a faulty decision, it could have serious implications for NATO's security posture. In some cases, these errors could even lead to accidental conflicts or escalations that could threaten regional stability and security. To mitigate these risks, it is important for NATO to adopt a comprehensive approach to AI security. This could include investing in advanced cybersecurity measures and threat intelligence capabilities, as well as developing protocols and procedures for assessing and addressing the risks associated with AI. NATO should also prioritise the development of ethical and transparent AI systems that can be audited and monitored for potential vulnerabilities or biases.

While AI has the potential to enhance NATO's security capabilities, it also poses significant risks that need to be addressed. As the use of AI continues to grow in the security sector, it is essential that NATO takes a proactive and comprehensive approach to AI security to ensure the safety and security of its member countries. By doing so, NATO can leverage the power of AI while minimizing the risks and vulnerabilities associated with its use.

# Chapter Seven

**M**ontego Bay, Jamaica

Dave Lomu stared at the four men in turn. They were young and wiry and jittery. Coming down from a high and in need of another fix. The whites of their eyes were yellowed and streaked red with burst blood vessels. Tatty, dirty jeans, scuffed trainers and shirtless – the ripped T-shirts tucked into the back of their jeans and hanging loose like a chef's oven cloth in their apron band. They were ethnic Jamaicans. Darker in colour than Lomu, who as a Fijian had Indian, East African and Polynesian heritage. Four against one wasn't good odds, but then again, Lomu was six-feet-four and eighteen stone of solid muscle.

"Four of us and one of you, *bumbaclot!*" the lead youth shouted.

Lomu grinned. He had heard the insult many times since arriving on the island. Someone told him it was the same as motherfucker, others said douchebag, but a creole Jamaican assured him it meant blood cloth – the man was literally calling him a used sanitary towel. Names did not worry the ex-SAS trooper. He had been called worse by scarier men than these.

"W'at funny *coconut*?" another said. Coconuts were brown on the outside and white in the middle. He may well have been from the other side of the world, but he was a proud island race and could trace his heritage back in the South Pacific since 1500 BC. He was a black man and he never pretended to be anything else.

"You're in my way," said Lomu, glancing at the edge of the dock and the oil slicked water ten feet below. A far cry from the crystal-clear sea lapping at the white sandy beaches. "I've asked you to move, and now I'm telling you..."

Two of the young men pulled knives out of their pockets. The other two flexed their muscles and stepped forwards. The lead youth, or Alpha sneered. "And we told you that you pay us insurance. Without it, your boat may just go up in flames..."

"Whoosh!" another jeered, making a gesture of an explosion with his hands, his eyes wide, as large as golf balls.

Lomu had arrived in port three days ago. He was not a natural sailor, despite living on the ocean in small boats and canoes for his entire childhood, he had discovered that modern, open water sailing was a different entity, and he had almost jumped ship in Darwin and again in Cape Town, but for the fact he never liked to quit. What was one more crossing of open water? Everything, as it had turned out. Thirty-foot waves sometimes double stacked to form sixty-foot faces, and always utterly relentless. Jenny had been in her element. An experienced captain and helmswoman, she had made sailing and small craft her life.

They had taken the yacht from Cairns to Jamaica, and she had painted a pretty picture of ocean life. They had outrun pirates in Thailand, narrowly missed running into a blue whale in the Indian Ocean and hit a submerged log off Durban, forced to dry dock for a week while the boat underwent repairs, but not before he had to carry out a running repair on the hull in water renowned for Great White sharks. With every port Lomu had forced himself not to walk away. He had fallen for Jenny while in Fiji, but he already knew that they were poles apart. He didn't want to walk away from her, but she had already secured a lucrative contract to deliver a Sunseeker power yacht from Jamaica to Cape Breton, France with fuel stops via the Azores and Madeira, and he knew he was going to have to sit this one out. Jenny had been quite breezy about it, but she couldn't turn down ten-thousand dollars for just ten day's work. She would leave the day after tomorrow, but until then when they completed the handover, the yacht was their home and their responsibility. And that included not having it torched as the consequence in turning down a local protection ring.

"Let's take a moment to think about all this," Lomu said. "It's not going to work out like you think it is."

"Pay the fucking money, *bumbaclot!*" one of the men shouted, his eyes glaring wildly.

"Make me."

It was a red rag to a bull and the man charged forwards - his companions still a beat behind and unready for physical confrontation. Lomu took a massive pace forward and rammed his right knee into the man's sternum. The wind was driven clean out of the young man, but Lomu grabbed him by the testicles and a handful of dreadlocks and lifted him clean off the ground and threw him over the edge of the dock and into the water. Without pausing a beat, he took two strides covering the space between himself and the group of men and launched a front kick into one of the men holding a knife, the ball of his right foot driving through the man's stomach and folding him in half. He yanked a handful of the man's hair and heaved him out over the edge. Both men sunk under the surface, making no attempt to swim.

"Decision time, lads," Lomu said staring at them both. "Three choices. Fight me and lose, run away or save your pals from drowning..."

One of the men leapt into the water and the other ran. Lomu shrugged and walked on. He hadn't anticipated that, and as he passed a life buoy hanging on a post with a coil of orange rope underneath, he unhooked it and tossed it down into the splashing melee below. He didn't stop to see who was struggling or who was drowning. The thrashing could have been bull sharks lurking near the boats in hope of fish guts and scraps from fishermen for all he cared. It was never a good idea to swim in harbours.

"Same old Big Dave..."

Lomu spun around at the familiar voice. Caroline raised her sunglasses and left them perched on the top of her head, keeping her sun-streaked hair out of her eyes. She rushed forwards and hugged him, and he reciprocated warmly. When she pulled away, he held her by the shoulders looking down at her. "What the hell are you doing here?" he asked, then looked around and said, "Where's King, is he ok?"

"He's on an errand," she replied.

"What's wrong?"

"Nothing," Caroline sighed. "And everything..."

Lomu nodded. "I'm off to get some breakfast," he said. "Want to tell me while we eat?"

"You and your food!" she smiled. "I'm so jet lagged, I don't know which way is up. So, yeah, I suppose breakfast won't hurt. I'm not even sure what meal that was on the plane."

Lomu led the way to the café. It was a converted working boat permanently moored to a quiet jetty. Somewhere between a fishing trawler and a small cargo vessel. Inside, the nautical theme continued with coils of rope, anchors, oars and boathooks affixed to the timber walls and various photographs of Jamaica and Jamaican life over the decades. The tables were four-seat booths and in American diner style, mayonnaise, ketchup, chilli sauce and other condiments nestled in holders along with paper napkins, cutlery, and menus.

"I'm not really a fan of Caribbean food," Caroline said as she perused the menu. "Or anywhere that serves fish for breakfast..."

Lomu laughed. "You're telling that to a Fijian?" He paused. "You and King lived in Cornwall for a while. Did you ever eat a Cornish pasty?"

"Of course."

"And you liked it?"

"Yes."

Lomu looked up as the waitress meandered over in the way only Jamaicans can truly master. Somewhere between the speed of a slow walk and sitting on the sofa. "I'll handle this, then," he told her, and ordered Blue Mountain coffee, coco bread, beef patties and buns and cheese, which he pronounced *bun'an cheeeeze*. He smiled at Caroline as the waitress took a full minute to reach the kitchen twenty feet away, looking all around her and out the porthole windows as squeezed her considerably wide frame between the tables.

"What the hell are we eating?"

"Trust me," he replied, glancing at his bulky G-Shock watch. "It's time for brunch, anyway." He paused, looking at her across the table. "So, go on, then. Why are you here?" Caroline relayed what Stella Fox had told them on board their yacht. The yacht that was now moored in Stintino, and apart from King's motorbike and Caroline's Mini Cooper covered with bedsheets in a lock-up in a quiet London mews, and Caroline's flat in Camden Lock which she had rented out on *Airbnb*, the yacht represented their life savings. When she had finished, Lomu asked, "How good is this man that will impersonate this Ahmadi character?"

"No idea," she replied honestly. "He was recruited solely on his appearance. I understand he is being taught all he needs to know."

Lomu nodded, then shushed Caroline as the waitress headed towards them and when she eventually made it across the room, she put down two large trays of food and when he asked about their coffees she smiled and ambled vaguely in the direction of the counter and called, "Yeah, man..." over her shoulder.

"So, are we getting our coffees or not?" Caroline chided.

"This is Jamaica. *Yeah man* can mean right away, maybe or anytime tomorrow..."

Lomu helped himself to one of the beef patties which was a mix of beef, onions and potatoes with chilli and spices and wrapped in a cornflour pastry. "I'm told that Jamaicans eat them like this," he said and took a slice of coco bread and folded the pie inside to make a thick sandwich. He took a bite and grinned. "And it's bloody delicious!"

Caroline tried some of the pastry and smiled. "That is pretty good, to be fair." She tried it the same way as Big

Dave with the coco bread and said, "Bloody hell, I haven't eaten so many carbs in years..."

"Wonderful, isn't it?" Big Dave paused. "I've had a few of these. I've given up trying to find a good fry-up. The last one I had was in Cape Town."

"Well, it won't do you any harm. I don't think you're about to fade away..."

The coffees arrived and the woman smiled as she put them down on the table. "You're eating them like a true Jamaican," she said.

Caroline smiled. "So, how do we eat the buns and cheese?"

The woman grinned and picked up one of the buns, broke it open with her fingers and picked up a slice of yellow cheese which she pressed inside. She took a mouthful and as she chewed, she said, "Like that, man..." and sauntered back towards the counter, barely squeezing between two tables.

Caroline's mouth had fallen open and Lomu laughed, "It's not often *you're* lost for words!"

"Wow," she said, shaking her head. "So, what the hell is bun and cheese, anyway?"

"It's not all that complicated," said Big Dave as he copied what the waitress had done and made the cheese roll. He took a bite and frowned. "Well, that one's a bit weird," he commented. "It's like a hot cross bun with unre-frigerated mild cheddar..."

"I'll pass." She took a sip of her black coffee. "That's pretty good, though."

"Wait for the after kick..."

"Right," she replied. "Tobacco overtones. Strangely, not unpleasant considering I don't like smoking."

"World renowned coffee, apparently."

"So, how's the love life?" She paused. "Jenny, isn't it?"

Lomu nodded. "I met her in Fiji when I went out for that family thing," he said quite casually. The rest of the team had known that he had some problems, but Big Dave wasn't the sort of man to dine out on them. Things went down and Lomu had resolved the situation. "We get along great, but she's married to the sea..."

Caroline laughed. "I thought you were born on the beach, learned to catch sharks from a canoe before you were five?"

Lomu smiled. "I did, and I love it. But Jenny is a professional powerboat and sailing instructor and as well as that, she makes the bulk of her money delivering vessels all over the world. Believe me, two months at sea is enough even for this Fijian." He paused. "Besides, I spent twenty years in the British Army. You don't tend to spend a lot of time at sea when you're with the infantry."

"Have you told her this?" she asked, then shook her head not waiting for the answer. "Of course, you haven't. You're a man."

"She's taking a boat to France. I just want to feel dry land under my feet for a while."

"Then tell her."

He shrugged. "A week or two won't hurt," he said. "I'd like to get back in the game and this Ahmadi thing sounds intriguing. Who else is in?"

"Ramsay is behind the admin and planning aspect. Alex has gone to Ukraine to find Rashid..."

"What the hell is he doing out there? He's not back with the regiment, is he?"

"No. I believe he went out there to instruct snipers, but it looks as if he got a bit more involved."

"Yeah, slippery slope."

"He's no mercenary. I just think he witnessed some things that put him deeper into the fight." She paused. "Took hold of him emotionally."

"It happens." Lomu tucked into two of the meat patties and some of the cheese. Caroline watched incredulously. Known as Big Dave to his friends, he usually ate four or five meals a day, and never left food on his plate. Caroline finished the one patty and concentrated on her coffee. When Lomu had finished he said, "How is it going down?"

Caroline put down her coffee. "Alex will try to get recruited."

"Easier said than done."

"He thinks he's found a way in. But until then, he plans on making some history." She paused. "A verifiable history to go with the potted history that will be left out in the ether. Ramsay has already started on it. Names, aliases, work history, banking history. King will take on several scenarios to get his name checkable."

"What like?"

"You know Alex," she replied a little tersely. "Knowing him, something spectacularly over the top, no doubt."

"For god's sake..." Lomu shook his head despairingly. "Ok, I'm in."

"Just like that?"

"Well, someone has to save King from himself."

Caroline shrugged and sipped some more coffee. "Fair enough," she said. "That's as good a reason as any." She paused. "How will you tell Jenny?"

"She's taking on a contract, she's going to be busy," he replied matter-of-factly.

"For a couple of weeks at best!" Caroline retorted. "You'll be gone for months."

"I'll swing it," he said. "Absence makes the heart grow fonder and all that crap..."

Caroline handed him an envelope and finished her coffee. "Ticket for one to Heathrow the day after tomorrow, one-thousand pounds and a smartphone. Our new head-quarters, Ramsay's, King's and my number have already been entered into the contacts. Text Ramsay when you land, and he'll have a car waiting for you in arrivals by the time you clear border security."

"You knew I'd say yes, didn't you?"

Caroline smiled. "You're not the retiring kind," she said. "I guess, deep down, none of us are."

"So, you finally bought the yacht and started out around the Med?" He paused. "I got your e-postcard, by the way. I find it hard to believe that you just gave up on all that."

"I might say the same about you."

He chuckled and said, "It was work. The most direct route possible with ration packs and zero sightseeing. Ok, some of it was fun, but it wasn't the idyllic picture you and King painted. But you? You two were living the dream."

"I thought it was all I wanted," she replied. "And right up until halfway through the conversation with the new director, I thought I still did. But then it dawned on me that the world needs people like me..."

Lomu bowed mockingly and said, "We're not worthy..."

"Dickhead!" she chided. "Alright, it sounded a bit lame when I just said it out loud, but it's all I've ever done. I joined the army because my father fought in the Falklands, and he never had a son to continue the tradition for men in my family. His father was in the Suez crisis, then again in Malaya. His father before him was in Korea and World War Two, his father was in the Great War, his father fought in the Boer War and Zulu uprisings..." She shrugged. "There was a Darby at Waterloo and another in America in the War of Independence. I could probably go on."

"Please don't..."

Unperturbed, she said, "I was recruited into army intelligence, and then again into the Security Service. Hearing Stella Fox talk about the Iron Fist made me think that it will never be over. There will always be someone who wishes us harm." She paused thoughtfully. "And besides, what chance have I got with Alex? He hears of a new threat and he's ready to get into a fight."

Lomu nodded. "I get it," he said. "But let's just hope our luck holds out."

# Chapter Eight

H ampshire, England

"You've got time on this aircraft?"

"No."

"Don't worry, I'll take you through it."

"Ok."

"I'll take the left-hand seat, leave you in the driver's seat. I'll get us up and hand over control when we're straight and level."

"I'll be fine."

"It's the company's bird, so I'll decide if it's fine or not."

"Right..."

"It's quite a step up from the R-22 and R-44 Robinsons."

"Death traps."

The pilot shook his head. "A very popular bird! And that is why civil aviation crash investigations have given them a bad name. But they sell ten times more than any other manufacturer, hence the high crash stats." He paused. "I have a twenty-two, myself." He looked at the thirty-year-old black man beside him dubiously. "Do you own a helicopter, Leroy?"

"No."

"I didn't think so. But you can do well with the company. Build your hours and you'll climb through the promotion ladder." He paused. "I have almost four hundred hours, so you should pick up a thing or two from me. I had fifty hours when I certified as an instructor. How many hours do you have?"

"Almost twenty thousand. Thirteen-hundred of those were combat hours."

The pilot stared at him, his mouth agape. He soon realised and pursed his lips. "Which aircraft?"

Flymo shrugged. His moniker had come about because nobody could hover lower or better. Like the brand of lawn-mowers of the same name that floated on a cushion of air. "Lynx, Gazelle, the Apache AH-64E attack helicopter," he replied. "Dauphin 2 and Gazelle AH1 helicopters while I was with 658 squadron in support of the SAS." He paused. "Oh yeah, and some time in Chinooks, as well as a dozen or so different models in civilian life."

The pilot said nothing as he started the engine and the rotors and tail rotors turned slowly into life, building to a crescendo above their heads. Flymo tried not to smile, fearing he'd only make matters worse. The pilot raised the collective and kept positive yoke to counter the crafts desire to flip over to the right, all the way onto its rotors. Take-off was smooth, but Flymo had experienced better. The fact that a civilian pilot needed only twenty-five hours after passing their private pilot's licence to take their instructor's exam seemed ludicrous to a pilot of Flymo's experience. He had regularly flown double that in a week while in Afghanistan. They headed east at an altitude of three thousand feet, the pilot outlining his route to the control tower. Slowly and steadily, they gained height and settled at five-thousand feet. Flymo did not know what the pilot wanted from him, but he was getting bored now and starting to regret applying for the instructor's post, let alone this wearisome interview, and he was wondering whether civilian flying was even for him. The sudden splutter from the engine and dip in height snapped Flymo from his thoughts. The pilot looked at the instruments and frowned.

"Carbon build up," said Flymo. "Take her higher and prepare for a shut off..."

"A what?"

"You have to clear the carbon from the heat exchange."

"How."

"Manual shut down," Flymo replied. "Take her up!"

The pilot shook his head and lowered the craft. "We need to land!"

"For fuck's sake, gain height or we won't have enough altitude for the rotors to free turn if we have to glide or autorotate."

"We can't glide, it's a fucking helicopter!"

Flymo took the yoke collective and said, "I have control..." He felt some fightback, but snatched over the control, which from the righthand seat – where primary helicopter pilots sat, and the opposite to an airplane – he could override the man next to him. The aircraft lifted and surged with power, and Flymo shut down the engine and the sound of the unpowered rotors scything through the air was eerily quiet and quite unnatural for the split second before they started to fall.

"Oh my god!" the pilot cried.

Flymo eased the yoke forward and the helicopter nose-dived, but as it dropped, the rotors – now acting as little more than fans – rotated more quickly and Flymo nodded towards a field in the distance that was far greener than the others around it. "That's our heading!" He dropped the nose further and as the helicopter accelerated rapidly, Flymo banked right, and the field filled their immediate view, the attitude level (like a spirit level and not to be confused with altitude) lined up on the furthest third of the field. With the aircraft at close to maximum speed had the engine been running at full throttle, Flymo raised the nose and switched the engine back on. The speed of the rotors caused a tremendous backfire and Flymo smiled. "That's the carbon gone," he said calmly, noticing the pilot's white knuckles as the man gripped the edge of his seat. Flymo raised the nose and climbed steeply, then dropped into a dive and when he climbed back up, he used the momentum to victory roll. The pilot screamed and Flymo grinned as he banked hard and gained a thousand feet of altitude. He switched off the engine again and the pilot screamed as loudly as before. "Keep your eyes on the south helipad," he said. "We're going to glide the whole way."

"We can't!"

Flymo chuckled. "Watch this, then..." The rush of air against the cabin buffeted them, the rotors spinning rapidly in the air, the soft hum of the rotors just loud enough to hear. Flymo lifted, shaving off some of their speed, then dipped again, this time banking past their intended landing spot. He lifted the nose again, dipped once more and they were right on target. At an altitude of five hundred feet, he raised the nose until they were almost vertical and when he dipped back down, when the craft levelled once more, they were showing an airspeed of ninety knots, an altitude of two-hundred feet and looking as if they were about to over-shoot. The pilot screamed again, but Flymo ignored him. He was having too much fun. Another rise of the nose, another dip and the helipad was looming up on them. Flymo banked hard, this time losing sight of the helipad altogether. They were travelling backwards now, no more than twenty feet from the ground, the airspeed indicator had glitched and as Flymo dipped the nose, the skids touched the grass and they slid backwards ten feet or so before the rear part of the skids touched the ground and they skidded to a halt. "And that, sunshine, is how you glide a chopper..." He pulled off his headphones and unbuckled his harness. "I'm not sure this is for me," he told the pilot before opening the flimsy door and making his way across the grass to the carpark. Several people who had been watching the landing stared at him, parting like the Red Sea as he drew near. As he climbed over the wooden post and rail fence, he glanced back and saw that the pilot was still in his seat and couldn't help smiling to himself. He hadn't really wanted to teach middle-aged businessmen to fly, but with his skillset and unrelated work experience, he hadn't thought there to be much else for him to do.

"What on earth was all that?"

Flymo turned and stared at Ramsay. "A bit of fun and games with a right tosser," he said dryly. "What on earth are you doing here?"

"Offering you a job," Ramsay replied. "Perfect timing, from the look of it..."

# Chapter Nine

E xmoor, three days later

The farm had been unoccupied since its previous owner had blown his brains a with 12-bore shotgun three years previous amid frustrations of supply and labour during the Covid Pandemic. The farmer's wife had sold off the stock and gone to live in Minehead with her sister. She worked at Butlins now, cleaning cabins and serving on the bar, but it was better than a farm tenancy and ongoing debts. Their children had not been interested in a life of farming and when they had dispersed to different cities for jobs and new lives, five generations of farmers had ended as swiftly as a slaughterman's dispatch.

Occupying three-hundred acres in the middle of the moors, with hills to three sides and glimpses of the Bristol Channel to the north, the farm comprised of a large farm-house, two concreted yards and six outbuildings. Nobody wanted the farm tenancy, so MI5 had bought the farm from the landowner with undeclared funds seized from Islamic terrorists. A team of tradesmen had decorated inside the house and as well as a well-equipped kitchen, luxurious lounge and an office suite, the house now boasted seven ensuite bedrooms and a comfortable lounge. A team of MI5 communications experts had supplied secure internet, coded landlines and sat phones. There were cutting-edge firewalls installed to allow secure browsing of the surface internet, deep web and dark web, and a CCTV system that covered three-hundred and sixty degrees, with split-screen monitors in every room. Stella Fox had wanted a safehouse and that was exactly what she had got. A panic room had been constructed in the cellar with air-filtration, supplies of tinned food and bottled water, and an underground fibre-optic cable connected to a battery cell power supply and a satellite phone that would ensure that the property's back-up power and emergency communications could not be cut. The Security Service was not officially permitted to carry weapons in the United Kingdom, but the new director general knew that this had been skirted for decades. She was putting together a department to fight terrorism, and foreign agents from nations that would do them harm. From what she had discovered about the Iron Fist, there was no time to waste worrying about mandates and the niceties of a rule book. Charles Forrester had started down a different path, and Simon Mereweather had taken up the mantle. Both men had made such significant difference that they had been killed during their service. Forrester as deputy director and Mereweather as director. Howard, Forrester's boss and Mereweather's predecessor had been killed in his office by a Russian agent. Stella Fox had not entered her service with MI5 and her directorship lightly. Regarded by commentators as a business guru and career civil servant, she was taking her foray into intelligence seriously. She had asked King what the team needed, and she had procured it. On the table in the open-plan kitchen and living area five hard, black plastic boxes rested in a neat line. Each box had a combination code, and on each box the name of the recipient was labelled neatly along with a serial number to match that of the item inside.

Stella Fox stood behind the table with Ramsay to her left and David Garfield to her right. King walked in first, a mug of builder's tea in his hand. Caroline followed with Big Dave, Flymo and Rashid bringing up the rear, still catching up on what the others had been doing since they had last seen each other at the Special Forces Club where they had drunk themselves into near oblivion after Simon Mereweather's funeral.

"Good morning," Stella Fox smiled, although it wasn't the warmest smile they had ever seen. "This is day one, ground zero. What we do now will never be widely known, nor publicly for that matter. But it will be vital." She paused. "You all know Neil, of course, but for those who don't already know, this is David Garfield, and he will head this department. Formally with those shits across the river, he knows the inner workings of the Secret Intelligence Service and will bring that knowledge to the Security Service."

King stared at the man in front of him. He knew who the man was, had watched him rise through the ranks of MI6. Hopefully the man would not remember King, but he seriously doubted that.

"There's no name for who we are," said Garfield. "No remit for what we do. There are forces at work against us, and there are departments within our own government and intelligence services that wish the Security Service to fail, wither and perish. *We* won't allow

that to happen. We will accept no reward, claim no responsibility nor acknowledge any fanfare. Likewise, we will not hold our hands up to failure. Failure happens. It's inevitable. We dust ourselves off, lick our wounds and march stoically onwards."

King would never admit it, but he was feeling buoyed by the man's speech. Their work, their effort and their risk was being acknowledged. Stella Fox and David Garfield were making a good impression. However, only time would tell. He had been around the block enough to know that it was easy to promise something, but altogether more difficult to deliver. He had been left in enemy territory by the empty promises of others more times than he cared to remember.

"We took recommendations from the best range instructors in both the police and military and have supplied you with Glock model nineteen pistols."

"I don't do guns," said Flymo. "I plan on staying in whatever helicopter I'm flying at the time."

Stella Fox nodded. "King already told me this. We aim to add to your duties, but we will respect your beliefs."

Flymo shrugged. "I just can't shoot straight, that's all," he replied. "I only just scraped through basic infantry training because of weapon handling and marksman scores. Don't like them much, either. Anyway, I prefer missiles and cannons and a nice big digital display in front of me, so if you can get hold of some for my next whip, that would be great."

"Whip?" she queried.

"Yeah, like my ride." He paused. "My chopper..."

She smiled. "We'll bear that in mind," she replied

coolly. "But right now, it's your flying instructor skills that we're after."

"Good luck..." Ramsay quietly mused.

"Each firearm is personally registered to you. A ballistic sample has been taken for our own records. The weapon's serial number has been laser etched onto the head of the firing pin, so each spent case will have your own unique signature. You will enter your own combination into the case. Inside each box is your primary weapon, three magazines and a box of fifty rounds of nine-millimetre ammunition." She looked at King and said, "Anything you want to add?"

King shrugged. He wanted to say that he doubted that he'd ever use his. An illegally obtained weapon could do its job and be tossed into a canal without anything coming back on him, but he wasn't about to voice that. He was simply used to covering himself in a world where nothing seemed genuine or straightforward. "The model nineteen is a compact version of the popular seventeen that most of us are familiar with, but has no real discernible difference in muzzle energy, velocity or accuracy despite using a barrel that is a whole inch shorter. The SAS, SBS, US Navy Seals and Delta Force have all adopted the model nineteen, so that speaks for itself. You're all familiar with the Glock family – no external safety – just the trigger hinge, no double action option, or first round firm trigger pull. It will not fire if dropped. Never. Because the firing pin is disengaged until the moment the trigger is pulled. It also has the best sights in the business – three luminous dots, two on the rear vee, one on the foresight. Line up all three and hit pretty much what you aim at. Good for up to fifty metres, quite possible to get accurate shots at over a hundred, dependent on the shooter." He paused. "Fifteen rounds in a flush-fitting magazine makes it a hell of a package. I thought they would be the best all-round weapon for our work. Incidentally, the boxes are x-ray proof, and we have the advantage of putting them in a diplomatic bag when we travel by air. This will be a game changer, as in the past we've procured weapons from the criminal underworld and the weapons would obviously have been tainted. The last thing we want moving forward is to have crimes and murders connected to any weapon we have in our possession..." He just hoped they could all keep a straight face, because like King, he doubted they would ever truly trust the establishment once the bodies started stacking up on a mission.

"And you'll only need them when the job dictates," Stella Fox added.

"No," King replied emphatically. "Murphy's Law dictates that when you don't carry a weapon then that's the time when you'll need it the most."

"The man's got a point," Garfield commented. "I mean, the people on the ground are the one's best to judge what they do and do not need..."

Stella Fox thought on this for a moment, then conceded. "Very well. Just don't make me regret it."

Ramsay expelled his breath loudly, and all eyes were on him. He frowned and looked away, but it was clear he hadn't been behind the idea. Never a man of violence, or indeed action, he had found himself pulled into their world on more than one occasion. He checked his phone and said, "He's on his way in. I told Jack to message me when they were close." Everyone looked up at the CCTV monitor fixed to the wall and watched as a dark blue, old model Range Rover Sport pulled in through the open agricultural gateway and proceeded up the lane, its progress followed on the various cameras indicated on the split screen. Finally, it was seen to park next to the other vehicles. A solid-looking young man got out of the driver's side and waited for the man in the passenger seat to get out. The younger man led the way and reached the door, all of them turning around and looking towards the sound of the knock on the front door. "This is where it will get interesting..."

King looked at Ramsay and frowned, but the chief analyst was not forthcoming. Garfield made his way to the door and let them inside. King watched the younger man exchange a few words with the intelligence chief. He looked under thirty and extremely fit. King estimated him to be around six-foot in height and thirteen stone in weight. Strong arms and chest, and a trim waist. King recognised a fellow combative when he saw him. The man paid no attention to King or the rest of the team and headed through to the kitchen half of the open area where he started to make himself a coffee.

The second man needed no introduction. King had seen the photographs of Ahmadi in the file, which he felt he knew almost by heart now. The man now talking to Garfield was Ahmadi's double. Apart from his haircut and an unkept moustache and beard where Ahmadi sported a pencil-thin shaped and sculptured moustache and goatee, it was if the Iranian arms dealer was in the room. King watched Garfield shepherd the man towards them, noticing the fear in the new arrival's eyes, the hesitant gait to his movements. The man was clearly terrified. As Garfield made the introductions it clearly did nothing to relieve the man's worries. Finally, he walked the man towards King and said, "This is..."

"Wait!" King snapped irritably and both men visibly flinched, Garfield looking incredulously at him, and for a moment Stella Fox looked about to step in. "I will be using a cover name. Our asset should only know this. Anything else could force him to make a mistake, and a mistake will cost lives. I don't want to know his name, either. From now on, I will call him Ahmadi and nothing else." He paused. "This isn't the start I wanted. Our asset doesn't need to know the rest of the team, or their names. We have already put him in a position where he can compromise himself."

Stella Fox nodded. "Very well," she said, looking awkwardly at Garfield. "We can still make this work, can't we?"

"One of the barns has been converted to accommodation and offices. If... the asset... takes up residence there, Ramsay and I can undertake the briefing. I was going to task Caroline with instructing him on undercover work, she has a solid record with The Det before joining the service." He paused, looking at her. "You can take *Ahmadi* across the yard and to the furthest building, Ramsay and I will be along later. Get him settled in. He has no experience, so start with what you were first taught..."

"I get the idea," she replied tersely. "But I'm not babysitting, when it comes to the operation, I expect to be front and centre in the field, or I walk..." She walked past King and he winked at her as she raised an eyebrow. When she reached the door, she looked back at the asset and said, "Well, are you coming or not?"

King watched the man hesitantly follow. He had already established that the man was terrified, and he hadn't seemed to gain in confidence. If anything, the man looked more scared now than when he had first stepped inside. King couldn't begin to contemplate how he would fair in deep cover. And he still had to convince Ahmadi's wife and son. It wasn't looking promising.

"He'll be ok," Stella Fox said reassuringly.

"Just because you want it to, it doesn't mean it will be," Big Dave commented. "The guy's shitting himself already."

"Getting him in is one thing," said Rashid. "Remaining in play is quite another."

"The dude's got to learn to fly a helicopter when he isn't learning how to be a bloody spook," Flymo added. "I'm not sure if you know, but helicopters aren't the easiest things to learn to fly."

"Evidently," Ramsay said without realising he had made the others laugh.

"Well, this is all *very* encouraging," Stella Fox said exasperatedly. She looked at King and said, "Do you want to add anything?"

"Plenty, but it's not the time." King paused. "The way I see it, we've got a few months to train him. We can do that, no problem. Caroline will start with the tradecraft. The real Ahmadi is an arms dealer, so our asset needs to live and breathe weaponry. He needs books and web browsing, but more than that, he needs to be tested. The poor guy is about to undertake the mother of all night schools. Ahmadi is a snappy dresser, extremely fashion conscious. Again, he needs to learn Ahmadi's wardrobe. Start by getting him to shave and groom and dress like the man every day. Get him the clothes, shoes and toiletries he needs. It says in the file that Ahmadi practises Brazilian Jujitsu. We all know a bit, but it's quite a popular and specialised sport. We need an instructor here most days for at least a couple of months. There's a chap that works in the basement at Thames house who has won competitions, so maybe he can be sworn in to help?"

"We need to keep this department tight," Garfield said pointedly. "The less who know, the better."

"I believe he's a competent analyst and researcher,"

replied King. "I think we need more people on board, given the few things I've pointed out and the multitude of details yet to be discussed."

"I agree," said Ramsay. "And while King is away, with whomever is assisting him, our asset will be slogging away here becoming Ahmadi." He paused, looking at his watch. "I suggest we take a tea break, get settled into our rooms and reconvene in an hour."

King smiled. All he needed to do was toss his bag onto his bed. He glanced at the young man drinking his coffee with apparent disinterest with the goings on around him. "Who's the kid?" he asked, just loud enough for 'the kid' to hear him.

"Jack Luger. He will be working with us," Ramsay replied. He waved the young man over and he ambled over still holding his coffee.

"S'up?" the young man asked then sipped his coffee.

"What's your story?" King asked.

"What's yours?"

"Too long to go into here," King replied.

"I'm not interested in stories," Luger said. "Either hearing yours or telling you my own." He paused. "I get it, I'm young and you're this older guy with all the experience. You don't need to know what brought me here. My story is my own."

King smiled. "That's ok, son. I think I've got yours..."

"Really?" He raised an eyebrow. "Go on, then."

"No, it's alright. I prefer to have some skin in the game."

"What?"

"A stake. First rule, don't ever do anything for free."

"You mean a wager?"

"Of course."

"Will a twenty do you?"

"A hundred would be better..."

"Fine. It's a deal. Want to shake?"

"Of course." King held out his hand, keeping it rigid. He expected some show of dominance, and he got it. But he gave it back, too. He watched the young man's eyes, saw a flicker of pain, or perhaps uncertainty. King gave him an out and pulled his hand away. "Late twenties privately educated then university followed by a gap year. Spent someplace exotic, but with needy kids so you could feel good about yourself doing some charity work along the way. Mum and dad together, stable home, an older sibling and a couple of younger ones, so you're not the doted older child, but mum and dad just kept going after you, so you never really felt truly validated." King paused. "When you came back from your gap year, you thought the military would be an exciting life. RAF? No, navy. Guaranteed travel, which keeps you interesting and away from your siblings. Great uniform, too. For officers, that is, which was the path you naturally took."

"Naturally?"

"Yes. Instant respect and privilege. After training, that is." King paused. "But, considering you're just in your twenties, I'm guessing it didn't work out. Although you got someone's attention, hence your recruitment into the Security Service. So, you have some skills and qualities that will be useful to us. Even if you come with little experience..."

"Ouch..."

King smiled. "How did I do?"

Luger shrugged. "Close enough, although you managed to make having a family and parents still together sound something terrible. We all know it isn't of course, so I suppose that's jealousy on your part." He paused, regarding King closely. "So, that means you had a shitty childhood.

I'm guessing it was worse than I could imagine, so I won't dwell on that, even if you still do. Yes, so far, I've had a decent privileged life, but I'm not going to apologise for that." He put his coffee down, took out his wallet and dropped a fifty, two twenties and a ten-pound note onto the table. "Are you Flymo?" he asked, looking past King. Flymo nodded. "Great, you're meant to come with me to pick up the helicopter. I'm a bit of a glorified taxi driver for now, but I look forward to working with you all."

King watched the young man walk towards the front door without further word. Flymo followed, a spring in his step as he realised that he would be getting in the air soon. King looked at Big Dave and Flymo and shrugged. "Well, that didn't feel as good as it should have..."

"You hit the nail on the bloody head, though. I don't know how you did it," Big Dave said quietly. "No protest, paid up like a decent sort. Even sussed you out, too."

"Amazing," Rashid agreed. "How the hell did you work all that out about him?"

King shrugged. "Garfield sent me his file last night," he replied.

"Shit!" Big Dave laughed, but Rashid pulled a face that told King he had overstepped the line. Big Dave said, "Well, I like the kid. You had a file, but he got your number with just a handshake!" he laughed raucously.

King shrugged like it was no big deal, but as he swept the money off the table and slipped the notes into his pocket, the victory seemed a hollow one at best.

# Chapter Ten

rticle in the Daily Mail

## RUSSIA DEFIANT AMONG ECONOMIC
## UNCERTAINTY

The ongoing war in Ukraine has driven food prices to an all-time high, yet despite the citizens of Russia living through economic sanctions, the Kremlin remains defiant and is planning a new offensive. Dismissing casualty figures as Western propaganda, the Russian president has warned of NATO's support of Ukraine through weapons and military equipment as a dangerous precedence, that will not be without a heavy consequence.

The ongoing conflict between Russia and Ukraine has been a major point of tension in the global political arena for years. Despite multiple diplomatic efforts to resolve the crisis, Russia continues to defy the international community with its aggressive stance towards Ukraine. In recent months, Russia has implemented food and economic sanctions against Ukraine, further escalating the conflict and sparking debates about Western propaganda.The latest round of sanctions imposed by Russia on Ukraine has caused significant economic damage to the country. Russia recently announced a blanket ban on Ukrainian food imports, including meat, dairy, and vegetables. The move has been widely criticised by Ukraine and its Western allies, who argue that the ban is an attempt to punish Ukraine for its pro-Western stance and to undermine its economy.

Russia has also imposed economic sanctions on Ukraine, including restrictions on the transit of Ukrainian goods through Russian territory. This move has caused major disruptions to Ukraine's economy, which relies heavily on exports to Russia. The sanctions have also had a negative impact on Russian businesses, which have lost access to Ukrainian markets.

However, Russia has remained defiant in the face of Western pressure, with many Kremlin officials dismissing the sanctions as propaganda. The Russian president has repeatedly accused the West of spreading false information about the conflict in Ukraine, claiming that Western governments are trying to isolate Russia and weaken its global influence.

Critics of Russia's stance argue that the country's aggressive behaviour towards Ukraine is motivated by a desire to expand its territory and influence in the region. They point to Russia's annexation of Crimea in 2014 and its support for separatist rebels in eastern Ukraine as evidence of its territorial ambitions. Meanwhile, supporters of Russia's actions argue that the country has been unfairly demonised by the Western media, which they claim has been spreading propaganda against Russia. They argue that the conflict in Ukraine is a complex issue that cannot be reduced to a simple narrative of Russian aggression.

Despite the ongoing tensions between Russia and Ukraine, there have been some signs of progress in recent months. In March Ukraine and Russia agreed to a prisoner exchange, which was seen as a positive step towards resolving the conflict. However, the food and economic sanctions imposed by Russia have caused significant setbacks in the efforts to reach a peaceful resolution.

Russia's defiance over Ukraine has created a major point of tension in the global political arena. The food and economic sanctions imposed by Russia have caused significant damage to Ukraine's economy, and media propaganda has further complicated the situation. While there have been some signs of progress towards resolving the conflict, it remains to be seen whether Russia will continue to defy the international community or whether a peaceful resolution can be reached.

# Chapter Eleven

rticle in The Times

## IRAN'S BELLIGERANCE CAUSES NEW TENSIONS

In recent days, tensions have risen between Iran and the international community as the country has defied calls to halt its support for Russian forces in Ukraine. Reports have emerged that Iran has sent missiles to Russian forces in Ukraine, a move that has been widely criticised by Western powers and the United Nations.

Iran's support for Russia in Ukraine has been a point of contention for months, with many in the international community calling for Iran to cease its support for Russian forces. Despite these calls, Iran has continued to provide support to Russia, with reports of missile shipments being the latest example of this defiance.

The Iranian government has not commented on the reports of missile shipments, but officials in Western governments have expressed their concern over Iran's actions. The United States, in particular, has condemned Iran's support for Russia, with Secretary of State Chuck Pliskin stating that, "Iran's actions only serve to escalate the conflict in Ukraine and threaten the security of the region."

The United Nations has also expressed its concern over Iran's actions, with the organization's Secretary-General, Antonio Guterres, calling on Iran to "refrain from any action that could escalate the situation in Ukraine and to respect the sovereignty and territorial integrity of Ukraine."

Despite these calls for restraint, Iran has shown no signs of backing down from its support for Russia in Ukraine. The move has led to fears that the conflict in Ukraine could escalate further, with Iran potentially becoming more involved in the conflict.

The international community has called on Iran to cease its support for Russia in Ukraine and to respect the sovereignty of Ukraine. However, with Iran showing no signs of backing down, it remains to be seen how the situation will unfold in the coming days and weeks.

# Chapter Twelve

rticle in the Daily Telegraph

## CHINA'S DOMINANCE IN WORLD TRADE WILL ROCK THE FOUNDATIONS OF THE WEST

As the world becomes increasingly interconnected, China's dominance in world trade has become more apparent than ever before. In recent years, China has established itself as the world's leading exporter and second-largest importer of goods, and its trade volume is now more significant than that of the United States and the European Union combined. The West's reliance on the East for trade has also become more apparent, with China becoming an essential trading partner for many countries worldwide.

China's success in international trade can be attributed to several factors. The country has a vast population and an abundance of cheap labour, which has allowed it to produce goods at a lower cost than many other countries. China has also invested heavily in infrastructure and technology, making it easier for companies to do business there. In addition, the Chinese government has pursued a policy of export-led growth, which has led to the development of specialised manufacturing zones and the promotion of high-tech industries.

The West's reliance on the East has grown significantly over the past few decades, with China becoming a critical supplier of goods and services to many Western countries. China is the primary source of many products, including electronics, clothing, and household goods, and is also a significant provider of services such as tourism and education. As a result, many Western economies have become increasingly dependent on China for their economic growth.

However, this reliance on China also comes with some risks. For example, the recent COVID-19 pandemic highlighted the vulnerability of global supply chains, with disruptions in China causing significant disruptions to many industries worldwide. In addition, there are concerns about China's human rights record and its trade practices, such as the alleged theft of intellectual property and the manipulation of currency values.

Despite these concerns, China's dominance in world trade is unlikely to diminish anytime soon. The country's rapid economic growth and increasing global influence mean that it will continue to be a major player in international trade for the foreseeable future. The West's reliance on the East for trade is also likely to continue, as many countries seek to take advantage of China's low-cost manufacturing and growing middle class.

China's dominance in world trade and the West's reliance on the East are complex issues that have significant economic and geopolitical implications. As global trade continues to evolve, it will be essential to find a balance between the benefits of international trade and the need to address the risks and challenges that come with it.

# Chapter Thirteen

rticle in The Observer

## WILLING ALLY OR STRATEGIC GLOVE PUPPET?

Russia and Belarus have maintained a strong relationship since the collapse of the Soviet Union. Belarus has been a staunch ally of Russia, and the two countries have enjoyed a long-standing strategic partnership. Belarus has been a crucial source of support for Russia, providing it with a buffer zone in the west and a friendly government on its border.

One of the most significant ways that Belarus supports Russia is through economic ties. Belarus is a major importer of Russian oil and gas, and Russian exports to Belarus account for a significant portion of its overall trade. Belarus also serves as an important transit hub for Russian energy exports to Europe. This has allowed Russia to maintain its position as one of the world's leading energy exporters, despite the challenges posed by international sanctions and political pressure.

In addition to economic support, Belarus has also been a critical political ally for Russia. The two countries are part of a political and economic union known as the Eurasian Economic Union, which also includes Kazakhstan, Armenia, and Kyrgyzstan. This union aims to promote economic integration and cooperation among its member states, and it has helped to strengthen Russia's influence in the region.

Belarus has also been a key supporter of Russia's foreign policy goals. For example, Belarus has supported Russia's actions in Ukraine and has refused to recognise the annexation of Crimea as illegal. This has allowed Russia to maintain a united front in the face of international criticism and to continue pursuing its strategic objectives in the region.

Furthermore, Belarus has also provided military support to Russia. The two countries have conducted joint military exercises, and Belarus has purchased Russian military equipment and weapons systems. This has helped to strengthen the military ties between the two countries and has enabled Russia to maintain a strong presence in the region.

Despite the close relationship between Russia and Belarus, there have been some challenges in recent years. The Belarusian government has sought to balance its ties with Russia and the West, and there have been tensions between the two countries over economic and political issues. However, the overall relationship between Russia and Belarus remains strong, and Belarus continues to provide crucial support to Russia in a variety of ways.

In conclusion, Belarus plays a crucial role in supporting Russia's economic, political, and military objectives. Its support has allowed Russia to maintain its position as a major global power, despite the challenges posed by international sanctions and political pressure. While there have been some challenges in the relationship between the two countries, the overall strategic partnership remains strong and is likely to continue well into the foreseeable future.

# Chapter Fourteen

rticle in The Guardian

## RUSSIA'S RELATIONSHIP OF CONVENIENCE

The ongoing conflict between Ukraine and Russia has been a topic of global concern for several years now. While many nations have condemned Russia's aggression and annexation of Crimea, North Korea has emerged as a surprising supporter of Russia's actions. This support has raised questions about the relationship between North Korea and Russia, as well as the motivations behind North Korea's stance on the Ukraine crisis.

North Korea's support for Russia in the Ukraine conflict is primarily rooted in their shared history of Soviet-style communism. Both North Korea and Russia are former communist countries, and North Korea has long viewed Russia as an ally and supporter of its own communist government. This shared ideology has created a strong bond between the two nations, and North Korea's support for Russia in the Ukraine conflict is a true reflection of this relationship.

Additionally, North Korea has historically had strained relations with the United States and its allies, including Ukraine. As a result, North Korea may see supporting Russia in the Ukraine conflict as a necessary way to demonstrate its own strength and defiance against the Western powers. This is in line with North Korea's broader strategy of isolation and self-sufficiency, which seeks to limit the influence of outside powers on the country.

North Korea's support for Russia in the Ukraine conflict has taken several forms. The country has issued statements condemning Western sanctions against Russia and has expressed support for Russia's annexation of Crimea. In addition, North Korea has reportedly provided military assistance to Russia, including sending military advisors and possibly even supplying weapons.

This support has raised concerns among some countries, including the United States and South Korea, about North Korea's motivations and intentions. Some fear that North Korea's support for Russia in the Ukraine conflict may be an attempt to strengthen its own military capabilities or gain favour with Russia in exchange for support in its own conflicts with the West.

Despite these concerns, it is clear that North Korea's support for Russia in the Ukraine conflict is rooted in a shared ideology and history, as well as North Korea's broader strategy of isolation and defiance against the West. While this support may create tensions with other countries, it is unlikely to significantly shift the balance of power in the conflict or have a major impact on global politics. Nonetheless, it is a reminder that North Korea remains a key player in international relations and must be taken seriously in discussions of global security and stability.

# Chapter Fifteen

King tossed the copy of The Guardian onto the pile of strewn newspapers and sat back with his mug of tea. He had woken early and taken a run around the perimeter of the farm. There was no security fence around the perimeter, just hedges, rustic post and rails and barbed wire strands on top of sheep wire. It had been a working farm, after all. The run had taken King up steep hills and along a stream at the bottom of a valley. He had assessed that logistically speaking, the property was only safe from where the CCTV picked up on all sides. If anything, the land provided would-be attackers enough cover to get within three hundred metres of the farmhouse. He decided that he would advise Ramsay or Garfield on some procedures that they could implement, but with the Exmoor wildlife so prevalent, it would be easier suggested than done. He had showered and had a brew and started on the papers. He wondered whether people had started to pick up on the five countries that made up the Iron Fist. Certainly, the papers had singularly covered them, although so far, they were not making the connection. In a world where faceless people on social media pedalled or believed all manner of conspiracy theories, it would be all too easy to discount the Iron Fist as fanciful propaganda.

King checked his watch. It was still only six-thirty-am, but he could hear movement upstairs. Somebody had collected the papers, but there was still no sign of life downstairs. He had left Caroline sleeping, which was unusual, but they had broken their usual stance and talked about the operation into the early hours. King had left out conning Jack Luger out of a hundred pounds. It hadn't been his finest hour. It wasn't like him to ride a new recruit like that. And in the small hours, as Caroline had finally fallen asleep beside him, he thought back to his relationship with his old mentor, the tough, no-nonsense alcoholic Scotsman Peter Stewart. A man who put King through hell. A man who taught him everything he knew about being an agent and assassin. He had dragged King through the hardest of times, moulded him into a formidable operative. Stewart had always had King's back, but he had dished out a great deal of vitriol as well. The Scotsman had once set King up. He hadn't had much choice in the matter, but years later he had taken a bullet and died for King and that had set things right by him. Had King seen something of himself in Luger, and subconsciously taken the role of Stewart? It was a reach at best. But it left him wondering if he was starting to feel his age and indeed, felt threatened by the man's youth.

"Coffee?"

King looked around and saw Luger standing behind him. He hadn't heard the man approach, and it unnerved him. *Jesus!* He thought. *Get a grip...* Had a few months swimming and fishing and sailing dulled his edge that much? "No, can't stand the stuff," he replied holding up his mug. "I'll have another tea, though. White with one sugar..."

He got off the sofa and walked over to where Luger was starting to make what looked like an impossibly strong coffee. "That's going to taste like tar, isn't it?"

"Sets me up for the day. Coffee all day, then dinner. Suppresses the appetite."

"Don't tell Big Dave. He won't know what to do with that information."

"Likes his grub?"

"And then some." King tossed the hundred pounds onto the counter. "We got off on the wrong foot yesterday."

"You won, fair and square."

"No, I didn't. I stacked the odds in my favour. You'll learn that's what we always try to do, but not among each other."

"Ok..."

King held out his hand. He was damned if he was going to morph into his former mentor. "I apologise."

"Ah, you two kissing and making up?" Big Dave commented as he walked in. "What's for scran, new bloke?"

"Scran?"

"Yeah, food." Big Dave opened the fridge and started to systematically empty it onto the counter. "Hungry?"

"No," Luger replied. "I've got a coffee."

"Can't eat coffee," Big Dave replied, looking at his cup. "Although that does look thick enough to chew." He opened two packets of bacon and set about laying the dozen or so rashers into a pan. He then repeated the process with a whole packet of sausages and put both pans on the gas rings. "Breakfast, King?"

"No, I might try this fasting lark. A couple of mugs of tea and see how long I can last."

"For fuck's sake..."

"Are you cooking for everyone?" Luger asked, looking at the mountain of meat now sizzling in the pans.

"The shitest Muslim in history might have a sausage sarnie," he replied. "Caroline will hit the muesli and Ramsay will have toast, butter and marmalade. Don't know what Garfield eats of a morning…"

"So, that's all for you?"

"Is Flymo here?"

"No. He's bringing the helicopter down later."

"Then yes. This is all mine, so hands off…"

"Jesus…"

King watched Big Dave turning the bacon in the pan. It smelled divine. "Fuck it, do us a bacon sarnie, will you?"

"Not fasting?" Big Dave chided.

"I think you need coffee to do it…" He paused. "Ask the kid." King could have cringed but managed to do so only on the inside. He was in his early forties but starting to sound old to his own ears, so Christ knew how he was sounding to others.

"It's Jack," Luger threw it out there.

"What the hell kind of name is Luger, anyway?" King asked but found himself wondering if it was a pseudonym just like his own. He had been Alex King for so long now that he genuinely forgot his birthname until he was reminded.

"It's nothing to do with the gun," Luger replied. "Or, it might have been, but nothing shows in my family history. My great grandfather fought in the Second World War with the Desert Rats in North Africa, and his father was at the Somme." He paused. "But it is Germanic in origin, something about people from the marshes or bogs in the north-east of the country."

"Boggy?" Big Dave asked, looking at King.

"It has a ring to it..."

"For fuck's sake, you're not calling me Boggy..."

King laughed. "No, we'll save you that fate," he said.

Big Dave dished up his meat feast and with an open bag of sliced white bread, started to turn everything into a folded sandwich, packing bacon and sausage inside. It was quite a sight to behold. A disappearing assembly line. King saved enough for a bacon sandwich and ate it while they both watched Big Dave like an eating challenge inadvertently viewed online.

"Bloody hell, Dave. That's half a pig!" Caroline appeared and made her way to the coffee machine. She worked the buttons confidently and after a few minutes sat at the table with a lungo, which she drank black and unsweetened.

"What's happening today?" Jack Luger asked.

"Best not to ask in this game," Big Dave said through a mouthful of bacon and sausage.

"Exactly," Garfield said as he walked in with Neil Ramsay following. "Coffee would be my first port of call. Caroline, I would like you to babysit the asset for the next two hours, after which, you will get your tasks and targets set."

"Babysit..." she glared. "I said that's not what I'm going to be doing..."

"Figure of speech. Keep him busy with some continuation of tradecraft," Garfield said, quite unperturbed by her indignation. "King, we'll see you first. Afterwards, Jack and Lomu, you will be given your orders. Where's Rashid?"

"Here," Rashid said as he walked in. "Crickey, it's all morning people here..."

"I've saved you a sausage sarnie," Big Dave commented. "Or half of one."

"Nice..."

"You're a Muslim?" Jack asked incredulously.

"It's complicated."

"He chooses the best bits," Big Dave chided. "Like not going to the Mosque on Sundays."

"Fridays," Rashid corrected him.

"And drinking..." Caroline interjected.

"You're worse than my mother..." Rashid retorted, but he was almost drowned out as the sound of a helicopter engulfed the house. "Sounds like he's putting it down on the roof!"

Everyone made their way to a window, but King walked to the front door and stepped outside. When he stopped at the edge of the garden, Rashid and Caroline were at his shoulder watching Flymo banking the Sikorsky 109 just fifty feet off the ground. The helicopter spun one-hundred-and-eighty degrees and ended in a hover. A few seconds later and it was on the ground, the rotors winding down.

"Slow and steady are two words he's never heard of," said Rashid.

"Thank goodness for that," King replied. "Because whenever we need him, we need to get the hell out of there..."

# Chapter Sixteen

I stanbul, Turkey

Ahmadi put down the sheet of paper and sipped some of the superbly rich and thick coffee which had been served black and loaded with sugar. The coffee had come with tall glasses of iced water, which was needed every now and then to slake the caffeine on the palate. The hotel coffee bar was open-aired, and decked in teak with chrome fixtures, and their table was separated by the water by just a few feet of elevation and a thin balcony of glass.

There was fifty-million dollars' worth of armaments on the list, and Ahmadi knew that he could provide half of the equipment with just a few emails. The rest would take a few days to figure out. Some items were being held in other countries, and there would be a few bribes to make to the usual customs people, but he was confident that he could provide everything to meet his client's needs.

"My organisation can no longer rely on state-sanctioned funding," Sergei Koromiko said quietly. "But I find it strange that they send me to an Iranian. In Turkey, no less."

Both men spoke in English. The common language they shared, as well as their love of the US dollar. There should have been some irony in there somewhere, but neither man seemed to pick up on it. Beside them the Bosporus, choppy and dark, did not mirror the bright azure-blue sky and orange glow of the sun to the west.

"The Wagner Group has grown too politically sensitive, too volatile, even for its own orchestrators. But you can still do good work for Mother Russia, even if they distance themselves from the original orchestrators, as well as the financial end, and use only intermediaries like myself." Ahmadi paused. "I can supply all the small arms. Chinese surplus Type-95 rifles, as they are currently replacing them with the new QBZ-191."

Koromiko nodded. "I do not like the ammunition..."

Ahmadi nodded. The Chinese saved money by pressing their 5.8x42mm ammunition out of steel instead of brass cartridges. Like other countries now favouring smaller, high velocity bullets, China had come up with something in between Russia's 5.45x39mm and NATO's 5.56x45mm. However, steel cases required a lacquer to prevent rusting and tarnishing, and this lacquer had been proven to become sticky under high temperatures. Like the climate in hot countries, or somewhat more importantly, the heat generated under heavy automatic fire. "I can over supply," he said confidently. "The Chinese has a thousand times more ammunition in storage than the rest of the world combined. And for you, more weapons mean more spare parts, and more ammunition is, well, better in every way."

"Even so..."

"It is a solid weapon," Ahmadi interrupted the Russian mercenary. "The bullpup design is light, easy to wield and because the working parts are behind the operator's cheek, a longer barrel can be used for enhanced velocity and range, and still keep the weapon compact. The British have favoured their SA80 since the nineteen-eighties, even though it underwent twenty years of battlefield testing and development before it was eventually corrected and turned into a decent weapon system. The French favour such a design also, with their FAMAS."

"Wagner soldiers prefer Kalashnikov rifles." He shrugged. "But then again, more is more. Say, twenty percent more?"

"Agreed."

"And the other items?"

"Rocket launchers, mortars and grenades... no problem. The mobile missile launchers will be Russian, Chinese, or Iranian made and can be towed by civilian four-by-four pickups or whatever military vehicles that you have to hand. I can get you field guns, but it will take more time. The helicopters, also. But it can be done. When the US pulled out of Afghanistan, they left us many great things. Even a few Black Hawk helicopters. These have been dismantled, stored in shipping containers and will set sail for Crimea the moment you transfer the funds. Iranian battle helicopters will follow soon afterwards. They are Italian made Augusta aircraft that have been retro-fitted with American missile systems and Russian gatling guns."

"It will be like no other offensive ever seen in the Ukraine," the Russian grinned wolfishly.

"How many men has Wagner got?"

"Fifty-thousand and counting," the Russian said confidently. "The Kremlin has granted any Russian prisoner freedom and a clean record. All they need is to commit to six-months' service to Wagner. They will be paid as well, and many will stay on. From our last batch of former prisoners, over seventy percent of survivors remained in service with Wagner. Many of the men simply love to rape and kill... it was why they were in prison in the first place."

"And the casualties? Were they as heavy as the media reported?"

"It's not good to believe everything your see or hear in the media..." The Russian shrugged. "Russia has lost forty-thousand men. The Wagner Group have lost more than sixty-thousand men. But there are many willing to take their place. What's better? Serving twenty-years for rape or murder in a gulag, or giving six months of your life to fighting in the Ukraine?" Ahmadi did not answer. The man's question had been purely rhetorical. Most people would have taken the deal given to the Russian prisoners, even if basic military training for prisoners without military experience was usually around three days. An indication, perhaps, to why the casualty rate was so high in the early days of the war. He remembered when the Wagner Group were real soldiers, often operating for the GRU or FSB under a civilian mercenary flag, but now many of those men had perished and Wagner was simply a group of killers who enjoyed their work. "And the other items?" the Russian asked.

Ahmadi nodded. "From China," he said. "But my Chinese contacts will want to relabel the merchandise first."

"And you can get enough of the stuff?"

"Enough," Ahmadi replied. "Enough to make a world of difference."

# Chapter Seventeen

Seven hundred metres away, from the fourth storey window of an apartment building, Ahmadi's head was in clear view through the powerful Zeiss field glasses. Former SAS major Scott MacPherson made notes beside him, not moving his eyes from the rest-mounted binoculars as he scribbled shorthand on the notepad with a pencil. He could only see a partial view of Sergei Koromiko's profile, so he could only lip-read half the conversation. But he had enough. The Russian had given the Iranian a shopping list, and it looked like the arms dealer was going to deliver everything on the list.

The silenced pistol rested on the table beside him. He had pulled the table up to the window and was now seated on one of the chairs with the binoculars focused on Ahmadi and his associate, locked into position on the small camera tripod. Behind him, a woman and her two children were seated on the other three chairs, their wrists and ankles bound in the same duct tape that sealed their mouths shut. He had needed their apartment and when she had seen the pistol the woman had complied. The man was a professional, and if they continued to cooperate, and just as long as her husband did not arrive home early from work, then he would untie them and leave them unharmed. But if it did not work out like that, then he would lose no sleep over silencing them permanently.

MacPherson worked for an intelligence department that answered only to the serving Prime Minister of the day. There was no name for this organisation, although recent events had brought the department to the attention of the world's media after more than a hundred years of anonymity. The man unveiled as its boss was Sir Galahad Mereweather, although he had rigorously denied and deflected the attention. The Prime Minister had denied all knowledge, too. The department had ridden out the storm, although because of Mereweather's first name, the department had been referred to by the media as 'The Round Table', from Arthurian legend. There had been much speculation about Sir Galahad's son, the late Simon Mereweather, who had been the head of MI5 at the time of his murder in Switzerland. Officially, Sir Galahad had distanced himself, an easy thing to do with an organisation that did not exist. He was still in charge, but there were going to be some changes and restructuring. They would continue the work they had done for almost a century without detection. Sir Galahad was still accountable for a quantity of gold being discovered and filmed by a journalist, but considering the links that the gold had to former members of the Royal family who had been sympathetic to the Nazi's cause, follow-up stories would appear to have been suppressed.

MacPherson's brief had been simple. Gain as much intelligence on Ahmadi and avert action that would harm the United Kingdom. As ambiguous as the second half of that brief read, the man would not be assembling his sniper rifle today. Britain was a friend of Ukraine, but that would not cover his brief. It was still early days. A man like Ahmadi would have many friends and those friends would be Britain's enemy. Sooner or later one of those enemies would fit the brief, and Ahmadi would step into the man's sights.

# Chapter Eighteen

**P**aris,
**Three weeks later**

King gazed out at the view across the city, the Eiffel Tower in the distance, the sounds of Paris playing out on the streets below. He checked his watch, then sipped his tea and ate his croissant and thought about the man he was about to become. King had spent until the early hours reading up on the man, night upon night, day upon day. He could answer just about anything when asked, felt he had become the man in more ways than one. There was more than a passing resemblance to the man who had been selected. In keeping with the character, King had cut his hair short with a grade 4 buzz-cut and dyed his light brown hair – which was now a little salt and pepper at the sides – a darker shade of brown all over. His eyebrows that were lighter, almost fair in the summer, had been given the same treatment, and thinned out considerably. The memory of Caroline plucking them with tweezers while Rashid and Big Dave ripped him apart was one that would live on with him forever.

Jon Wood had a good history from a 'legend' perspective. Orphaned at seventeen, he joined the British army at eighteen and had an unremarkable five-year career, although he had served a tour in Iraq and had been mentioned in dispatches for a firefight lasting three hours that had taken heavy casualties. Corporal J. Wood had dragged a wounded colleague to safety and engaged three of the enemy single-handedly. If it hadn't been for an incident in camp involving a fight and vandalism, he would have received a medal, but not all things in the British army were easily forgotten or forgiven. Disillusioned, Wood had left the army and after a string of jobs and minor public order offences, he had been arrested for handling stolen goods and served six months in Belmarsh prison. An assault outside a pub saw him back inside, this time serving time in three different prisons for a total of nine months. King had found himself easily understanding, even empathising with the man. After all, it had mirrored much of King's youth. A string of failed businesses had landed Wood in trouble with HMRC for VAT misappropriation and back taxes. He could not pay the fines, so amid bankruptcy he had served another six months in prison for his lack of judgement. Wood's history and record took a pause after he worked overseas for a few years on oil rigs and in the merchant navy. After a few scrapes and sackings, he ended up protecting ships in the Red Sea and Arabian Gulf from pirates. The work had been easy. Three meals a day, a cabin to himself and twelve-hour shifts watching the horizon for small boats or manning the radar at night and sweeping the darkness with powerful searchlights. Smoke grenades and water cannon were the first deterrents, but live ammunition was often used, targeting the engine and below the water-line, followed by live targets when all other options had failed. It was good work for a man who had military experience and didn't want to work hard for his money. Wood did this work for a few more years then travelled the world for a year with money he had saved. He popped up on the radar with a speeding fine in Queensland and a drunk and disorderly charge which was later dropped in New South Wales. He was hospitalised in California after stepping in front of a car in Long Beach, and with no travel insurance, left the hospital without settling his bill. There was another couple of years with no information on Jon Wood until he was employed by an events security company in London. This time, he was paying national insurance and tax and saving some of his money in an ISA. His current account was usually down to double figures by the end of the month, but that was nothing unusual in these times. The private security industry asks civilians to do much of the work of the police but without the authority. It was only a matter of time before Jon Wood would find himself on the wrong side of the law while going to the aid of fellow nightclub security staff being attacked by a gang of drunks. Wood was later charged with assault and later manslaughter when the unfortunate victim who had hit the pavement a little too hard later died from a blood clot. Nothing out of the ordinary, but pavements were hard, and skulls were not. Wood was sentenced to six years but got out in three. Only he didn't. The man known as Jon Woods was stabbed in prison over an argument about a bag of sugar and died from his injuries. With no living family, no partner and few friends his body was claimed by a man from MI5 with all the right paperwork and Official Secrets Act papers for the governor and prison officers to sign. Wood's body was disposed of in the prison incinerator, and after entering the prison from the back of a van in the deliveries yard, Alex King had walked out of the gates and into the life of Jon Wood, former soldier, convicted criminal and the man about to infiltrate the Iron Fist.

# Chapter Nineteen

Ramsay had ensured that Jon Wood's bank accounts had remained open and he had back dated monies into the account with the cooperation of the bank. More Official Secrets Act documents signed and dated, then filed where they could be lost and denied if necessary. King now had an operating capital of twenty-thousand pounds, with access to another twenty thousand in Wood's ISA. This now put pins in maps that could trace King's movements and provide a trail for Ahmadi's people to follow when the time came – if they could be that lucky. The next three months would be checkable and easily confirmed. Wood's time in prison would account for the gaps. Jon Wood's life was laid out like a road, only after his death, MI5 had taken another turn and staged the rest of the journey.

There were various people in MI5's clasp. Often referred to as 'assets', some were people who had cut a deal for their freedom, others were targeted and recruited because of their position. Position could be their employment, or their husband or wife's social circle, the friend or relative of somebody influential or compromised. Assets were guided and instructed by a handler known as an 'agent'. Some assets were willing participants and had approached the Security Service out of feelings of patriotism. But most were not. One such asset was a man named Jordan White, a career criminal in south London who simply could not do the time for his crime. He had cut a deal with the police and when the criminal outfit he worked for crossed paths with terrorists – no more than a supply and demand issue – MI5 had become involved and taken Jordan White under their wing. The criminal organisation that Jordan White worked for did not have a name. Its leader was a fifty-year-old south London gangster called Ronnie Vickers who had kept himself out of prison for ten years and was always well-distanced from any crimes or associations. Under constant surveillance by the National Crime Agency, Vickers had escaped their clutches by becoming an excellent planner. Jordan White had become the man's right-hand man, and now he was easily manipulated by the Security Service because once he crossed the line to avoid jailtime, he was controlled by simply implying that it would be the easiest thing in the world to send Vickers transcripts, photographs, and film footage of their association with the gang leader's second in command. Simply put, there was nothing that Jordan White would not agree too, because to risk the alternative was to guarantee his own gruesome murder at the hands of his fellow gang members. Jordan White was now a valuable asset and when Ramsay had met with the MI5 agent handling him, he had left the meeting having secured King's first iteration of Jon Wood's new record.

# Chapter Twenty

Paris

King was aware that he was being watched. Not by Rashid and Big Dave, who were shadowing him as back-up, but by unknown forces. He did not have communication with the team for security reasons – he could not risk being seen to talk into a mic and if he was searched and found to be wired, then it would all be over. In more ways than one. But he knew that the criminal gang that Jordan White had put him with would be doing their own surveillance. The asset had told Ramsay as much. King did not try to spot Rashid or Big Dave. He doubted he would, anyway. Rashid had procured a silenced M4 assault rifle with a decent optic set-up. King did not know the details, but Rashid had assured him that it was zeroed and would be close to hand, which meant that he would be mobile. Most likely inside a van with Big Dave driving. King thought about this as he walked, choosing a route which did not go against one-way systems. The pair would have to keep up with him, but he would do everything in his power to make sure that they did not have a tough time doing so.

King saw the CCTV cameras ahead of him, and alien as it was, he made no effort to avoid his image being captured. He had used his debit card in an ATM and withdrawn two hundred euros for walking around money. It was all to create a trail, a checkable history for the man he had become. Jon Wood. A clumsy criminal who used his own debit card and got himself captured on video, despite being on his way to meet a criminal gang.

# Chapter Twenty-One

"We will have one minute," Macron said in faultless English. There were two British, a Pole and a German in their gang of eight and English was the only practical answer. King had refreshed himself with enough French to understand when he was being spoken about, which he had been but so far, they trusted him because of his contact in the form of Jordan White. Of course, they were rude about him, but the French and the English had never truly got along. "One minute to stop the armoured car, kill the two guards in the cab, blow the doors and kill the three guards in the back."

"And... *zey 'ave* to be killed?" a tall, thin French man asked in poor English somewhat meekly. "I mean... armed robbery *iz* one thing, but five murders *iz* quite another..."

Macron stared at the man, then looked at each man in turn. "Does anyone else have a problem with killing some fat ex-cops working for minimum wage?"

King shrugged, thinking that he might as well set the tone. "Not me. I'll take out the guys in the front. Anyone worried by the messy visuals can take the rear, chances are the charges will do the job for them."

Macron smiled. Jon Wood had come highly recommended. "Anyone else want to volunteer for the guards in the front? No?" He looked back at King and said, "Very well, Wood. The job's yours..."

King nodded, the other men looking at him uncomfortably. He had shown his hand as a killer and he could already tell that the other men were not only wary of him, but secretly hoping that what he had said about the charges would be true. The scenario of killing men inside a ten by six metal box was akin to shooting fish in a barrel. Not only was there no sport in it, but it was up close and personal. The rear of the van would be full of acrid smoke and phosphorus from the charges, the guards would be blinded, likely deafened from the blast and clawing to escape the smoke and heat. King had seen worse, and they would all assume that Jon Wood had.

"What's the take?" the other Brit asked. His name was Riley, and he was a career criminal out of the Eastend who worked for Ronnie Vickers.

"*Quoi*?" Macron frowned.

"How much?" Riley said loudly, as if volume was all that was needed in the first instance.

"Ten million euro, guaranteed." Macron paused. He had done a deal with Ronnie Vickers and other crime bosses across Europe. "It splits equally, however, your respective bosses get half of your... *take*."

Riley shrugged. He was pleased with anything over a hundred thousand for just a few days work. King nodded, mirroring Riley's enthusiasm. But he had other plans.

# Chapter Twenty-Two

They had gone over the plan a dozen times. Each time with the same conclusion. They would strike hard, strike fast and show no mercy. The underpass would provide them with the cover they needed, and they knew that they would have no more than a few minutes to blow the doors, kill the guards and unload the money into the waiting vans. There would be two guards in the cab, three in the back. In accordance with new legislation in 2018, the guards would not only be armed with batons and pepper spray, but one of the guards up front, and one in the back would be armed with a .38 revolver. Enough to present a problem for them.

King had been given a pistol, but he knew that he may not get through the toughened glass with such a weapon, so had argued the case for a sawn-off shotgun and solid slugs. The cartridges contained a 1oz lead and copper rifled bullet designed to spin inside the smooth bore of the shotgun. Initially designed to tackle large game in areas of human population where high-powered rifles could be a concern, and for American woodsmen who may just have a shotgun for everyday small game, but needed something appropriate for deer, or threat from bears. There would be no bears today, but two blasts from point blank range would punch through any armoured glass rated for security courier firms. From there on in, it would be quite another matter.

King drew a steady breath, the incessant smoke from the two men chain-smoking in the front seats getting to his chest. He already had the window open a crack, and he told the driver to open his own.

"*Non,*" the Frenchman replied. He was a man named Jacques and he was a former French Foreign Legionnaire.

King could eat legionnaires for breakfast, but there was only another five minutes to go. Besides, he already knew how the man's day was going to pan out. Instead, he opened the breach of the sawn-off and loaded a cartridge into each of the two barrels. The .380 Beretta automatic nestled in his inside jacket pocket. Thirteen rounds. Enough to do the job.

"Don't close the breach of that shotgun while you are sitting behind me..." Jacques said coldly.

"Well, that depends."

"On what?"

"On whether you open your fucking window or not..."

The Pole in the front passenger seat shook his head and said, "Open the window, Jacques."

The Frenchman begrudgingly opened his window a touch and the smoke started to waft outside. King checked his watch. Another minute and he'd take up position. Beside him, a Frenchman called Jean checked his watch also, and opened the bag resting in his lap. The tension was high, almost tangible inside the car.

"You guarantee that these charges will give us five seconds to get clear?" Jean asked King.

"Absolutely," King replied. He had made the charges

himself and they had tested them on an old van in a quarry fifty miles to the south of the city. "Just wait until I have taken care of the guards in the cab. I'll shout clear, then attach them and walk briskly away."

"*Briskly?*"

"Quickly. But don't run. You don't want to slip on the wet street surface. And get down behind something or walk behind the blast. Ninety degrees should do it."

Jean nodded. He was a thief, but this was well outside his comfort zone and lived experience. In practice he had been tentative handling the charges, but they had been shaped expertly and blew the rear doors inwards. It was all in the shaping of the plastic explosive and the position of the detonator. These ones were RDX, and the plastic explosive was American $C_4$ liberated by the Taliban in Afghanistan after the American's withdrawal and sold on to both terrorists and criminal gangs alike.

King snapped the barrels shut and smiled as Jacques flinched in the seat in front of him. He slipped the weapon inside his jacket as he got out, looking all around and catching the eye of the driver in the BMW X5 SUV on the other side of the road. The vehicle had bull bars fitted and reinforced steel bars running back on either side of the engine, welded to a roll cage inside the cabin. The traction control and ABS had been switched off at the fuse box and the airbags had been disconnected. King watched as the Audi A6 saloon pulled out of a turning, cutting in front of a blue and white armoured security van. The Audi accelerated up to forty-miles-per-hour and when it had passed King and entered the shadow of the underpass, it hammered on its brakes. The brake light bulbs had been removed and it was enough to ruin the armoured van driver's reaction time. The van broke suddenly, but too late.

It crashed into the rear of the Audi as the powerful BMW SUV accelerated and slammed into the rear quarter of the armoured van and drove it across the road by a car's width. King was running hard. He had the shotgun out and as he skidded to a halt he fired twice through the windscreen as the other men crowded around the rear of the van and took the charges out of two bags. King dropped the shotgun to the pavement and thrust his gloved hands into his pockets and retrieved two grenades. One was a flashbang developed by the SAS. A blindingly white light, followed by a terrific 'bang' that would render anyone in the vicinity temporarily blind and deaf. The grenade was instantly followed through the holes in the glass by another which was a canister around the size of a soft drink can. The canister was activated by a 12g $CO_2$ gas capsule that released pressurised chloroform in a mist that filled the cabin with the incapacitating agent. King drew the pistol and fired over the bonnet of the van and into the offside front and rear tyres of the Audi, then emptied the magazine at the front wing, sending bullets into the engine bay where they cracked the engine block, severed pipes and wires, and damaged everything from electrical fuses to coolant reservoirs. King just hoped that he'd got lucky and that the vehicle would be put out of action. He shouted 'clear' and ducked down while the men, thinking that he had killed the men inside the cab, attached the charges. The five seconds he had given them in practice was now little more than one, and as he cupped his ears to the tremendous sound of the explosion, the vehicle rocked forwards and the bodies of the gang were blown into the air. The effect of the explosion was all about the shape of the charges, and King had changed the charges to suit his objective. He took a far smaller charge out of his pocket, attached it to the door handle and stepped aside as it blew the lock away. He then slipped a mask over his mouth and nose and set about moving the unconscious driver over to his companion. As he drove away, he watched the driver get out of the ruined X5 and survey the carnage of bodies and vehicle parts in the road. The Audi did not follow, either.

He knew that he had around five more minutes before the guards regained consciousness. Ramsay had assured him that the technicians at the UK Government's military test facility at Porton Down were confident in the incapacitating agent, but that it depended on several factors, which he could not recall right now. Weight, blood pressure and peak flow lung capacity were in there somewhere. He could see that size mattered, as the largest of the two men was already starting to stir. The space of the cabin would have played a vital part as well.

King saw the large Renault van ahead and checked his mirrors. Nobody on his tail, but that would not last long if he travelled much further. He slowed, pulled in front of the lorry and into the alleyway. It was a dead end, and when the van pulled into the entrance boxing him in, the alley darkened, and the noise of the street was partially blocked out. Big Dave leapt down from the cab and jogged down the alley. King switched off the engine and unlocked the front doors, then set about pulling the large man's hands behind his back. Big Dave opened the passenger door and handed King the heavy-duty cable ties, which he took and fastened tightly around the man's wrists. Big Dave removed the .38 revolver from the man's holster had the other guard trussed up similarly and they pulled both men out and eased them over their shoulders.

"Something's wrong here," said King. "You've got the light fella."

"You're not exactly small, mate."

"Even so..." He watched as all six-four and eighteen stone of Dave Lomu tossed the unconscious man unceremoniously through the sliding side loading door of the van. King followed suit but managed to rest the man down with a little more empathy, even if his fall was broken by the smaller of the two guards.

"Now for the guys in the back..."

King nodded and took out another chloroform canister. "This may be tricky," he said. "At least one of these guys will be armed with a revolver, and all of them have CS gas and batons."

"Did cruising around the Med make you soft?"

"Piss off!"

"Let's get it done then," said Big Dave as he put on his mask.

King attached his own mask, then set the charge and stepped around the vehicle to wait out the three-second fuse. There was a flash of light and a dull thud, and he swung around and dropped the canister into the rear of the van and waited until the hiss of the $CO_2$ initiated mist of chloroform did its work. There were three thuds and the vehicle rocked on its springs as the guards hit the metal flooring. King opened the door tentatively, the small automatic in his hand as he waited for the mist to clear. All three men were out cold, and King picked the revolver off the floor and helped Big Dave secure their wrists. They each carried a man back to the van, and Big Dave made the next trip while King stacked the cases of money near the rear doors.

"Will these have dye canisters inside?" asked Big Dave.

"Undoubtedly," replied King.

"What about trackers?"

"It's a possibility. Have you got the bag I left?"

"Yes."

"Go and get it," King snapped. "Hurry!"

Big Dave rarely did things at the double, but he jogged to the van and picked up the bag. King looked around as he heard a terrific 'thump' and then a hollow 'bang' and echo from the van. When Big Dave got back, he said, "The big guy was awake and moving around."

"Was?"

"He's gone night-night now." He paused, inspecting his knuckles. "What's in the bag? It's about as heavy as one of those blokes back there."

King winced at the thought of a Big Dave-sized fist giving the good news without being able to block it. What his mentor Peter Stewart had referred to as a battlefield anaesthetic. He opened the bag and took out several heavy black vinyl bags. "Lead lined. Xray proof and thick enough to kill the signal of a tracking device." He put the first case into one of the bags and started on the rest as Big Dave took his cue and ferried the bag back to the van. There were six cases in all, and King brought the last of them with him, and after he threw it through the open door he leapt inside as Big Dave got behind the wheel. "Let's get the hell out of here," he said. "Head for the drop-off point. And keep it steady, there's no reason for anyone to suspect anything."

# Chapter Twenty-Three

C hequers Court, Ellesborough
         (The    Prime    Minister's    official
         country residence)

They had been served pan-seared scallops and buttered
samphire from Cornwall, smoked salmon and fine-milled
oatcakes from Scotland and the Herefordshire beef with a
show-stopping horseradish ice-cream. The chef had served
the beef fillet as a classic Wellington, with the twist of slow-
braised shin of beef mini cottage pies on the side and chilled
slithers of carpaccio of sirloin with braised red cabbage and
buttered carrots, along with a show-stopping horseradish
ice-cream. As usual with such occasions, the food was
under-appreciated by virtue of the conversation and political and social agenda. A classic Eton Mess was served for
dessert, but as an inside joke, as the Prime Minister had
attended Harrow and the classic dessert was always served
by Eton College at the annual cricket match with Harrow
School. The notion was lost on many of the guests. Cheese

and port followed and when everyone had returned from toilet breaks or cigars on the patio, the first of the speeches started.

"Ladies and gentlemen," Stella Fox said confidently. In her previous career in finance and as an actuary she had given speeches all over the world. "I stand before you today to talk about the dangers of Artificial Intelligence, or AI, when given a specific destructive task with no switch off code written into the programming. I fear that AI is the biggest threat to our nation, and the most dangerous and utterly unpredictable enemy the intelligence services face today." She paused, reading the room. Predictably, the group of men and women representing the country's technology sector seemed bemused. "While AI has the potential to bring about tremendous benefits to humanity, such as improving efficiency and productivity, there are also significant risks associated with the technology, particularly when it is not properly regulated or monitored. One of the most significant dangers of AI is when it is given a specific destructive task with no switch off. This is often referred to as terminal degradation. This means that the AI system is programmed to carry out a certain action or set of actions, and once it begins, it cannot be stopped. This could have catastrophic consequences if the AI system were to malfunction or if its actions were to have unintended consequences.

"Consider, for example, an AI system that is designed to control a nuclear power plant. If this system were to malfunction or be hacked by our enemies, it could cause a catastrophic nuclear meltdown that could have devastating consequences for human life and the environment. Similarly, an AI system that is programmed to control a military drone could potentially carry out lethal attacks on innocent civilians if it were to malfunction or be hacked. The problem with these kinds of AI systems is that they are designed to act autonomously, without human intervention. This means that if something goes wrong, there is no way to stop them from carrying out their destructive task. Once they are set in motion, they will continue until their task is complete, even if that means causing harm or destruction in the process.

"To prevent these kinds of scenarios from occurring, it is essential that we regulate and monitor AI systems carefully. We must ensure that AI systems are designed with fail-safe mechanisms that allow them to be shut down or overridden in the event of a malfunction or unintended consequence. We must also ensure that AI systems are subject to rigorous testing and quality control measures before they are deployed in the field." The technology table were talking among themselves, apparently uninterested in her concerns. She scanned the room, the Prime Minister and Defence Minister giving her their full attention. "In conclusion, while AI has the potential to bring about tremendous bene-fits to humanity, it also poses significant risks when it is given a specific destructive task with no switch off. It is up to us as a society to ensure that we regulate and monitor AI systems carefully, to prevent them from causing harm or destruction. I see current technology trends pushing us too quickly, too confidently towards a precipice from which there will be no return. Legislation is needed desperately, and indeed, immediately. Thank you."

Ninety minutes later and Stella Fox had taken to the patio where she nursed her gin and tonic and one of her rare cigarettes. Bankers, technology gurus and social forecasters had all spoken and if there was one thing to be garnered from the speeches, it was the rise in technology and unprecedented speed in development. There were notable points she considered. The wristwatch, for example. Developed in the First World War by soldiers wanting a more practical application than the pocket watch, it was already technically outdated. Every mobile phone had a clock – undoubtedly more accurate thanks to the atomic clock – and smart watches could take your pulse, read your blood pressure, and be used to text and email. The classic automatic wristwatch existed only for status and for people who enjoyed the analogue. There were doubts that the wristwatch would even exist in the next fifty years. Cars had developed from single horsepower units more akin to a motorised carriage, to exceeding two-hundred-miles-per-hour in less than a hundred years, and man first took flight less than sixty years before orbiting the earth. So, what of computer technology? The history of computers can be traced back to the 1800s when the concept of a programmable machine was first proposed by mathematician Charles Babbage. However, it wasn't until the mid-1900s that computers as we know them today began to emerge.

In 1936, Alan Turing introduced the concept of a universal machine that could simulate any other machine's behaviour through a series of instructions. This laid the foundation for modern computing and the development of the first electronic computers. In the 1940s, the first electronic computers were built, including the Colossus, which was used by the British to crack German codes during World War II. In the United States, the ENIAC (Electronic Numerical Integrator and Computer) was developed for military use. These early computers were large, expensive, and used vacuum tubes for processing.

The 1950s saw the development of the first high-level

programming languages, such as FORTRAN and COBOL, which made it easier for programmers to write software for computers. The 1960s saw the emergence of minicomputers, smaller and less expensive than their predecessors. In the 1970s, the personal computer revolution began with the introduction of the Altair 8800, the first affordable computer aimed at hobbyists. This was followed by the Apple I and II, which helped popularise personal computing. The 1980s saw the emergence of IBM-compatible PCs, which dominated the market. The introduction of graphical user interfaces (GUIs) and the mouse made computers more user-friendly, leading to their widespread adoption.

The 1990s saw the rise of the internet and the World Wide Web, which transformed computing and led to the development of web browsers such as Netscape Navigator and Internet Explorer.

Since then, computers have become an essential part of our daily lives, and the development of mobile devices and cloud computing has continued to revolutionise the field. The future of computing is likely to involve further advancements in artificial intelligence, quantum computing, and other emerging technologies. But simply put, the technological advancement in less than a hundred years went from basic calculating to artificial interfaced programming that could allow a robot to 'think' thousands of times faster than a human and to learn from its responses.

"Mind blowing, isn't it?" Stella Fox turned, familiar with the Prime Minister's voice. "To think that everything we heard in there, from computing to transport to medicine, all got from the very basic beginnings to where we are now in less than a hundred years."

Fox nodded. "We could add film technology to that as well. Silent movies to CGI in less than a hundred years."

"Makes one believe in *The Matrix*, doesn't it?"

"Not quite," she replied somewhat awkwardly. "But I get the reasoning. Like a Fibonacci number, a program in and of itself. But why a hundred years?"

"We could well ask." The Prime Minister sipped his whisky from the cut-crystal tumbler and smiled. "How goes the intelligence business?"

She returned his smile. They had met for briefings, of course, but she had yet to deliver a victory or a clear objective. *Finding her feet*, was a phrase that could not be bandied about for long before she would be held to account. "Another one of the hundred-year rules," she commented somewhat cryptically. "From Kell and Cummings, to where I stand now. A hundred years, give or take. From dead drops and spying to fearing computers making *their* own decisions and wondering what the fuck you can do about it."

"So, rather like my job," the Prime Minister smiled wryly. "Throughout history, academics have feared, and predicted a plateau to human development. In a way, I suppose they were rightly justified. However, I see it more as a pinnacle. Yes, there have been incredible successes, and indeed mysteries around certain civilisations. The Egyptians, for example. Many civil engineers marvel, and in some cases, doubt their ability to engineer such structures. Pyramids are found on two other continents as well. The Aztecs did not benefit from trade routes and the passing of knowledge from other cultures, so their development is even more incredible. Especially when one considers that they built their first pyramids two hundred years after Oxford was already established as a university. Certainly, civilisations that came afterwards were less ingenious." He paused, finishing his whisky, then said, "I'm not sure a plateau would be how our time will be seen. I think it may well be the pinnacle."

"Sir?" She frowned. "But that can only mean that what comes next is our demise..."

He nodded. "Great societies lasted hundreds, if not thousands of years. The Roman Empire lasted for a thousand years. The Egyptians, well, they were around for three thousand years. Togas and swords. Horses and chariots. Barely anything more complicated. Yet within just one hundred years we have had the first motor vehicles, the first manned flight, the first film footage, the first computer, the atomic bomb... We have put man in space, to the moon, even. We have a rover on Mars and can see other galaxies. I have no doubt that in the past hundred years we have developed technology at an alarming, and possibly dangerous rate. Our question now, is where will it end? Because on our current course, we are developing beyond our capabilities. Take your fears of AI, for instance. It is developing exponentially, beyond that of our ability to control it. A virus without a vaccine."

"My fears exactly," she concurred. "But we can't slow it down."

"No. And nor should we. Our destination is our fate, not our design. But in the hands of our enemies..." He shrugged. "Well, it simply does not bear thinking about."

# Chapter Twenty-Four

E xmoor

"Before we get started, let's go over a few things. Firstly, do you have any experience with aviation?"

"I've flown, obviously. But I've never taken control."

"I'll take that as a no, then," replied Flymo.

"This is crazy..."

"Yep."

"I can't do it."

"Well, that kind of depends on me." Flymo paused. "We'll start with the basics. The first thing you need to know is that the controls in a helicopter are different from those in an airplane. Instead of a yoke, we use a cyclic stick to control the helicopter's movement. And instead of rudder pedals, we have anti-torque pedals."

"Right..."

"To control the helicopter's altitude, we use the collective lever. Pulling it up increases the altitude, while pushing it down decreases it. To control the speed, we adjust the angle of the blades using the cyclic stick."

"That sounds... complicated. How long does it take to learn how to fly a helicopter?"

Flymo shrugged. "It varies from person to person, but it typically takes ten hours to become comfortable with the controls and around forty to fifty hours of flight time to become proficient and get your licence. After a few solo flights, of course. But you won't need a licence. You already have one in the mark's name. You just need to be able to fly if the moment arises. Don't worry, we'll start with the basics and build up your skills gradually."

"Great..."

"It is what it is. Listen, I've been told to get you flying. It can be difficult, or it can be easy. But that sort of depends on your attitude. At the moment we're on the near impossible side of fucking difficult. I don't mind difficult but *fucking* difficult is too much. Near impossible is a waste of both your time and mine."

"Got it."

"Have you?"

"Yes."

# Chapter Twenty-Five

**P**aris

The guards had been left in the rear of the van with the door open. Big Dave had called the location into the police anonymously from a phone box and taken the money to where Ramsay had been waiting with the equipment needed to kill the transmitters and deactivate the dye canisters inside the cases. Rashid drove the hired Citroen saloon with Big Dave beside him. He had covered the alleyway, armed with the rifle if it was called for. He had seen nothing of the gang, nor the police.

"How long will it take?" asked Rashid.

"As long as it takes," Ramsay replied gruffly. He had hoped that with his position as 2-IC of the newly established unit that his field days would be over. He had never been a field agent and had gradually been pushed into the role. He enjoyed his old office at Thames House, relished using a computer to do the work of a dozen agents in the field, but had learned that having people on the ground was vital. "The scanners are already dead," he said. "Electromagnetic pulse. Short frequency, about a fifty-metre radius. Oh, I should have said, check your watches and phones..."

Rashid glanced at his Breitling. It was a perpetual automatic movement, but when he took out his phone he frowned. "It's dead..."

Big Dave checked his chunky G-Shock and pulled a face. "Nice one, Neil..." He unfastened his watch and tossed it aside. "My phone's gone, too."

"Whoops," Ramsay said without any sense of feeling. "I switched mine off. If the power source is off, EMP doesn't affect circuitry."

"Now he tells us," Rashid said sardonically.

"This one is done," Ramsay announced, sliding the case towards them. "And I'll get you both new phones."

"What about my watch?" asked Big Dave.

"There's a clock on the phone, just in case you didn't know..."

"You open it," Rashid said to Big Dave, who was still scowling at Ramsay's comment.

"No, be my guest..."

"Oh, for heaven's sake!" Ramsay niggled. "Just open the ruddy case!"

Big Dave lifted the lid tentatively and stared at the twenty-euro notes, packed and banded in thousands. "Jesus, Allah and Buddha..."

"Still hedging your bets, I hear," Rashid chided.

"That's a hell of a lot of dough."

"And all sequentially numbered," Ramsay declared. "It

would take days to shuffle the notes in that case alone to avoid detection. Only somebody reckless and slightly unhinged would spend it in one place. The chances of being caught are simply too high to get away with it."

"When does King spend it then?" Big Dave asked.

"As soon as we get it to him..."

# Chapter Twenty-Six

M onte Carlo, Monaco

Jon Wood had hired a car using his passport and debit card and driven across France using two filling stations along the way for two fuel stops, a plate of *steak frites* and some bottled water, using his card not only for the fuel and his food, but also for an ATM withdrawal of a hundred euros. Or at least, that is what either police checks, or anyone with a competent investigator behind them would discover. King had played it casual throughout. He did not seek out the CCTV systems, but it was safe to assume that they were there, and he did nothing to avoid them.

The Iron Fist were an amalgamation of five countries, and those countries all had a fearsome reputation for their security and intelligence services, not least their secret police. Although MI5 knew little of the organisation, it would be safe to assume that they had a competent security and intelligence network, and the fact that MI5 had only recently discovered its existence was testament enough to that.

King had parked on the cliff road of Mont Agel to take in the view. The glistening Mediterranean, the wonderful architecture of Monte Carlo and the billionaire's playground of Port Hercule. The marina, and one of the few places on earth where a millionaire could feel impoverished. King liked Monaco. He had driven the mountain road from France to the principality and taken time to reflect on the last time he had been here. A young agent working with his mentor Peter Stewart as they had planned and instigated a coup in a central African nation. If he closed his eyes, it seemed such a short time ago, but it had been almost twenty years. He still regarded it as his best work, although MI6 had been far from pleased by the outcome. But he could live with that.

The sea breeze was warm. A hot wind blowing over from the Sahara that brought with it a sense of change. He wondered if it was a euphemism for the operation. The temperature rising along with the risk. He would soon find out.

He drove the mountain road rapidly, enjoying the downward gradient and the tight bends. He would have liked to ride the road on a powerful motorbike or be behind the wheel of a fast car, but he soon realised that the gradient, inertia and the tight corners was pushing the vehicle's capabilities and he slowed down, realising that the drop was sheer, and the barriers looked flimsier than anything on British roads, and in some cases were twisted and damaged from earlier and unfortunate encounters. When he entered Monte Carlo, he was reminded of what a millionaire's playground it was. Stylish, elegant women walked the pavements like a catwalk, and young brassy girls accompanied overweight men bringing the age-gap into speculation. People ignored mainstream Ferraris and Lamborghinis but took pictures on their phones when a Bugatti or Zonda warbled past, hoping to identify the millionaire sportsman or social media star behind the wheel, or marvelled at classic open-topped cars worthy of Concourse awards, and the unassuming billionaire on his morning jaunt. Quite simply, Monte Carlo was in a league of its own.

King had checked into the Hotel de Paris. At over twelve-hundred euros a night for a modest suite, he would blow through his funds before long, but he didn't expect to be here long. The receptionist had photocopied his passport and swiped his card. All in the name of Jon Wood.

King tipped the bellhop in cash, but it would remain untraceable until his funds arrived. His tip would not have been the largest the man had ever seen, but it was undoubtedly not the smallest. Enough to be remembered for the right reasons. He looked out across the water, the bay windows affording him one of the best views in Monaco. For the first time in days he thought about Caroline, and how they had been sailing those waters, and what had become of their dream. But dreams seldom lived up to the reality, and he knew that this was what he wanted to be doing. Rolling the dice against an enemy and seeing how it played out. He smiled as he thought about her training the asset while he was in a luxurious five-star suite. A gin and tonic on the balcony, and this would have been right up her street. And, as he thought about his time here with Peter Stewart all those years ago, and their operation that would later take them to the highlands and jungles of Burindi, he thought of just how far he had come. His earlier work with MI6 had seen him sleeping under the stars in the Middle

East or huddling under his jacket in torrential equatorial rain in damp, stiflingly hot jungle.

The text tone snapped King from his thoughts. He stepped back inside the room and picked his phone up from the dresser. *We're here.* Short and sweet, but that was Neil Ramsay's way. King typed out and sent his reply and returned to the view from the balcony while he waited. After ten minutes, he heard the knock at the door, and he walked across the large room and checked the spyhole. Ramsay waited patiently, with Big Dave standing to the side and slightly back from the door, twice as wide and a head higher than the analyst and now second in command of their new department. King opened the door and stepped aside.

"Nice digs," Big Dave commented.

"Get a suite and put it on expenses," replied King as he closed the door and slipped the security chain in place.

"He most certainly will not!" Ramsay bristled. He looked around for somewhere to place the case, then simply rested it on the bed.

"Here, take this," said Big Dave, handing King his Glock 19 and two loaded magazines.

King knew that the others had brought the weapons in using the diplomatic bag. "Cheers, mate," he said as he took the weapon, checked the chamber and inserted one of the magazines before making it ready. The Glock was safe to carry in this manner because of its ingenious hinged blade safety on the trigger. Until the little blade was depressed flush with the trigger in the simple act of pulling the trigger, the trigger remained locked.

"You won't get into the casino with it, though," Big Dave told him. "They have a metal detector and bag search at the foyer."

"How many security guards?"

"Eleven. Four in uniform, the rest in monkey suits doing their best to blend in."

"Except for the fact that they're all hideous bulging beasts," Ramsay commented as he opened the case. "Like Lomu, here."

"None taken..."

"I meant..."

"Yeah, we get what you mean, Neil," King replied. "Are they armed?"

"Like security has been all over France after the Charlie Hebdo attacks, some security officers can be armed with a .38 revolver, but it must be carried openly. Bodyguards can apply for a permit to conceal-carry a 9mm automatic." Ramsay shrugged. "Not all will be armed, but it's a safe assumption that there will be access to firearms inside."

"Given that it is the law for a casino to carry enough money to cover all possible bets, you can bet your white ass that there are a few men carrying weapons," Big Dave added. "So, good luck with that."

"Cheers." But as King watched Ramsay stack the bundles of twenty euro notes on the bed, he knew he was going to need all the luck he could get.

# Chapter Twenty-Seven

V ienna, Austria

The *Figlmueller Backerstrasse* was the quintessential purveyor of the veal schnitzel, some said the best in all Vienna. The veal loin had been flattened with a kitchen mallet until it had six times the surface area and was just a few millimetres in thickness. The breadcrumb coating was light and had puffed with air as all the great chefs achieved with the dish, and it tasted rich and buttery from the frying in clarified alpine butter and was served simply with a wedge of lemon and a fresh, aromatic tomato sauce. More than half the diners had opted for the dish, the rest choosing from the dozen other dishes on the menu.

"What do you think?" Hendricks asked.

Ahmadi nodded. "It is good," he lied. He preferred his food to be spiced with chillies and aromatic spices, and fragranced with coriander and fenugreek. In his opinion there were no better spice blends than baharat, berbere, ras el hanout, sumac, za'atar or harissa. The heat, the sweetness, the bitterness, the smokiness. Nothing could beat heavily spiced goat cooked on a wood fire. He doubted that the veal was halal, slaughtered in accordance with his faith, but he would pray and ask forgiveness, for when one walked his enemy's land, one could not always tread the path of the righteous. That was what the Quran had taught him.

"I meant the... er, shipment..."

Ahmadi looked at the South African and shrugged. "Small arms, not a problem."

"The deadline is short," Hendricks said somewhat irritably. "The villages need clearing before the mining can start."

"And what of the structures when the people and animals have gone?"

"Bulldozers. It will be like the places never existed."

Ahmadi nodded. He knew that the South African was chief of security for a cobalt mining concern operating in Namibia. Three remote villages were in the way and the company were not going to pay for relocation. Mercenaries from the Wagner Group were going to handle the situation. A caveat in the land rights said that when people no longer inhabited the area, then the mining concern could open the cut intersecting the three villages. The Hiano people had clashed with many tribes in the region, and the 'soldiers' from Wagner would provide witnesses that it had been a case of inter-tribal retribution. Wagner had been briefed that not a single man, woman or child – or even a goat, for that matter – would be left alive. When it went down, Hendricks would be visiting relatives in Holland, and the directors of the cobalt mining company would have similar alibis. They had decided that it was a small price to pay for supplying companies with the precious cobalt they needed to power mobile phones and electric cars.

"We have a ship in the region," the Iranian said matter-of-factly. "There are containers on board with weapons and ammunition inside. A phone call could have the ship rerouted to Angola or Namibia. Engine repairs, or something along those lines. Perhaps a propeller repair."

"What are we talking about?"

Ahmadi knew that the South African had a military background, so he wouldn't have to over-explain. "Kalashnikovs and Chinese type ninety-fives. Ammunition for both. Makarov pistols as well." He paused. "Some heavy machineguns, too."

"Enough for fifty men?"

"Absolutely."

Hendricks wedged another piece of veal into his mouth and chewed sparingly. As he swallowed all too soon, he said, "The payment will be with you within an hour. That is, unless you would care for dessert?"

Ahmadi couldn't think of anything he would care for less. He yearned for baklava and its syrupy sweetness, the delicate and buttery filo pastry and the sweet fruit with bitter nuts. "That would be delightful," he conceded. Hendricks was about to spend good money and would recommend Ahmadi's services to other mining concerns across the troubled continent, and like all operators with the Iron Fist, Ahmadi kept thirty-three percent of his fee, the other sixty-six percent was split evenly between the Iron Fist, and the respective country of that operator. The one percent remaining was diverted to a separate Swiss bank account by all five nations, and the identity of this account remained a mystery to all members. By Ahmadi's reckoning of his own transactions, there would be several million dollars sitting there, and he had no idea what funds had been diverted by the other four nations. Like everyone within the Iron Fist, there was no collusion, no knowledge of other operators – simply emailed instructions every few weeks. The emails always came in the form of a draft folder via a shared mail provider. Simply open, type out a reply and save without sending. No email ever entered the ether, and the practice remained impossible to trace. All the relevant parties needed was an email account and a shared username and password.

Hendricks sipped some of his champagne and grinned. "Without people like you; people like us, Africa would be very different place indeed."

"Better or worse?" Ahmadi asked somewhat cynically.

"I think we both know the answer to that, my friend." He paused. "But there's simply too much money to be made to get sentimental over such things."

# Chapter Twenty-Eight

M onaco

King bought his Scotch and soda using the Jon Wood debit card. He did not care much for the drink, but it had been Wood's tipple of choice and accuracy could only add to the strength of the legend. He wandered through the casino, drink in hand, marking out the high rollers from the timid amateurs. The security guards were easy to spot once inside. Large men, scowls upon their faces. They looked tough, pugilistic. Outside, the two uniformed guards carried batons and the two tuxedoed bouncers on the door politely and efficiently eyed the clientele with scrutiny. It was a message. Do not misbehave in this establishment, because these men will be the consequence. Once through the foyer, smart men and women greeted the guests and directed them towards the cashier the coat check and the bar. They wore the same uniform as the croupiers and hospitality staff -

crisp white shirts with black skirts or trousers and burgundy waistcoats.

King wandered over to the cashier kiosk. A tuxedoed bouncer stood behind the cashier, a bulge under his left armpit. Undoubtedly armed with a .38 revolver in line with France's new legislation for private security. He showed his passport and changed ten-thousand euros to chips. The money went through an electronic counter and the woman slid the piles of chips over without pausing a beat. He walked away, Rashid's voice in his ear, the earpiece no larger than a paracetamol capsule, but with a flanged end to prevent it going too deep into the ear canal.

*"So far, so good..."*

King said nothing. He had a microphone in his collar but would avoid talking until necessary. People tended to take notice of people apparently talking to themselves. He hadn't spotted Rashid, which was a good thing he supposed. He reached the roulette table and placed a thousand on red. A call for no more bets was stated, and the croupier spun the wheel and flicked the ball. When the ball settled, it was black 15. King watched his chips get swiped back to the croupier, but he dropped another thousand on red. He was only playing fifty-fifty. Flip of a coin stuff.

The roulette wheel has numbered pockets, alternating between red and black, with a single green pocket for zero (European roulette) or both zero and double zero (American roulette). King had only ever played a European table, like the one before him. Players place bets by placing chips on the roulette table, indicating their chosen number(s), colour (red or black), or other betting options. There are two main types of bets in roulette: inside bets and outside bets. Inside bets involve specific numbers or small groups of numbers, while outside bets cover larger sections of the wheel. Once

A P Bateman

all bets are placed, the dealer spins the wheel in one direction and rolls the ball in the opposite direction along the wheel's track. As the ball loses momentum, it eventually lands in one of the numbered pockets. The winning number is determined by the pocket in which the ball comes to rest. If the ball lands on a number or group of numbers that a player has bet on, they win a pay-out based on the odds of that specific bet. The pay-out varies depending on the type of bet and its likelihood of occurring. Losing bets are collected by the dealer, and winning bets are paid out accordingly. The game then starts anew with new bets placed. Certainly, it was a game of chance, but the more one played, and the more one explored the coverage of bets, a tidy profit could often be made, just as long as the player knew when to stop. Beating the odds only lasted so long. King often thought about his work as a game of roulette. He had stepped away twice before, and as he watched the ball spin in the opposite direction to the wheel, he wondered if he had put all the luck in his enemy's favour.

Luck favoured the house tonight and he watched his thousand disappear. Another bet on red, and this time luck was favourable to him, and he was paid out his thousand. He switched to black and after the spin he had another thousand and was back at scratch. No winners, no losers. He finished his scotch and headed to the bar.

*"Lucky bugger..."* Rashid commented.

King looked around but still could not spot him. "OK, I give in..."

"Your drink, Sir..." Rashid's voice distorted as King heard the man in real time, and with a split-second's delay in his left ear. He stood before King in a waiter's uniform, and a single Scotch and soda in a tumbler on a silver salver.

"Got in through an employment agency," he explained quietly.

King took the drink and sipped, before dropping a fifty euro note onto the tray. "Don't spend it all at once," he said. "In fact, don't spend it at all..." He turned and headed over to the blackjack tables. He knew that Rashid would pool the tip, and that would only add to the story once the sequencing serial numbers were discovered. He decided to speed up the process and dropped a few thousand on a blackjack table, only it was called *Vingt et Un* in Monte Carlo.

The objective of the game is to have a hand value as close to 21 as possible without exceeding it. Each player is dealt two cards, while the dealer receives one card face up. Numbered cards (2-10) are worth their face value, face cards (Jack, Queen, King) are worth 10, and an Ace can be worth 1 or 11, depending on the player's choice. Players can request additional cards (hits) to improve their hand's total value. If the total value of a player's hand exceeds 21, it results in a bust, and they lose the round. Once all players have finished their turns, the dealer reveals their second card. The dealer must follow a specific set of rules: they must hit on a hand total of 16 or less and stand on a total of 17 or more. If the dealer busts, all remaining players win. If neither the player nor the dealer busts, the hand with a total closest to 21 wins. If a player's first two cards are an Ace and a 10-value card (10, Jack, Queen, King), it is called a black-jack and pays out at higher odds. The game is typically played with multiple decks of cards, which are shuffled together. Players can make additional bets, such as doubling down (doubling the initial bet for one more card) or splitting pairs (separating two cards of the same value into two separate hands). Insurance is an optional side bet that protects against the dealer having a blackjack.

King played recklessly, his aim to get through his chips as quickly as possible, but the odds favoured him, or his recklessness, and even asking for hits on eighteen and in one case on a nineteen, he still beat the dealer and was soon five thousand up. He downed his drink and ambled over to the roulette table.

*"You've got eyes on you."*

"Thought so..." King replied. "The ape on the steps to the poker tables?"

*"Yep. A tall thin man near the baccarat as well."*

*"Have him,"* Big Dave's deep voice played into King's ear.

King had to remind himself not to nod, but knowing he had two extra pairs of eyes – and hands and feet if the need arose – buoyed his confidence. Now to see how far he could take it. He dropped five thousand on zero and waited for "no more bets" to be called. Unsurprisingly, the ball followed somebody else's luck and King watched the chips get swept back to the bank. He placed another five-thousand euro bet on zero, already drawing a crowd to the table and gasps of both excitement and disappointment as he bust. King strolled to the bar, ordered another Scotch and soda, tipped with another fifty and strolled back to the cashier's kiosk. The woman glanced behind her at a man who had joined the bouncer but looked to be half the size. His tuxedo was a far better cut and fit, and quality than the ape beside him. King showed his passport, asked for twenty-thousand, and dropped two bundles of notes into the drawer, which the woman slid towards her and waited for the man to agree, which he did with a simple and discreet nod. King slipped his passport back inside his jacket pocket.

The tuxedo had been a gift from someone who had attempted to recruit King. He smiled to himself that it had come into use so soon. It was possibly one of the most expensive suits in the room, and that was certainly saying something in Monte Carlo. He could tell that the bouncers were closing in on him, and right on cue Rashid's voice crackled in his ear. *"More than a few pairs of eyes on you now, my friend."*

*"Yeah, you're becoming really popular now..."* Big Dave said sardonically.

*"I'm parked outside, across the square in a grey Range Rover Velar if you need a fast getaway,"* Jack Luger's voice came over the net.

King did not reply, but he was glad they had his back. No two men in the room would be a match for Big Dave, and Rashid was an agile and dirty fighter. King knew that Luger had come highly recommended – Stella Fox would not have brought him into a new section if he was anything other than brilliant – and he was pleased at the thought of a getaway vehicle being on hand if needed. And, as he surveyed the room, he imagined he would find out soon enough.

King put five thousand on red and doubled his money. He was paid out under the watchful eyes of the ever-present bouncers and slid the ten thousand euros onto black. Fifty-fifty. As the wheel slowed and the ball bounced between numbers, a gasp went out as the ball finally settled on black 26. Ten thousand euros in chips was pushed across to his pile and he moved them to zero and retained twenty-five thousand. The wheel spun, the ball rolled the other way and bounced across the numbers, finally settling on red 18. The crowd gasped and sighed, but King remained impassive and as other players laid their bets, King waited and watched. The odd glance told him that five bouncers were positioned around him, but Big Dave was stood behind the two largest men. Rashid, tray in hand was hovering near the next largest man. That left two for King, the two between himself and the exit. The house cleaned up and as the other players worked out their system, or calculated the bets already placed – not that luck behaves rationally for the gambler – King slid his entire stack of chips onto black 24. The age he had been when Peter Stewart had given him an ultimatum, sprung him from prison and changed his life forever. Twenty-five thousand with odds of 36 to 1 on the French wheel. Eight hundred and twenty-five thousand euros if he won. Eight-hundred and fifty with his stake back. Or nothing. It was all in the spin, and all in the luck. He didn't really care which. Several other players slid their chips towards his pile and called 24.

"No more bets!" said the croupier as she spun the wheel, then gave the ball a hard spin in the opposite direction.

The air was tense with anticipation and as the wheel started slowing down, and the ball dropped and bounced its way across the numbers, King looked up and saw some of the bouncers cupping their ears as they received their instructions, and the woman behind the kiosk was talking animatedly with the casino manager and showing him a wad of banknotes. King looked back at the table as the ball bounced and settled, and the onlookers gasped and applauded, and the wheel slowed to a halt with the ball resting in black 24. The gasps turned into cheers and the croupier looked unsure what to do next, but high rollers came and went with the seasons, and she started to pay out, piling and sliding ten-thousand-euro plaques across the table. The bouncers closed in, and King smashed the palm of his left hand through the chips and plaques and shouted, "Votre prochain pari est sur moi!" *Your next bet is on me!* Winners, losers, the rich and the pretenders. Every casino was full of them, and they all had something in common by being there – everyone loved money, and everyone wanted more of it. A rugby scrum of tuxedoes and chiffon erupted as everyone scrambled for the chips.

King looked up to see Big Dave slamming the two men's heads together in front of him. He looked set to follow up, but King had his own problems now, and the two men between himself and the exit squared up to him but were not ready for the complete lack of pause King gave to the situation. He came in low, kicking one of the men in the kneecap, and straightening up with a solid uppercut under the second man's chin. Neither man needed a follow up blow, but they each got a savage punch in the middle of their faces. One-two. King leapt over them and caught sight of Rashid using the edge of the silver salver against a bouncer's windpipe – a blunt axe that dropped the man onto his backside, clasping his throat and choking for precious air. The melee of people were bustling one another and grabbing at the chips and plaques, because the bet had been won fair and square and the house had no choice but to pay out whomever held a chip or plaque bearing the casino's name. King dodged people sprinting towards the tables, and as he ploughed through the doors – all polished wood, etched glass and polished brass – he bounded into one of the guards and narrowly missed being clubbed by the other with his baton.

Blue and white strobes filled the square and as King looked for Jack Luger waiting in the Range Rover, he had no choice but to give up on that idea and he sprinted downhill and darted into a narrow alleyway. There were gunshots behind him, and he heard the bullets strike stone and ping off into the night. Reckless shooting for police officers, and he wondered whether the gunshots had come from one of the security guards. When he emerged from the alleyway, it was between the auditorium and the Monaco yacht club. He could hear shouts and racing footsteps behind him, and he headed for the quay and was aided by the dull orange glow of the ornate streetlights along the promenade. King risked a glance and could see police officers looking around them as they raced out of the alley and into the open street. King leapt the whitewashed wall, slid down the three-metre concrete slope and into the water. There was a slight chill, but he ignored it and he started to stroke away from the seawall and when he had put in fifty metres he ducked under the surface and swam as far and for as long as he could, exhaling before he surfaced, breaking the water with little more than his eyes and nose and taking a steady breath through his nose, his eyes on the orange glow of the promenade. He saw police officers scanning the water with torches, but they did not look for long, and took off in two directions along the seafront. King smiled to himself. He had always felt comfortable in water, and his training had taught him to head for water when in danger, because you played to your individual strengths. King had trained with the SBS and completed their underwater demolition program, which pulled on canoeing, scuba diving and swimming skills, as well as piloting submersibles and being dropped miles from shore by helicopter and swimming to shore.

King trod water easily. Half floating on his back, gently sculling with his hands and feet, he could see distant and white flashing lights, but was so far out to sea that he could not hear anything other than the lapping of water from his rhythmic movement. He kicked off the shoes, regrettable given their value and quality – a gift along with the tux – and he switched his wallet and passport to his rear trouser pocket, then took off the jacket – which he found easier to do fully submersed. King then unfastened his tie and undid the first three buttons down his shirt and fixed his gaze on the shore. He found a marker and used the streetlamps to establish distance. The current was gentle, but significant. There was no sense working against it. Work smarter, not harder. King checked his watch, then started out with a powerful freestyle stroke parallel to the shore.

# Chapter Twenty-Nine

**T**hree Days Later, Exmoor

"Jon Wood is now a blip on the radar. Your escapades have ensured that both the London and Paris criminal fraternity are aware of him. Ronnie Vickers has put a price on his head, and that sort of action makes people sit up and take notice. Congratulations. The person to kill you will receive a hundred thousand pounds..."

"Nice," King commented flatly.

Stella Fox ignored his glibness. "The police in both Monaco, France and Italy are on the lookout for Jon Wood. Many criminals on the run head straight for Italy from the principality, so that's another avenue to be explored. Either way, it's only a matter of time before the Paris gangs migrate down that way and start asking their own questions." She paused. "And the beauty of it all is by driving to Toulouse and using Wood's cards, not only have you given them yet another false trail, but by travelling back as Alex King, Jon Wood has simply disappeared into thin air..."

"For now," King nodded and sipped his tea. "So, what's next?"

"Planning and recruiting."

"Recruiting?"

"You said that Ahmadi's son was the way in..."

"That's how I see it."

"Care to enlighten me?"

King looked up as the noise of the helicopter grew steadily louder, suddenly enveloping them completely. "How's he getting on?"

Stella Fox shrugged. "He'll get there. Flymo said that he's able to take off and land, fly straight and steady. There's a lot to take on board."

"A crash-course, so-to-speak."

"Let's hope not."

King smiled. "I was unaware that straight and steady was an option with Flymo in the cockpit..."

"So, I've heard."

King stood up and walked to the window, where he could see the helicopter making a slow and somewhat deliberately careful landing. The rotors started to power down at once. After a full minute, he watched the asset climb out of the cockpit. The man's image had changed drastically. Haircut, facial grooming, even the way he dressed. It was like Ahmadi was standing in front of him. "What do you have in store for the Iranian once we make the switch?"

"We leave him in play."

"I meant Ahmadi. The real one."

"Not good things..."

King already knew the answer. The man would be held captive for as long as the asset remained in deep cover. He would be interrogated constantly, or until he yielded nothing more. There were methods for that, and King knew them all. But there would be no happy ending for the man. No reunion with his family. He had long ago learned to deal with these operations as an assassination assignment. The man would ultimately die, so it paid those involved to view him as nothing more than a corpse. What the minds of MI5 – or indeed Stella Fox's new department – did with him was not King's concern. He simply had a job to do, and he would do it well or die trying.

"He'll never fool Ahmadi's wife."

"He's putting in the work."

"But in the bedroom?"

"Our asset will have to think on his feet," she replied, unperturbed. "Perhaps he'll have to develop a headache."

"What footage have you of Ahmadi at home?" King asked. "His mannerisms, the way he talks, even."

"Caroline has worked him relentlessly. It's been like a stage school in there. Walking, talking, sipping tea, eating... whatever footage we have of Ahmadi, the asset has re-enacted it. Convincingly, too."

"Inside his home?"

"We have plenty of footage."

"But, not of inside his home..."

"Why is that so damned important," she asked, irritably.

"Because we don't know if the real Ahmadi beats his wife, has her tickle his arse with a feather duster, sleep in separate bedrooms, or if he has a penchant for home baking..." King shrugged. "We can train the asset all we like, but without knowing what the man is like in his own home, then it's a fool's errand!"

"Then, what do you suggest?"

"We need eyes and ears inside his castle."

"Castle?"

"Figuratively," King sighed.

"I would say that's damn nigh-on impossible."

"I'll settle for nigh-on. I've had a hell of a lot worse odds in my time."

"I don't like your chances," she said derisively.

"Not me," replied King. "I can't risk being seen until I make my play towards Ahmadi."

"Then who?"

"The new guy," said King. "Jack Luger. I've read his file several times over."

"And?"

"Impressive."

"I'm glad you approve of my recruiting judgement," she replied somewhat tersely. "Tell me what else you know about him. What didn't make the file..."

# Chapter Thirty

**T**wo Weeks Later,
   Casablanca, Morocco

Jack Luger looked like just about every other tourist in the city. Cargo shorts, a collarless shirt and sunglasses. He drew the line at sandals but wore a pair of well-worn boat shoes without socks. He was seated askew to a small, round table so that he could get the full warmth of the sun, and with his leg crossed in a masculine manner, he leaned back confidently watching the golden hue of sunlight on the choppy Atlantic Ocean. He sipped strong, black coffee and occasionally helped himself to mini baclava dusted with powdered sugar that had melted to a sticky syrup in the sun. Gloriously indulgent.

At the seafront wall, two men each teased two pairs of cobras that hissed and struck at their tormentors, fascinated tourists whooping in fear and delight, dropping coins on a blanket as they watched and filmed and tried for selfies with the snakes in the background. The snakes were large and fast, but the men had the routine down pat, and Luger wondered whether the reptiles had been milked of their highly toxic venom, or de-fanged altogether. Ahmadi was seated at the next café with his wife and son. The couple shared sweet tea while the boy drank a bottle of local cola that had copied the Coca-Cola branding, but from where Luger was sitting, the Arabic writing looked like the word *Isis*. He knew it didn't, but it didn't give off the best vibe to the casual and uninitiated spectator.

Leaning on the seawall a large bodyguard did his best to look inconspicuous. Luger could see a large bulge under the man's armpit and rather than a pistol, he suspected a mini-machinegun like a MAC-10 or a Mini-Uzi. A lot of fire-power up close. At the next table two more bodyguards sipped glasses of iced water and parked on the road a luxury S-Class Mercedes waited in the shadow of the close protection team's Range Rover Sport. He spotted at least one handgun bulge above one of the men's right hip. Luger sipped some more of the thick, black coffee and ate another tiny piece of the baclava. Ahmadi clicked his fingers at the waitress indicating that he wanted the bill and finished his glass of tea. The man's wife did the same and the boy picked up his bottle of cola. Ahmadi dropped several notes onto the dish in the waitress's hand, not bothering to look at the bill and as he stood up and adjusted his lightweight suit jacket, Luger saw that he was armed with a small pistol in a suede holster. The set-up was so small that it reminded him of a tiny cowboy pistol and holster he had played with as a child complete with chaps and miniature Stetson.

*"Sit rep..."*

Luger ignored the voice in his ear. It was vital that he did not speak and give himself away. He tapped the side of his cup twice with the teaspoon, then picked it up and sipped. "Target is mobile," he whispered with the cup to his mouth. "Wait out..." He watched as the men closed in on the Iranian and his family and shadowed them to the Mercedes. Luger left three 20-dirham notes underneath the saucer and walked back along the seawall in the opposite direction. "Target is in the vehicle and mobile," he said more urgently.

*"Have that,"* Big Dave acknowledged.

*"Heading towards me,"* Rashid said. "Berk at the front, hedgehog at the rear..."

"Berk?" Luger queried.

*"Mercs for berks,"* Big Dave chided. *"Never heard that saying?"*

"No."

*"Beemers for dreamers, Mercs for berks..."*

"Then what the hell is a hedgehog?" Luger asked, getting into the Jeep hire car.

*"You don't know the difference between a Range Rover and a hedgehog?"* Rashid laughed. *"Well, a hedgehog has pricks on the outside..."*

Luger shook his head in exasperation as he started the car and followed the cars from a discreet distance. He'd just part-exchanged his Mercedes for a BMW back home, but wasn't about to tell them that, although he suspected they already had an inkling as it seemed quite random. He slowed for the traffic, and it happened so quickly that all he could do was intake a sharp breath. The man had opened the door, slipped into the passenger seat and jammed the barrel of the Uzi machine pistol so firmly into his ribs that he thought he had heard one crack. He certainly felt the pain to accompany the sound as the wind was driven from his lungs.

"Keep driving..." the man growled. Luger had not seen the man get out of the Range Rover ahead of him, could not think when he would have had the opportunity. "Who the fuck are you...?"

"Who the fuck are *you*?" Luger protested, making sure that the other two men would hear the exchange in their earpieces. "Get out of my car!" The muzzle of the Uzi pressed deeper, and he winced. He steered towards the kerb and slowed. "Fine, take the fucking car... It's a hire car, though. They'll find you pretty quickly."

"*Stay casual,*" Big Dave said quietly and reassuringly into his earpiece. "*I'm en route...*"

"*Same,*" Rashid added. "*Just ride it out while we work out what to do...*"

"I don't want the car," the man replied menacingly. "Keep driving! Follow the Range Rover." He paused. "As you were doing so, before I got in..."

"Look, who the hell are you?"

"You were watching us on the seafront."

"I was," he admitted. "The man looked important, rich. What is he, a Bollywood film star?"

"Bollywood?" the bear of a man asked exasperatedly. "Shut your fucking mouth!" he snapped vehemently, yet somewhat still incredulous at Luger's assumption.

"Look, I don't know who he is. I'm just on my way back to my hotel."

"Where are you staying?"

"The Four Seasons," he lied, having earlier trawled through a list before choosing *The Hyatt*. Both Big Dave and Rashid had chosen two separate Airbnb. The two seasoned hands had laughed at Luger's choice, but Luger was new to this and had been taken in by the proximity of the wonderful golden sands and glistening sea, and the novelty of an expense account for the first time. He suspected the other two men enjoyed the change from their accommodation limit, as much as the anonymity such places afforded them.

"We shall see..."

"I don't know that man."

"We know." The man paused. "But it is his opinion that you wish to learn more about him. And if you have any idea who he is, which I am sure you do, then you will know that cannot be allowed to happen..."

Luger said nothing. In his rear-view mirror, he could see the giant figure of Big Dave sitting somewhat comically behind the wheel of a preposterously small electric Hyundai hire car. Pulling out of a side turning ahead of them, Rashid boxed the Jeep in. His white Toyota Corolla looked anonymous and bland in the traffic, which ranged from luxury brand SUVs with blacked-out windows, to horse and carts, with almost every conceivable mode of transportation in between.

"I'm just a tourist," he replied. "I don't know who that man is. I was interested because he clearly had armed body-guards. But I'm not following him, I'm going back to my hotel."

"Save it."

Luger listened to the voices of Lomu and Rashid in his right ear. They were with him, front and back, and he found some comfort in that. The road wound around to the right, away from the seafront and through an area of waste ground ripe for development. Rashid slammed on the brakes and Luger bumped him from behind. Right according to plan. "Bugger!" Luger snapped, exasperated.

Rashid got out; hands stretched to each side, his expression and body language leaving no doubt to his utter disbelief. Of Pakistani heritage, he looked like a local, or enough to pass muster. He walked up to the window and started to bang on the glass. Luger lowered it a touch, feeling the muzzle of the Uzi grinding against his ribs. "Look what you've done!" Rashid shouted through the crack, his English this time heavy on Arabic accent, rather than his midland drawl. "Get out and look at the damage!"

The man glared at Rashid, lifted the Uzi just enough to show him the sight of the gun, and when he did, Luger lashed out and chopped the man in the throat with the edge of his hand. He then caught hold of the muzzle of the weapon and pointed it safely down to the footwell as the passenger door was torn open and Big Dave ripped the man out of his seat. He tried to struggle, but even being such a big man, he had nothing on the Fijian, who yanked him out by a fold of fat on his stomach and a handful of his hair. There was a sickening crunch and the man dropped life-lessly to the dusty ground, blood pouring out from his nose. Luger made the weapon safe and dropped it down behind his seat.

"Open the boot, Rashid, let's get the fucker out of view..." growled Big Dave.

Rashid darted to the Toyota and lifted the boot lid as Big Dave dragged the man over and tossed him into the empty boot space. He unfastened the man's boot laces and used them to expertly secure the man's hands behind his back before closing the boot lid.

Luger joined them, looking all around them earnestly. "Bloody hell, I think we've got away with it..."

"Hardly," replied Big Dave. "What the hell are we going to do with him now? Ahmadi will know that something went wrong. And we can't let him go, or they'll know for sure that they had a tail."

Jack Luger looked at Rashid, then back at Big Dave. "You're not going to kill him, are you?"

"Well, *I'm* not," Rashid replied. "I don't kill in this sort of scenario. Not unless I can help it, and I can."

"That goes for me, too, bro," said Big Dave. "It's different in the heat of a contact. I'm not lifting the boot lid and killing a tethered man. Anyway, you're the one who let down his guard," he said staring at the young agent. "So, how are you going to do it?"

"I didn't sign up for that shit," he replied defensively. "Not my skillset."

"Would you have killed him earlier if you had the chance?" Rashid paused. "When he held you at gunpoint, if you could have turned the tables?"

The young man thought about it for a moment, then said, "Yes, I suppose so."

"You've got your pistol..."

"It's different. The guy's trussed up like a chicken."

"We could set him free to run if that would help?" The big Fijian suggested. "Make it a bit more sporting, like?" He watched the indecision on Luger's face and said, "Get back in your car and follow me." Lomu waited until Luger was seated back behind the wheel then turned to Rashid and said, "So, what do we think?"

"He won't make the same mistake again in a hurry."

"And about the twat in the boot?"

"Luger isn't a hot head. That's good. I don't want to work with a gung-ho killer." Rashid paused. "King said that Stella Fox told him that she recruited Jack because of some less obvious qualities that she thought a unit like this needed. And now we know that it isn't because he's an obvious killer."

"I'll let Ramsay know that he's ok. I mean, so far, so good."

"He wanted to know?"

"He's dubious about the remit this new unit will have, and what Stella Fox is planning for us all."

Rashid nodded as he mulled on this. "So, what about the bodyguard?"

"It's a good opportunity to learn more about Ahmadi," Big Dave said thoughtfully.

"Where's King when you need him?"

"Really? He doesn't strike me as a sadist."

"Far from it. But he has made people talk in the past."

Big Dave nodded. "Well, he isn't here. But we are, and this guy may be the link between getting the result we want or blowing the entire operation."

# Chapter Thirty-One

"This is highly irregular..."

"Everything we do is highly irregular," Big Dave replied. "That's why we're always in and out of favour."

Ramsay raised an eyebrow and sighed. "So, where is he?"

"Jack's guarding him inside an empty shop."

Ramsay handed Big Dave the aluminium case, no larger than a thick hardback novel. "Well, I hope it works," he said somewhat dubiously.

"It'll work," said the big Fijian. "I can't see why it wouldn't."

Big Dave made his way out of the hotel foyer and walked to the Toyota. He opened the door and slid in beside Rashid.

"Do you think it will work?" he asked.

"Jesus! It's going to work!" he replied exasperatedly. "You're as bad as Neil..."

Rashid pulled a face like it wasn't the best compliment a man could have and pulled out into the traffic. "The camera and recording equipment are all set." He paused. "I can see part one and two working, but part three? What if he merely confesses to his people?"

"I have a feeling he won't."

"So, the entire operation is based on a feeling?"

"We've won before on less..."

"We've fucked up on more, too..." He watched the ramshackle streets for the turning, wondering whether every North African or Arab town had a dead dog in the gutter. "Bousbir was the red-light district during the French occupation. About a thousand prostitutes plying their trade. Many from France, but plenty of Arab women, too. It's where the term dusky maiden came from. More French servicemen were hospitalised for venereal disease than from wounds suffered in battle during the whole North African *and* Southeast Asia campaigns of Cambodia and Vietnam combined."

"Sounds about right. For French men, that is," Big Dave reflected humorously.

"Growing up, my neighbour was an Italian who fought at Tripoli in the Second World War. Next door to him was a Scotsman who fought in the same campaign. The two men became friends despite being on opposing sides and even had an allotment next to each other. They shared their harvests so that they could each plant different things." Rashid reflected nostalgically. "The Scot said that they were always begging for ammunition and uniforms, and the Italian said the same thing. The Italians had waited for weeks, down to a handful of rounds each. When they finally received an airdrop, it was full of condoms and nude magazines!" he laughed. "Someone back in Rome thought that the men would need these more than bullets!"

Big Dave smiled as Rashid manoeuvred the Toyota into

the alley. He already had his Glock 19 in his hand, his finger resting alongside the trigger guard. Nothing looked out of place. Luger's Jeep was parked facing outwards on the opposite side of the alley, Rashid avoiding blocking in the man's vehicle. Both men got out, Rashid had his weapon tucked into the front of his waistband, his untucked shirt concealing it from view. Big Dave looked around him then slipped the pistol into his pocket. Rashid rapped a pre-arranged tattoo on the rear door of one of a series of abandoned shops. The entire sector had been bought out for a development which had never happened. As he looked about himself, he saw two children watching from across the dusty waste ground. He stared at them and after a moment they sprinted down one of the many alleys between the derelict buildings. In Iraq or Afghanistan, that would have been a warning sign. Kids were the eyes of the enemy. In Morocco, it likely meant that the kids were nosey, or would come back with their friends for a bit of distraction and pickpocketing.

The door opened silently, Jack Luger standing to the side, the 9mm Glock held in his right hand, muzzle pointing to the ground.

"How's our guest?"

"Angry," Luger replied. "And thirsty."

"Did you give him a drink?" asked Big Dave.

"No."

"Good. He'll bargain for one soon enough."

"He keeps saying that Ahmadi will find him. That Ahmadi will make us pay..."

"Easy," Big Dave said measuredly. "Don't let him unnerve you."

"I haven't," Luger replied dismissively. "I'm just filling you in."

"And you checked him all over for a tracking device?" Rashid asked.

"Yes," Luger nodded. "Unless it's under his skin or up his arse..."

"I think we're safe," replied Rashid. He walked through the dusty room, the remains of a business selling and altering material still evident by the scraps of fabric and abandoned coils of measuring tape scattered on the floor. He opened the door and studied the man bound and seated on the floor before him. Luger had tied his hands in front of him but secured a broom handle through the man's elbows and along his back. It was a good technique because Luger had been able to keep an eye on the man's hands and the broom handle secured his arms tightly in place. The man's ankles were bound, too. There was a pool of urine under the man and all around him. When you had to go, you had to go. The room was hot and dark, slithers of light casting dusty beams from cracks in the boarded windows. "Name?" Rashid asked, staring at the man on the floor.

"Fuck you..."

Rashid nodded. He bent down and opened a case of water that had been placed in front of the man. He cracked the top off a bottle and drank down the tepid water grate-fully. He placed another near the man's feet. So near, yet so far. "Name..."

The man eyed the water, then looked defiantly up at the three men. "Ahmadi will get to you," he told them. "And when Ahmadi gets to someone, he knows how to hurt them. *And* their families..."

"We're no strangers to pain either," Big Dave said confi-dently. "And we don't scare easily."

"You know nothing of pain or fear..."

**159**

"I know that you're here, and we're the ones asking the questions," Rashid interjected.

"*Kafir...*" the man glared venomously as he threw the Islamic insult of a non-believer. "There is a place in *Juhannam* for a pig-fucker like you..."

"And you believe that there is no place for you in hell for a man who does the devil's work?" Rashid spat at him. "Ahmadi deals in death. His weapons kill children, make orphans and widows. You are the one who will scream through the gates of *Juhannam*, not me..."

The man sneered, but his eyes darted back to the water. The room felt airless and hot. The stench of urine was overpowering. The mercury was nudging forty-degrees centigrade inside and untouched by the sea breeze.

"Have some water, man," Big Dave offered. "Just answer a few questions and you can have a drink."

"I can hold out."

"Sure," Big Dave said sardonically. "But in ten hours' time? A day, maybe two? You'd lick hot dog piss off a lamp post if you got the chance..."

The man shook his head. "You know nothing about me."

"No," replied Rashid. "But we soon will." He looked at Big Dave and held out his hand. "Give me the case."

Big Dave shook his head. "Not yet. The water should be enough."

"Forget it. I want to cut to the chase. We all know how it works. You break a finger, you beat him for a while, you pull out a fingernail or two... sooner or later, they talk. They always do."

"It's too soon," argued Big Dave.

Rashid snatched the case from the big Fijian and knelt beside the man. He opened the lid revealing two syringes.

"Something to encourage you to talk," he explained to the man without looking at him.

"Not yet..." protested Big Dave. "We need to hurt him first..."

Jack Luger stared incredulously at the small aluminium case and the two syringes inside. The liquid inside one was a vibrant yellow, the other looked like maple syrup. He looked back at his two colleagues, unsure how this scenario was going to play out.

"What are you doing?" the man asked, his voice finally echoing concern. He was perspiring profusely, blinking through the stinging sweat. "What are they?"

"I can't be a part of this..." Big Dave said and strode decisively to the door and the storeroom out back.

Luger frowned, but he was planted to the spot. As much as he wanted to question Big Dave, he needed to see what Rashid was going to do next.

"Please..." the man begged as Rashid took out the syringe containing the vibrant yellow liquid. "I did not mean to call you *kafir*..."

"This is the perfect truth serum," Rashid explained, ignoring his pleas. "Or to be more accurate, the second ampule is technically the truth serum. Because once this is injected into your bloodstream, you will tell me what I want to know for the chance to have the other."

"What is it?" the man asked again, panicked.

"Egyptian Cobra venom," Rashid said casually. "And the latest antidote, or anti-venom approved by the WHO."

"No!"

Rashid took the cap off the needle, checked the syringe for air bubbles. "Do you know how cobra venom works?" Rashid shrugged. "Don't worry, it's a rhetorical question. Cobra venom is a potent neurotoxic substance. It contains a complex mixture of proteins, enzymes, peptides, and other bioactive molecules that work together to immobilise and kill prey or defend against predators. When injected into a victim, the venom targets various physiological systems, particularly the nervous system, leading to a cascade of harmful effects. The primary component of cobra venom is a group of toxins known as neurotoxins. These neurotoxins disrupt the normal functioning of nerve cells by interfering with their communication and signalling processes. They specifically target the neuromuscular junctions, where nerve cells meet muscle cells, impairing the transmission of signals and causing paralysis." Rashid paused. "Are you still with me? Good." He continued, "One of the key neurotoxins found in cobra venom is called alpha-neurotoxin, which blocks the action of acetylcholine, a neurotransmitter responsible for transmitting signals between nerve cells. By blocking the receptors that acetylcholine binds to, alpha-neurotoxins prevent the normal transmission of signals from nerve to muscle, resulting in muscle weakness and flaccid paralysis." He paused again, opened a bottle of water, and drank thirstily, watching the man's reaction to both the syringes and the water. He placed the water near the man and continued reciting what he had earlier read, "In addition to neurotoxins, cobra venom also contains cardiotoxins, which can disrupt the cardiovascular system by causing cell damage, disrupting heart rhythms, and interfering with blood clotting mechanisms. These cardiotoxic effects can lead to cardiovascular collapse and organ failure." He glanced up at Jack Luger, who was staring at him, almost transfixed. "You don't have to be here for this..."

The young man shook his head. "No, I want to hear the man's answers. I have questions for him, too."

Rashid nodded. "Very well." He leaned towards the man and pulled up his sleeve.

"No!" the man screamed. "Stop!" Rashid pressed the needle into the man's arm. There was no need to find a vein, snake venom was a fast worker without making it more so. The man flinched, but could not help watching the bright, yellow liquid drain from the syringe. "No, please..." the man managed, but it was too late. The syringe was half empty, and Rashid pulled it out and placed it back in the case.

"Shit..." Jack Luger said quietly.

The man started to perspire more than he already had been. His milky coffee skin started to grow pale. After another minute he slumped, his muscles relaxing.

"The anti-venom is right here," Rashid told him. "Let's start with how many security personnel does Ahmadi keep with him?"

"Fuck you..."

"No," Rashid replied coldly. "You're the one who is fucked, if you don't answer!" he yelled.

"Give me the anti-venom and I'll tell you!"

"Answer my questions and you'll get it!"

The man started to pant, then suddenly lurched and vomited on the floor beside him. "Please..." he croaked. Unable to wipe his face, the vomit dripped off the tip of his chin. "I don't want to die like this..."

"What do you know about the Iron Fist?"

The man shook his head. "I've heard the name," he said. "Ahmadi fixes things for them."

"What things?"

"He deals in weapons. In arms. He helps people win wars..."

"Or start them," Luger interjected. He picked up the bottle, bent down and shook water on the man's face. He allowed him a short drink, then took the bottle away. Rashid glared at Luger, but the young man merely shrugged. "It's not just weapons, though, is it?" Rashid frowned, but he said nothing. "Ahmadi has other ideas of weapons..." The man licked his lips, then spat on the floor. He was having trouble sitting upright and Luger caught hold of him and dragged him to the wall to lean on. "Tell me about AI cyber-botics..." Rashid looked at Jack Luger and held out both palms. The gesture was easy to read. He was in the dark and this line of questioning was all new to him. "Ahmadi works for the Iron Fist. Iran, Russia, China, Belarus, and North Korea. Five fingers, working together to make a fist to strike at the West."

"I don't know about that," he said, looking at the syringe. "Please, I can't feel my mouth..." And as if to add weight to his claim, he dribbled saliva and vomit, and had slurred the last sentence. He lurched again and vomited, this time down his front and onto his legs. When he had finished, he looked up pleadingly and said, "Give me the anti-venom and I will tell you everything you wish to know..."

# Chapter Thirty-Two

"Got it?"

"The kid set up the camera," Rashid replied. "The bodyguard is singing like a bird."

Big Dave nodded. "I thought I'd bail out. Give him the good cop, bad cop routine."

"Seems to have worked."

"Did you know that Jack had his own agenda?"

"No." Rashid paused. "But he's clearly been read into something above our paygrades..."

Big Dave nodded. "I think it's Stella Fox's management style. She clearly compartmentalises her agents and agendas." He paused. "Did the anti-sickness work?"

Rashid nodded. The man had been given a harmless emetic. Thorough, but harmless. The anti-sickness drug was *Metoclopramide*, widely used in the NHS. No harm had come to the man, although his mental anguish would have been immeasurable. "It did. He's feeling better, but he is extremely aware that we can inject him again." He paused. "Now it's a matter of what to do with him."

"We let him go..." Both men looked up at Jack Luger,

who was standing in the doorway. "You could have told me that it wasn't cobra venom..."

Rashid shrugged. "Well, your face certainly looked the part, and that made it more believable."

"We can't just let him go," Big Dave commented flatly.

"We can and we will." Luger paused. "He's terrified that Ahmadi will think he talked. If we let him go with the threat of letting it be known to Ahmadi that his bodyguard talked, then he's a dead man. He knows it, and we know it. Plus, if I spin it enough, then we may even have a short-term asset on the inside..."

"Sound's workable," Rashid commented flatly. "Any other agendas we could do with knowing about?"

"No," Luger replied. "You do you, and I'll do me..."

"Meaning?" Rashid asked, clearly rattled. "We're meant to be a team."

"And we are. But do you think right now we know what King has been briefed on, or what Ramsay is doing between sourcing emetics and analysing data? We all have jobs to do..."

Big Dave placed a hand on Rashid's shoulder, then stepped closer to Luger. "So, what is AI cyberbotics?" He paused. "We may not have been read in, but we want to be brought up to speed. Now."

Luger looked up at the giant of a man, who had four inches on him in height and at least five stone in weight. But to his credit, he did not seem fazed. The big Fijian got the impression that the man did not back away from conflict. Undaunted, Luger said, "Artificial Intelligence is theoretically in its infancy, but only because its applications are unbounded. So, we already have apps and websites allowing university students to generate dissertations. Businesses can use it for copywriting, saving millions. Integrated with search engines, AI can be used for in depth searches and produce passable copy. These are good things. But where it becomes a threat is if AI can be written into computer viruses, to self-generate and continuously evade anti-virus software."

"But how does this involve an arms dealer?" Big Dave responded.

Luger sipped from the bottle he was holding. The room must have been over forty degrees now, the sun beating down directly above the corrugated iron roof. "Because Stella Fox thinks that Ahmadi has found a way to weaponize AI..."

# Chapter Thirty-Three

MacPherson knew his capabilities with a rifle. There was no cover to speak of for two-thousand metres. The compound was situated on raised ground with mountain views to the east and distant sea views to the west. The perimeter wall cut most of the visibility needed for a long shot, and that was if he was lucky enough to catch a fleeting glimpse of the target walking from the house to the car. The gardens, terrace and pool were out of sight. The clearest shot would be the second floor, but he had neither established a pattern or routine, and without a firing position with suitable elevation, the distance created too much drop for the bullet unless he could guarantee the target stood behind his bedroom window or took a leisurely breakfast on his balcony. Having discounted a sniper scenario – unless he could utilise another location - MacPherson would focus on a thorough reconnaissance of the compound.

The drone was hovering a thousand feet above the compound, its underside painted various shades of blue and grey in a similar pattern to a tiger's coat. The craft was fitted with both a wide-angle and telephoto lens, with high resolution so that stills could be taken from the constant video stream. MacPherson watched the images on the controller, although he would scrutinise the footage later on his laptop. Below, the cavalcade of Mercedes and Range Rovers were parked on the gravelled driveway in a fan formation. Pathways of gravel lined with palms cut swathes through a rocky garden, and behind the villa a vast lawn to rival any golf green on the PGA Tour surrounded a sparkling blue kidney-shaped swimming pool, with shallow pools and fountains flanking one side with palms and olive trees provided shady sanctuary from the North African sun. A lithe woman in her thirties was reading in the shade, a metallic silver bikini accentuating her olive skin. She was reading a magazine and beside her, a jug of amber liquid and two glasses were perched on a small table. MacPherson assumed it was iced tea as Ahmadi presented as a devout Muslim and outside the compound, Ahmadi's wife wore a hijab, although it was one of the more stylised varieties that went with her designer wardrobe. In the pool a boy of eleven was using a mask and snorkel, diving for coins, and examining them on the pool edge as if they were gold doubloons having rested on the seabed for three-hundred years.

MacPherson broke the hover and piloted the drone so that he could first study the entrances and exits, then concentrate on the balcony and bedroom windows, although it only consolidated his hesitance to go for the rifle shot. Firstly, he would have to source a specialist weapon as he only had access to a Dragunov SVD sniper rifle, and while good for a thousand metres, there was simply not enough cover to take advantage of.

The vibration of the mobile phone in his pocket broke

his train of thoughts. There could only be one person calling him, and that person was not known for his patience. MacPherson put the drone into a hover and answered. "Hello?"

*"You may have company..."*

MacPherson frowned. Sir Galahad Mereweather was still lying low, weathering the storm. Even so, the man had connections. "Who?"

*"I'm not sure, but the new director of Box has been asking questions."*

"King and his chums?"

*"Doubtful,"* Sir Galahad replied tersely. *"I hear he's stagnating while living some idealistic dream sailing the Med. But Neil Ramsay is in Casablanca."*

"He's no agent!"

*"No, but if he is there, then he will be supporting some-body at the sharp end. I don't believe in coincidence. If the Security Service have a presence there, then you can bet they're after the same thing."*

"Point taken. Too bad they're late."

*"Quite. Are you still clear on the objective?"*

"Yes."

*"The target meets his maker with extreme prejudice. No accidents, no ambiguity. We send a clear message. But we do it soon, before a connection can be found."*

MacPherson nodded, his eyes on the compound in the distance. The heat haze making the structure look like a distant mirage against the featureless terrain. "Understood."

# Chapter Thirty-Four

The bodyguard was still bound, but now he was cramped in the boot of the Toyota with Rashid driving with both Big Dave and Jack Luger following in the Jeep. Rashid stopped the car near the marina and waited for both Big Dave and Luger to cover the boot before opening. Luger reached inside and cut through the man's bonds with a clasp knife. He folded the knife and slipped it back into his pocket before tearing the piece of duct tape from the man's mouth, the man grimacing as half his stubble was torn out. He rubbed his mouth, licking his lips. Rashid handed the man a bottle of water as Big Dave heaved him out and pressed him backwards so that he half perched, half leaned on the lip of the boot.

"You confronted our man here..." Rashid told him. "Satisfied that he was just a curious tourist, interested in what sort of man requires such a protection detail, he gave you the slip and left you stranded."

The man shook his head. "This will not go well for me..."

"If you tell Ahmadi that you were bested and made to

talk, then he will kill you." Rashid paused. "This way, you tell a small lie, but keep your head connected to your neck..."

"You do not know the man; you could not possibly know how he thinks."

"If you don't do what we want, then we will see that Ahmadi gets the video and audio of our... *conversation*," Rashid replied.

"I have told you what you wanted to know!"

Jack Luger shook his head. "You will receive a text message when we want you to act," he said curtly. "You know what we want you to do."

"They will kill me."

"We'll kill you if you don't," Big Dave added for gravitas. "Or we'll send Ahmadi enough footage of your betrayal for him to do the job for us."

"Pigs!" the man spat at them, but he knew that he did not have a choice. He had seen what happened to traitors of Ahmadi, the man's enemies as well. It wasn't pretty.

Big Dave stepped aside and gave the man a pull, jerking him abruptly to his feet. "On your way now, sunshine," he said somewhat jovially. "We'll be in touch..."

# Chapter Thirty-Five

The **Kakheti Region of Georgia**

It was difficult to imagine that a region so beautiful in its topography, flora and fauna could play host to such an awful crime as sex trafficking. Difficult, but not impossible. The war in Ukraine had fuelled supply and demand, as early refugees fleeing both Ukraine and the Russian Federation had flooded the Georgian border and girls and young women had been herded in droves and snatched into the underground sex trade by ruthless, opportunistic criminals.

Caroline Darby had history with this country. While on sabbatical with Interpol she hunted sex traffickers and brought them to justice. She had her own motives for such work, and since she had returned to MI5, she had always ached to do more, like she had unfinished business. But that business would be finished today.

The tip-off had come from Jordan White, just as the

bank job had in Paris. Ronnie Vickers had a stake in East European sex trafficking, himself owning a dozen or more brothels in London and taking fresh girls every couple of months. He then sold the well-used girls off to other criminal gangs around the country. By then the girls were addicts and compliant and seldom strayed because of their need for a fix and a roof over their head. Using trains and suitable *Airbnb* rentals, the girls simply turned up in a new town each week with their services advertised on internet selling sites and free ads. *These girls would not end up like that,* thought Caroline as she surveyed the farm through the powerful pair of Zeiss binoculars.

King watched from the other side. Between them, they had worked their way around the property in a clockwise direction, leaving no area unwatched. King had been on the Jon Wood passport since flying in from Bulgaria, a country that did not use European watchlists. He had hired a car using a debit card in the same name and had used it again to check into a cheap hotel. He had then met up with Caroline and they had wined and dined with cash and stayed together in a quiet country hotel using her details for the booking and heading to their room early to make up for lost time. The hours snatched had seemed more fulfilling, more intimate than when they had been on the yacht together. Absence really did make the heart grow fonder, and a good thing sometimes needed to be missed to be truly appreciated.

After hot showers and a cold breakfast of deli meats, cheese and bread, King had left for his own hotel and once again taken up the persona of Jon Wood. The two had met again near the farm, parked both cars off the road using the field hedges to hide them from the road and set out to the farm cross-country. Caroline had used her diplomatic bag to bring in both her and King's 9mm Glock 19 pistols and two loaded magazines a piece. King, who had flown from Bulgaria as Jon Wood, had not had the convenience of the diplomatic status afforded to the team by Stella Fox and the Foreign and Commonwealth Office.

"Three men so far," Caroline said into her phone using a Bluetooth ear bud and mic.

*"Just two this side."* King paused. *"Standard East European criminals. Tracksuits and cigarettes. Squatting while they chat. Don't look like they've washed in weeks."*

"Same this side. No visual on weapons, but they will have pistols for sure."

*"A couple of AKs inside would be a safe assumption. If they get to those then we won't have much of a chance..."*

"Ever the pessimist..."

*"Realist."*

She did not contradict him, knowing that he had a point. A pistol was no match for a rifle. But they had surprise on their side, and she felt fire in her belly when she thought about the girls being held and abused and degraded in this place.

*"We need confirmation on trafficked girls first."*

"The information comes from Jordan White personally," Caroline argued.

*"Ah, truly a man of integrity..."*

Caroline felt herself getting angry. They were here, they had good information. "We know this is the place," she protested. "We need to go in!"

*"Wait out,"* he said. *"You're too emotionally involved. I'm going in for a closer look..."*

"Alex, wait!"

*"Just a look-see..."*

Caroline cursed as the line went dead. She raised the

field glasses in time to see King moving down the side of a
hedgerow before disappearing behind a large outbuilding.
"Damn it!" she hissed. *How dare he say that!* she thought,
but to her annoyance she knew that he was right. She had
been held herself in a similar captive state, the ever-present
threat of ending up as a slave in the illegal sex trade hanging
over her until she had finally managed to escape. Other
women had not been so lucky. She slipped out from the
bushes and followed his lead, using the hedgerow as cover
as she headed for a closer observation post.

King had bypassed the two men, still squatting, still
smoking. He headed for the largest barn and knew instinctively that this was the right place because the bolt on the
door was shiny and well-used, and the padlock securing it
further was new and well-oiled. He had earlier picked up
some tools from a hardware shop, and he slipped the
Glock back into his jacket pocket and took out an
adjustable spanner. He slipped the jaws around one side
of the padlock and screwed the jaws together until they
clamped tightly, then taking out another identical spanner
he repeated the process, confidently crossed the handles,
and squeezed them together. He slipped at first and took a
sizeable chunk of flesh from the knuckle of his index
finger. Cursing under his breath, then sucking the wound
instinctively, he got a better purchase and squeezed with
all his might. It was enough to ease the shank of the
padlock from the lock inside and with his left hand he
pulled the body of the lock down and the padlock snapped
open. He looked around him, the final snap of the padlock
making more noise than he had anticipated. Still clear.

King eased the bolt back, sliding as easily and smoothly as a well-used bolt-action rifle. Inside, the barn had been converted into cells. Each cell door had a Perspex inspection window, and sure enough, there were two or three women per cell. The women looked bedraggled and unwashed. Emaciated. There was a fetid smell, and he could see toilet buckets in the first cell. The women barely glanced at him. He knew addicts when he saw them, and they had been conditioned into a state of compliance by drug addiction. Most likely heroin. They stared through each other, through the walls, through their own existence. For a moment, King was taken back to his childhood, his mother staring endlessly at nothing, her mind a million miles away, a near endless stream of men knocking at their flat door for fifteen minutes of her time and enough money for another fix.

"*Daagde iaraghi!*" the man shouted from behind him. King froze. He did not understand Georgian, but he knew when he was in trouble. He started to slowly turn around but was jabbed hard in the right kidney with something hard and narrow for the trouble. "*Bros' svoye oruzhiye!*" the man snapped at him again, but this time in Russian. King understood enough to get the gist, and he slowly pulled out his pistol and complied, dropping it to the ground with a clatter. With his hands raised, he slowly turned around and saw the man standing just a few feet from him, holding the AKM assault rifle which he had jabbed him with. The last inch of the muzzle had a canted end rather like semi-circular tray which helped keep the muzzle down by expelling the gases upwards under automatic fire. This was known as a compensator, but it also hurt like hell when it jabbed you in the kidney, although it is doubtful that was ever a factor in its design. "You... are... not... Russian..." the man smirked in passable English. He gestured with the rifle and added, "Outside..."

King walked ahead of the man. He heard the scrape of metal as the man kicked the pistol ahead of him and he glanced back to see the man bending down in the doorway to retrieve the weapon. King lunged backwards and kicked the muzzle of the Kalashnikov aside. A second kick sent it out of his hands altogether and it clattered on the muddy ground. The man lurched forwards and kicked at King, but he was not quick enough, and King blocked the kick and when he straightened, he caught the man with a left cross, grabbed hold of the man's jacket by the lapels and kneed him in the gut. The man was an experienced brawler and took the blow, punching and kicking King backwards. King went with the attack, giving himself some space, but the man reached behind him, and the next thing King knew, a blade was flashing back and forwards in front of him. The man stopped, panting and eyeing King warily as he started to move around King in a circular motion. King whipped out his own folding lock knife. A simple Opinal no8 that he had purchased in a filling station after hiring his car. It was nothing fancy to look at, but it had a rigid and unique twist-lock and was one of the sharpest blades he had ever purchased. The man flashed his saw-back combat knife, the blade somewhere over the eight-inch mark, but King could tell by the way that he held it that he had practised in the mirror and nothing more, and that this wasn't going to go the way the man hoped. King waited for the man to move and when he lunged forwards King swiped the knife across the man's forearm and he yelped and withdrew his hand, but King followed up with a massive front kick towards the man's stomach, designed to drive him backwards if he didn't get lucky and land the blow. The man stabbed out, but King blocked the attack, stabbed his own knife into the man's bicep and whipped the blade backwards, damn-near filleting the muscle from the bone. The man's face turned white, and he switched hands and staggered forwards. King slashed his blade across the man's forehead and darted back. The white gash, the blade scraping the man's skull, started to turn red, then cascaded down his forehead and showered the man's eyes in blood, forcing him to wipe it away with the back of his left hand, his right arm now hanging limply by his waist. The man made a half-hearted attack, but King smashed the edge of his foot into the man's right kneecap and was on him as he fell, his left arm wrapped around the man's neck like a python, his own blade plunging into the man's side, six, seven, eight times. When the man slumped to the ground, King stared for a moment catching his breath when the gunshot made him flinch. He turned around to see Caroline aiming her Glock, and a second armed man lying between them on the ground.

"Well, that was smooth," she said. "Just a *look-see*, my arse..."

"Mission creep," King said nonchalantly. He rushed over and picked up his own pistol and tucked it into his waistband as he picked up the dead man's AKM. Caroline was already checking the other man's Uzi. "Let's get this done," he said to her. "On me..." They did not have to go far. Two men ran around the edge of the barn, pistols in hand, and were cut down by a dozen bullets between them. King barely slowed his stride and when he rounded the barn a man was hurriedly getting into an old Opel saloon. King fired a short burst and the man dropped onto his knees and fell beside the vehicle. "I'm going into the house! Wait outside and cover the yard!"

Caroline was about to protest, but she knew that King

was the more experienced in this scenario and she filed back to a low wall where she could see anyone coming from across the yard, yet still watch the doorway to the house. She quickly ejected the magazine of the machine pistol. She had more in the Glock, so she slipped the Uzi over her shoulder on the sling and swapped to the pistol. She had put in many hours on the range with the Glock and decided it was better to stick to what she knew. Besides, the Uzi was a 'spray and pray' weapon and with King inside the house, she did not want to make any mistakes.

"Exiting!" King shouted. "One unarmed man ahead of me!"

Caroline found herself shaking. Partly because her adrenalin was starting to subside, and partly at her anger for the beast that was about to walk into her weapon's sights. The man stepped out with little care or regard for being held at gunpoint. His eye was swollen, and his lips were thick and split from where King had obviously punched him, and he spat a glob of blood and saliva at Caroline which splattered on her thigh. She turned her nose up in disgust as the mess rolled down her leg, and King jabbed the assault rifle in the man's kidney for his trouble. He groaned and screwed his face up in pain, but he quickly got over it and stood outside the farmhouse, taking in the sight of his comrade lying beside the car. He glared back at both King and Caroline.

"Who the fuck are you?" he demanded belligerently. "You will pay for this. My boss will slice the skin off your faces for this..."

"Where's the money?" King asked.

The man looked confused. "Money?"

King shrugged. "You guys don't look like you pay taxes

or file accounts for this venture," he said. "Where's the money?"

The man studied King for a moment and bartering out of his current situation did not take long to come to mind. "Kitchen drawer," he said. "Near the sink. Take it and let me go."

King nodded to Caroline, and she tucked her pistol inside her jacket and stepped over the front threshold into the farmhouse. He stared at the man, his hold loose on the Kalashnikov, but still aimed at him. There was a flicker in the man's eyes, a tightening of his lips. "Caroline! Wait!" King shouted, but it was too late. Caroline let out a shrill cry, and then a gut-wrenching scream. King turned towards the farmhouse just a second too long and the man lunged for the rifle. He caught hold of the muzzle, pushed it aside and held firm. King fired but the bullet thudded into the ground and showered them both with mud and debris. The man tried to swing a punch, but King blocked it with his left hand, and continued with a left jab, his right hand gripping the weapon firmly. The jab stunned the man, but nothing more from such short range. The man tugged hard at the rifle, the muzzle safely away from his body. King flicked the selector upwards into the 'auto' position and clamped his finger on the trigger. The rifle rattled away in fully-auto and the man released his grip on the barrel, his hand scorched from the heat. King dropped the rifle, his right hand already gripped around the Glock in his waistband. The man turned, bent down, and picked up the rifle but froze when he looked up into the muzzle of King's pistol. Caroline was still screaming inside the house, and the man smiled at the sound. King fired once through the man's right eye. The man slumped onto his knees, the rifle clattering to the ground and King didn't even see him fall as he turned and sprinted into the farmhouse.

Caroline had wrapped a kitchen towel around her right hand, but it had already turned almost completely red. Her blood was dripping onto the floor, and she had turned pale. King guided her to a chair. The table was cluttered with dirty dishes, fast-food wrappings and a coffee cup over-spilling with cigarette butts and ash. He cleared the table with a swipe of his forearm and laid a second kitchen towel on the table. It was the best he could do under the circumstances. He gently unwrapped the towel and was met by a surge of blood. "The drawer was spring-loaded..." she managed to hiss through her clenched teeth. "When it clamped shut around my wrist, I realised that there was a blade fixed to the top of the drawer..."

King shook his head. *The sick bastards,* he thought. The blade had sliced completely through her veins, and he suspected from the limpness in her wrist that the tendons had been damaged. But it was more than that. There must have been razorblades or scalpel blades mounted inside the drawer on its longitude as well, because two blades had sliced down her forearm as well as across it. The suicide cut. Attention seekers sliced across their wrists, but anyone serious about taking their life followed the artery for at least six inches down their forearm. He looked around for options. Caroline looked even more pale if that were possible, and he tore off his belt and strapped it around her upper arm, cinching it tightly and tucking the end in place to hold it firm. He then turned to the cupboards, tearing things out and assessing what could help him, and what could be discarded. Switching on the gas stove, he took a deep breath before placing a spatula on the flame. Caroline barely noticed. She looked nauseous and weak. King found some salt and sugar and he pinched a couple of fingers of salt into a dirty glass, tipped in a lot of sugar and filled it under the tap. "Drink," he said, helping her with the glass as she gulped down the liquid. He unwrapped the dressing, and before Caroline knew what was going on, he took the spatula, squeezed the wound together, and pressed the glowing implement tightly on the gash, cauterizing the wound. Caroline wailed, then slumped in the chair as she lost consciousness. King held both her and the spatula in place, the smell of burning flesh permeating the stale air. When he removed the spatula, the wound looked raw and blistered, but was no longer bleeding. She would certainly need hospital treatment, but King was confident that he would at least get her there now. He wrapped the lateral cut to her wrist with some strips of towel, that he tore quickly using his teeth. King took out his wallet, which contained fifty US dollars and five-hundred Georgian Lari. It also held a debit card in the name of Jon Wood. Caroline was a dead weight in his arms, but as he stepped over the body on the ground, he dropped the wallet next to it and kept walking.

He took Caroline's car, resting her in the passenger seat and belting her in, then he found the hospital on *Google Maps*, and he called the police on the way. He gave the address of the farm and told them what they would find when they got there. Then he memorised the route to the hospital, and the address and tossed the phone out of the window.

# Chapter Thirty-Six

C asablanca

Ahmadi looked out on the lawns and the pool beyond. His son was playing in one of the fountains, cooling off in the glaring sun. Ahmadi's wife was working out with her personal trainer under the shade of a ring of palms. Ahmadi always watched them. As did one of his bodyguards, who was sitting nearby and drinking iced tea in the shade. With a woman as beautiful as Alya one never fully relaxed. Especially when her trainer was a bronzed Adonis from Sweden who trained many women in the city. He watched the man arrange the dumbbells in order weight and repetition. He finished with the heavy kettlebell, then clapped his hands and Ahmadi watched as Alya started at the beginning of the chain.

"And you failed to find him..." It was a statement, not a

question. "He got the better of you and you let him get away."

"Sir, with respect..."

"People who start a sentence like that seldom show any respect..."

The bodyguard nodded, casting his eyes to the floor. "He did not know anything. He was just a tourist."

"You allowed him to best you."

"It was a simple mistake; I will not fail you again!"

"No. You will not," Ahmadi turned around and stared at the man before taking to his chair behind an expansive teak desk. He opened the top drawer to his right and took out a wickedly sharp-looking knife with an acutely curved blade. A khanjar. The knife looked ceremonial with mother of pearl bolsters and filigree gold inlays along the length of the hilt. On the end of the hilt – the pummel - a large ruby caught the light shining in through the window behind him. Ahmadi placed the knife down on the polished wood. "Your left little finger, if you please?" he said calmly. "As a reminder of how costly mistakes can be, and how to avoid repeating them."

Behind the bodyguard, the two men who had accompanied the man into the room tensed, readying themselves for the man to resist. Knowing it would be futile, the man stepped forward and picked up the knife, his right hand shaking and a bead of sweat running down a furrow in his brow and onto the tip of his nose. "Please, have mercy..."

"A finger from you, or I will take a hand..."

The man glanced behind him, but the two men – his friends and colleagues – each had an arm tucked inside their lightweight linen suit jackets and he knew that their hands would be wrapped around the butts of the pistols underneath.

Friendship and loyalty only went so far when a man was terrified of his boss, and everyone here feared Ahmadi, and especially the reach he had. The man turned back, took a breath, and placed his left hand on the desk. He formed a fist, then poked the little finger out as he hefted the dagger and got a feel for its balance. In a blinding flash, he brought the blade down but missed and drove the blade deep into his knuckles. He screamed and dropped the knife, clutching his hand, the blood oozing between his fingers and dripping on the tiled floor.

Ahmadi shook his head. "A finger, Malik. A finger. No more; no less..." The man bent down slowly and picked up the knife. His hands were shaking, and his left knuckle was bleeding from a deep gash. This time, he placed his hand on the desk, lined the blade up with the middle joint of his little finger and pressed down with all his might. The blade crunched through the bone like a chef jointing a chicken and he dropped the knife and whimpered, clutching his left hand. "Very good Malik. You have earned my trust again," Ahmadi said pleasantly. He looked at both bodyguards behind Malik and said, "Take our friend and see that he gets first class medical attention for his efforts." And without further word, he got out of his chair and continued his vigil on his wife and her personal trainer. As the men reached the door, the bear of a man whimpering, he turned around and said, "Oh, and leave the finger. I'd hate for you to forget this lesson in years to come..."

# Chapter Thirty-Seven

**E**xmoor
**Three days later**

"Is this how you work? Because if it is, then I'm not sure there's a future in this department."

King shrugged, sipped some more of his tea, and looked at the new director of MI5. "Situations change in the field," he said in a disinterested tone. "Very few variables can be planned for. But the mission is the mission, and we are on track for that."

Stella Fox looked at Caroline, her right arm in a sling and heavily dressed underneath. "You're not fit for duty..."

"Well, it's just as well that this is a department that doesn't exist," Caroline replied tersely. "I don't imagine health and safety will have much cause to check up on us." She paused. "And I'm fine, by the way. Nothing that a couple of weeks' restricted duties won't sort out." She paused. "That, and a course of skin grafts when all this is over..."

The MI5 director ignored her comment and looked at Big Dave and Jack Luger, no less irked by recent developments. "You were supposed to be on a reconnaissance. A surveillance operation, but already you have been compromised by the enemy."

"Shit happens," Big Dave replied without any apparent concern. "We turned it around pretty well."

"I'd say we did better than that," Jack Luger commented. "We have an asset in place. With the best motivation of all. Fear. He knows that if he tells Ahmadi that he broke under interrogation, then he's a dead man."

"He may be a dead man, anyway," Stella Fox countered.

"Is that our problem?" asked King.

"It's a life!"

"People know who they work for," Caroline stated flatly. "He knows who he's in bed with, we can't worry about that. I mean, Ahmadi's family shouldn't be touched, but his security? No, they're fair game."

"How about we concentrate on the mission?" David Garfield suggested tactfully. The department boss and second-in-command of the Security Service stood up and looked at Neil Ramsay. "Neil?"

Ramsay opened his laptop and squinted at the screen as he said, "King has planted another seed for his legend, Jon Wood. Our telephone intercepts have confirmed that Vickers is aware of *Jon Wood's* actions. He stole the money from the armoured van, won and lost a fortune in Monte Carlo, and ripped off a hundred-thousand euros from a sex-trafficking concern in Georgia, shutting them down in the process. Vickers had a man inside the local police in that region of Georgia and he reported back to Jordan White what the police thought had happened, and that Jon Wood's ID was found at the scene. Wood is a person of interest in France and Georgia, and now Interpol have an all-points on him. We know that Ahmadi has a person in Interpol, so he will find out all he wishes to know when King presents himself to him later." Ramsay paused, scrolling on his screen. "It is unfortunate that the reconnaissance party were compromised in Casablanca..."

"Whose fault was it?" Garfield asked.

"Nobody's," Big Dave answered emphatically.

"Mine," said Luger. "I was made while I was drinking a coffee nearby. One of Ahmadi's bodyguards backtracked and got into my car."

"Armed?"

"Of course," Luger replied. "An Uzi machine pistol."

"The kid never had a chance," Big Dave interjected. "But it worked out alright in the end."

"King?" Garfield looked at him. "What is your take on this?"

"I wasn't there."

"You're the one who's going to try and infiltrate Ahmadi's machine, you need to be happy with your team's performance."

King glanced at Jack Luger, who did not hold his stare. The young man looked dejected. "I'm happy," said King. "Because shit *does* happen, and if Big Dave says that it wasn't his fault and that Jack couldn't have done anything else, then nobody could have done anything differently."

"The situation has given us an asset," Ramsay offered. "In my view, this is not only the best possible outcome, but something it is doubtful we could have ever cultivated."

Luger looked up again, buoyed somewhat in confidence. The team acting like a team, and he the newest member. He caught King's eye, but King remained impassive. He didn't go in for gratitude. "So, what did you learn?" he asked.

"Situational awareness, I suppose..."

"That's not what I meant," said King. "You sat near the man and his family for forty-five minutes. He made you because of this. What did you learn while you were there? Every detail from his wife's order to whether he tipped the waiter. Everything." Jack Luger shrugged. "Come on, man! Close your eyes and remember the scene."

"Seriously?"

"Seriously." King watched the man close his eyes, and he held up a hand to everybody not to interrupt. "Go on, take yourself back there..."

"OK, well..." he started hesitantly. "Ahmadi wore a beige suit. Lightweight. A white shirt, open at the collar..."

"How many buttons?" King prompted.

"Three," Luger added adamantly. "Good leather shoes. Tan. No socks. He had three espressos. His wife had a cappuccino. The boy had two cokes, local brands. Arabic writing."

"How close did Ahmadi seem to his wife?"

"Reasonably," Luger nodded. "It's an Arab country and they're both Iranian, but they touched hands a couple of times. He touched her knee once, but she pulled away. She wore a hijab, but only just and it looked expensive." He paused. "Ahmadi seemed impatient. He jiggles his right leg. Toes on the ground, but his leg is going up and down constantly..."

"That's really helpful," replied King. "Could his impatience really be apprehension?"

Luger shrugged. "I don't see why. Casablanca's a pretty safe city and he had his security detail with him."

King frowned. "And how was he with waiting staff?"

"Ahmadi tells them what he wants, and he gets it. No please or thank you. He clicks his fingers for attention..."

"That's gold," said King. "Ramsay, are you getting all this?"

"Of course..." Ramsay replied. He wasn't writing anything down, and nor was he recording the conversation, but it was committed to memory, and he would recall it word for word in his minutes later."

"The bodyguards were all armed," Luger continued. "Obviously I can vouch for the man who got the drop on me, but the others all had pistols, some had more. My guy had a mini-Uzi."

"Where is that, by the way?" Garfield asked incredulously.

"Rashid has it," Big Dave replied quietly, his eyes on Jack Luger, whose own eyes had remained closed throughout the interruption.

"Ahmadi has a gun, also." He paused. "Really small and in a tiny leather holster. A strange butt or handle. Bulbous shaped, but with a flat profile."

"How small?" asked King, leaning forward in his chair.

"Toy-like..."

"A derringer?"

"I don't know what that is..."

"A gambler's gun, in the Wild West..." King turned to Ramsay and said, "Find an image of a classic double-barrelled derringer..." Ramsay had the image in a few seconds and tilted his laptop screen for King to see. "Here you are," said King. "Look at this..."

"No need," said Caroline. She fished out a small pistol from her purse. Everyone but King frowned. The little stainless-steel gun had two short, two-inch barrels, one above the other. A single hammer and a trigger without a looped trigger guard indicated the simplicity of operation. The grips were made from ivory and were flat in profile and pear-shaped for good dexterity in the hand.

"Explain, please..." Stella Fox said humourlessly.

"That submarine job we did off Svalbard..." King paused, but both Fox and Garfield looked bemused. "Well, do you remember the Iranian sub that went missing in the Arctic while there was an operation to raise one of our own stricken subs?"

Garfield nodded sagely. "The Iranian submarine imploded at depth, so I believe..."

King said nothing at first, then went on, "I came across an Iranian agent who had a small derringer pistol as a last resort weapon." He paused. "That one, to be clear..."

"It looks like a harmless toy..." Stella Fox commented incredulously. "What happened to the Iranian agent?"

"I can't comment on that. Not if Simon Merewether has done what he could to hide our involvement in the whole affair." King paused. "But it's not a harmless toy. It's point thirty-eight-special in calibre. The bullets are less than an inch shorter than the barrels. It's only good for a few metres, but it packs a mighty punch. This is a good thing," he said, looking at Ramsay. "You know where the file will be. Look back and find that agent's identity and who exactly he worked for. It means that there may be a link between the agency that agent worked for and Ahmadi. However small the link, I'm sure that pistol is the catalyst binding them together."

"It still doesn't explain the gun in your possession," said Fox.

King shrugged. "I gave it to Caroline as a souvenir..."

"Then Caroline can hand it into the police today," the MI5 director said decisively. "Is it loaded?"

"Not much good if it isn't," Caroline replied, slipping it back into her handbag.

"Where is Rashid?" asked Garfield, changing the subject and attempting to defuse the tension.

"In situ," replied Ramsay. "He's keeping up surveillance, working some of the angles the team have come up with."

"Why Rashid?" asked Stella Fox.

"Skin colour, baby..." Big Dave said casually.

"I'm not sure we can say that..." the MI5 director replied tersely.

Big Dave grinned. "See my face? I can say what the hell I like about skin colour when it ain't white." He paused. "If it was Central or Southern Africa, then it would probably be me staying behind. As it is, Rashid is better placed in Morocco."

"Fine," Fox replied. "But let me make one thing perfectly clear... call me *baby* again and you'll be patrolling ports and airports until you draw your pension, OK?"

Big Dave grinned but said nothing. As apologies went, that was as good as Lomu gave.

"Rashid is one of, perhaps even the best, sniper I've known," said King diplomatically. "If anyone is going to thoroughly survey Ahmadi's compound without being seen, then he's the man to do it."

"We have eyes and ears inside the compound," Jack Luger said. He looked at every eye on him, then said, "I texted the bodyguard a few hours after he returned. I told him to open a window at the rear of the building..."

Big Dave frowned. "You did what?"

"I wasn't sure it would work, so I took a chance. If it didn't work, then both you and Rashid could honestly deny all knowledge." Luger shrugged, glancing awkwardly at both Stella Fox and David Garfield. "It was a gamble, but I flew a drone inside. Quite a small affair, but it is equipped with a camera and has several fail safes, such as recall to the control unit and instant hover if signal is lost, or there's pilot error. I strapped a wireless camera and microphone to the drone. It's connected to a battery-powered receiver that I've hidden nearby. There is only a few days' battery life for the entire set-up, but at least we can see what Ahmadi is like around his wife, child and the staff..." He stood up and handed a smartphone to David Garfield. "It's recording to the cloud, there should be some helpful footage there. I've taken the passcode off for you to access. The bodyguard has been told to remove and discard the camera in three days."

"Risky," Ramsay said irritably.

"No doubt," replied Stella Fox. "But this is a game-changer. This drone of yours sounds like something we should deploy further." She looked at Ramsay and said, "Liaise with Jack and discuss the possibilities."

"We do have our own drone programme," he replied tersely.

"And has anyone else flown a drone through a window to deliver orders or equipment to an asset?"

Ramsay sighed. "Not that I am aware of."

"Well, it sounds like a vital concept that needs further exploration..."

"Where are we on a diversion?" David Garfield asked, casually changing the subject to keep matters on track.

"There are a group running around Syria that fits the bill perfectly," Ramsay said, opening a file on his laptop and scrolling as he spoke. "These chaps... *Prophets of Jihad*. They're a bunch of murdering scumbags. Started out aligned with Al Qaeda ended up with ISIS. They did the whole soldier of ISIS thing – took young brides, beheaded prisoners, killed innocent civilians. Then they started to do much of their killing for their own pockets. Raze villages to the ground, steal money and food, rape and pillage indiscriminately. Before long, they plied their trade for splinter groups who had various takes on Jihad, even got work through the Wagner Group which of course was exclusively mercenary and actively representing Russia and Assad's campaign." Ramsay paused. "Simply put, flash enough cash at these men and they'll do what we require."

"And no tears will be shed for their demise..." Garfield mused quietly. "And not before time, too. As we know, Wagner are putting killers in Ukraine, and the SIS are concerned that Wagner will send this Prophet of Jihad lot on sabotage missions against the UK, dressed up as Islamic Extremism. They brought these jokers to our attention, so we'll use them in any way we can."

"Who is making contact with them?" King asked.

"Well, it can't be you," Stella Fox said emphatically. "Jack?"

"I can do it," he replied.

"Take Ramsay with you," said King. "He can play the accountant to our enterprise."

"I'm not a field agent," Ramsay protested.

"So you keep saying," King grinned. "And yet, here you are..."

"I'm not going to bloody Syria!"

"Really?" King teased. "But Aleppo is so nice at this time of year..."

# Chapter Thirty-Eight

C asablanca

The last time Rashid had surveyed a place like this it had been in Abbottabad, Pakistan. He hadn't been in the country to look up family members, his parents having escaped Indian persecution when Rashid had been only a baby. He had been one of the few men on the ground to confirm that the man pacing around the compound, the man with the unusually long shadow that indicated him to be over six-feet four inches tall, when the national average was a mere five-feet-seven. Rashid had been ready to move. Ready to capture or kill Osama Bin Laden when his orders had come in to stand down. The Americans were running the show and their infamous SEAL Team Six were to have the glory. French commandos had the man in their sights two years previously, but like Rashid's team, they were stood down for an American Delta team to lift him, and the

World's most wanted evaded capture by a matter of hours. Rashid had remained out of curiosity. Holed up in a hide that had been his home for four days, he had seen the helicopters and the SEALs fast roping down, seen the infamous Black Hawk crash. He had heard the shots inside, seen the flash-bangs and grenades. The raid took fifteen minutes with the entire operation taking just thirty-eight minutes from wheels down to wheels up. But Rashid had seen more besides. More than anyone should have. He had seen a body taken from a helicopter and carried inside the compound and a tall, hooded figure dressed in white robes escorted out in handcuffs and whisked away. Some people asked why the Americans buried Osama Bin Laden at sea so quickly after his death, but Rashid knew. It was because the man hadn't been killed that night. He was likely still alive in a secret CIA prison and would die there of old age, or when he was no longer of any use. Rashid had never told a soul, and he never would. Some secrets should simply stay that way. He was only safe for as long as he remained silent.

Like the infamous compound in Abbottabad, the walls were ten feet high and made from blocks and cement render jutting out of a stark area of open, featureless ground. Unlike that far away compound, this one was luxurious inside. The house was in the style of a villa with Hollywood dimensions and an oasis of colour testament to money, horticulture skills and irrigation.

Rashid had spotted the man on day two. Or rather, he had spotted the drone and studied it returning to its operator. He had found his position and constructed his hide at night, and he had enough room to observe one-hundred-and-eighty degrees and have a good supply of water and cold rations for what he knew as 'hard routine'. *Eat cold rations and shit in a bag,* was also how his SAS instructors in

Hereford had described it. The reality was that Rashid being a specialist sniper, he could operate for days under these conditions.

He had built the hide into a hillock using stones to shore up a wall from which he could observe through the gaps and had laid out sheets of thick fabric over his excavation and covered it with stones and dirt to blend into the landscape. He had a powerful pair of Swarovski binoculars and a thermal imaging x4 viewer, as well as solar-powered webcams that he would fix in position when he thought he was safe enough to move. Although, that would have to wait, because avoiding Ahmadi's security was one thing, but avoiding the other observer was quite another.

# Chapter Thirty-Nine

Exmoor

"Do you think it will work?"

"It'll work."

"What makes you so sure?"

King shrugged, but as they ran alongside each other the gesture was lost on the man. "It'll work."

"But if it doesn't?"

"Then we're dead." The man stopped running and stood stock-still, panting for breath, beads of perspiration at his brow. King stopped and walked the few paces back to him. "Are you having second thoughts?"

"Second thoughts?!" the man started to laugh. "Second, third and fourth... a hundred, even."

"Look, Ahmadi..."

"Ismael! My name is..."

King shoved the man hard in his chest, and he stumbled back a few feet. "Ahmadi! Your name is Ahmadi!"

"It's bullshit!"

"It's life or death! You are Ahmadi, I am Jon Wood! And if you can't hold onto that under scrutiny, or God forbid, interrogation, then we are both as good as dead..."

The man stared at King. He was still breathing hard, but the real Ahmadi ran five miles every morning and in an impressive time, and if they were going to the extent of teaching the asset to fly a helicopter, then a simple five-mile run was what David Garfield had described as a 'no brainer'. King would have to admit that the man had done well. With Caroline's tutorage and help from the Brazilian Ju Jitsu champion working in the archives of Thames House, he was now adept at Judo and Ju Jitsu and handling small arms. He could field-strip a dozen different pistols and rifles and had become a proficient marksman at short range. He dressed like Ahmadi, walked like Ahmadi and now with the mannerisms mastered, he even looked and moved like the man. He still had to knock two minutes off his five-mile morning run, but King had suggested that if he did not get down to the same time, then he could easily feign a minor injury or strain or change the route.

Flymo had taught the asset well. He had undertaken two solo flights as a confidence boost, and the ex-army pilot was now passenger as the man built up his hours and was met with a series of theory tests each evening.

"I can't do it..." the man said, a finality to his tone.

"I don't blame you."

"You don't?"

"No."

"What should I do?"

King shrugged. "Well, it looks like you're caught between the devil and the deep blue sea, old son."

"I don't believe in the devil anymore," the asset said adamantly. "Because I no longer believe in a God..."

"It's not any of that religious or spiritual crap," replied King.

"Meaning?"

"Sailors in tall ships used to have to seal or caulk the seams of the ship with thick oil while on the high seas. The devil was the seam closest to the water, because if you didn't seal it, the ship would fill with water and sink. But if you did, then you had a good chance of falling in and being lost at sea." King paused. "Damned if you do; damned if you don't."

"You like history?"

"I suppose," replied King. "Especially the gory and sexy bits. It makes for an interesting read."

The man nodded. "Much of what is happening in my country will be studied as history," he said. "I am not sure about sexy bits, but there is much gore. I had two sisters and a brother. They were all killed. My mother and father also. Strictly speaking, my youngest sister disappeared within the machine of the regime. But I know that she is dead."

King nodded. He had a sister who had been murdered, so he knew something of the man's pain. "And that is your motivation for this?"

"It is."

"But Ahmadi is not part of that regime. He is something else entirely."

"He is cut from the same cloth." The man paused. They had reached the cliffs and the view down to Lynmouth was breath-taking. The sea was calm and blue, its tranquillity mirrored in the cloudless sky above. The coastline of Wales was clearly visible in the distance. King could tell that the view was both new and yet meaningful to the man. "He represents the Iranian regime, but either singularly or within this new group. A get-out for Iran. A stooge to deflect political pressure or criticism."

King watched the ocean, losing himself in its beauty and stillness. It looked so inviting. A distraction from the reality they both faced. Suddenly the yacht moored in Sardinia had never seemed so appealing. *Damn Ramsay, damn Stella Fox...* The Iron Fist was a proxy for enemies of The West, but the threat was both credible and, as yet unknown. "Then let's take the bastard down," said King eventually. "Let's hurt the regime, and others like it."

The man nodded, but he said nothing, his eyes focused somewhat dreamily on the sea, briefly wondering how many had stared at such a sight and wished for escape.

# Chapter Forty

R aqqa, Syria

"We were out here with the regiment when Russia committed forces to Assad's regime. Bloody unworkable. Everyone was against ISIS and ISIL, but the Russians were just too heavy handed for the West to work with. Besides, Russia made it perfectly clear that they supported Assad at all costs. When the people revolted against Assad, Russia merely bombed hospitals and schools and gave the Syrian regime unwavering support." Parker paused. "We couldn't side with that, so had our asses handed to us by the politicians, once again. Now we're freelance doing bits 'n pieces for MI6, the CIA and some of the Middle Eastern states."

Ramsay said nothing. He had the ability to concentrate on his laptop even when the roads were rutted, and the vehicle's suspension was due an overhaul, but like most Mercedes saloons in the region this two-hundred-thousand-mile vehicle hadn't seen a main dealer service for a while. Jack Luger nodded and said, "How risky is it?"

Parker laughed. "We don't get too close to the front-lines. But if we come across those Wagner butchers, then we'll give them the good news. We mainly keep up reconnaissance and get assets out of trouble." He paused. "And then there's hostage rescue. That used to keep us busy, but not so much now. ISIS aren't going in for the video beheadings so much these days."

Luger shook his head. Everywhere he looked there was evidence of war. That, and the aftermath of two tremendous earthquakes. Not a building, road or wall was left unmarked by bombs, bullets or natural disaster. He had researched and made notes on the country and its situation of constant political unrest over the past decade. Most notably he now knew that the Syrian Civil War began in 2011 because of anti-government protests and had since escalated into a multifaceted conflict involving various domestic and international actors. The war has caused immense human suffering, with millions of people displaced, widespread destruction of infrastructure, and a high number of casualties. The conflict has given rise to one of the world's most severe humanitarian crises. According to the United Nations, more than thirteen-million people inside Syria now required humanitarian assistance, including food, shelter, healthcare, and clean water. Millions of Syrians have become refugees, seeking safety in neighbouring countries and beyond. The conflict has led to massive internal and external displacement. Internally displaced persons in Syria have sought refuge in other parts of the country, often living in dire conditions. Additionally, neighbouring countries such as Turkey, Lebanon, Jordan, Iraq, and others have hosted millions of Syrian refugees, putting a strain on their resources and infrastructure. Because the conflict has fragmented Syria politically, geographically, and socially, multiple armed groups, including the Syrian government, rebel factions, extremist organizations, and Kurdish militias, now controlled different territories. This has contributed to a complex power dynamic, making a political resolution challenging.

All parties involved in the conflict have been accused of human rights abuses, including arbitrary detentions, torture, extrajudicial killings, and the use of chemical weapons. Civilian populations have often been subjected to indiscriminate attacks, resulting in significant civilian casualties. Everywhere Jack Luger looked there was evidence of poverty because the conflict had severely impacted Syria's economy, leading to widespread poverty, unemployment, and a decline in living standards. Basic services like electricity, healthcare, and education have been disrupted, exacerbating the humanitarian crisis. This provided the perfect conditions for the rise of extremist groups, most notably ISIS and ISIL. These groups have taken advantage of the power vacuum and instability to establish their presence, carry out acts of terrorism, and commit human rights abuses.

"Are you OK, buddy?" Parker asked.

Luger glanced up into Parker's vanity mirror, which he had kept down to look for a tail to aid the driver. The man's eyes were steely grey and cold. They reminded him of King's, and Luger recognised a killer when he stared into them. "Fine," he replied. "Just a bit of a culture shock, that's all."

By contrast, Neil Ramsay had not appeared to have noticed anything of the destruction or impoverished country that they motored through. His eyes were firmly on the screen of his laptop, a powerful dongle providing him with roaming coverage.

"These guys aren't the type you want to bargain with," Parker stated flatly. "Rather you than me. If you want them taken out, save all that secret squirrel bollocks in the middle, then have a word with your bosses. We can get the job done quick smart."

"Thanks..." Luger replied unenthusiastically without looking at him. He had the 9mm Glock in a jacket pocket and the two spare magazines in the other. He wasn't a fan of guns, but he had gone through the small arms training course at 'the farm' – a joint venture of MI5 and MI6 for agents and officers who may find themselves in hot water abroad. The course dealt with the likeliest weapons in the usual regions, so he had left the course reasonably proficient and familiar with the 9mm Browning Hi-Power pistol, the AR and AK platform of rifles and the ubiquitous Glock because it was carried by so many law-enforcement and security personnel. During his service with the Royal Navy, he had trained with the SA-80 A2 weapon system, but he had never taken pleasure from using firearms. He did, however, take great comfort from the feel of the pistol in his pocket, and the fact that both Parker and his driver, 'Digger', were armed to the proverbial teeth. As were the four ex-SAS men following them in the beaten and filthy Toyota Land Cruiser.

The team knew the location of the Prophets of Jihad, but they had no call to engage them. They worked on contracts brokered by a company occupying stylish offices at Canary Wharf. The company subcontracted many teams like Parker's, all around the world. Hiring only the very best ex-soldiers from elite regiments, the company was both hired and trusted by intelligence agencies and security companies alike. Parker and his men would get both Luger and Ramsay close enough to hire a go-between – a trusted (as much as they could be) local who would take them to the Prophets of Jihad leader.

As they approached the village of Rimsa – a bombed-out ruin of stone and timber surrounded by scrub and desert – Parker ordered Digger to pull off the road, and the white Toyota Land cruiser – now almost red with dust – pulled up behind them. Two of the men got out and jogged past them, one carrying a rifle, the other carrying a compact, belt-fed machinegun. "Dozer and Fred will cover us with the Minimi and the sniper rifle while we wait for my contact," said Parker confidently, pulling out a sat phone and entering the number from a slip of paper. He got out of the car while the phone dialled and then spoke quickly in a language that Jack Luger did not understand, but to his ear sounded Arabic. Parker was in fact speaking Levantine. He pocketed the large sat phone and adjusted the *shemagh* wrapped around his head and neck. "He'll be here in a minute and take you in."

"You're not coming?" Jack Luger asked incredulously.

Parker smiled. "Not the contract," he replied. "Deliver and arrange an intermediary. Job done, mate."

"And take us back to Aleppo," replied Luger. "Don't forget that part."

"Of course not." Parker smirked. "We're just a very expensive taxi service today..."

Luger did not reply. Instead, he gave Ramsay a gentle nudge and said, "Come on, Neil. Put that thing down and get ready..."

Ramsay tutted as he saved something on his screen, sent it to his cloud and logged off completely. He never saved anything to his laptop, and his passwords were legendary in their creativity. "Fool's errand," he said quietly.

"Go big on the bounty," said Luger. "They'll never see all the money, so do what you have to do to get us in and out unscathed..."

Ramsay sighed as he put the laptop in its well-worn leather messenger bag and opened his door. "I *have* done this sort of thing before," he said irritably. "Have you got your pistol?"

"Yes."

"Good. Leave it here."

"What?"

"Leave it here," he repeated. "They'll search you anyway, and then you'll only have to convince them of your intentions. I saw you put that old military clasp knife in your pocket..."

"My father's," he replied.

"Jolly nice. Now, leave that, too." Luger tucked the pistol and spare magazines into the door pocket, then dropped the penknife in as well. For good measure, he put his wallet and passport in the door pocket as well. Ramsay followed suit, wallet and passport and his wedding ring. He hesitated, then unfastened his slim, vintage Longines wristwatch and dropped it in as well. He looked at Luger and said, "That's a nice watch you have there. You might want to leave that behind, too. These men will be the worst you'll have ever met. There is little to do with Islam, and much to do with murderous villainy and banditry with men like these..."

Luger took the hint and unfastened his Tudor diver's watch, carefully placing it in the ever-filling door pocket. When he looked up, a white Lada circa. 1975 bounced across the road and performed a terribly executed five-point turn. Like the Toyota, the Lada was caked in red dust. A man wearing a ripped and dirty suit with an Arab headscarf got out and immediately sparked up a cigarette. He trudged unhurriedly across the road and was greeted warmly by Parker, who it was evident had put in much effort to cultivate local assets. The two men spoke for several minutes, Parker giving the man a carton of two-hundred cigarettes in cellophane wrap, the man handing him a small fold of paper. Parker then read the note and fished out a thick envelope and handed it to him. The man pocketed it as if daylight could evaporate it. Luger looked on. Parker had a solid source of information in this man, and he felt that if that were the case, then he should be able to trust him, even if he could not trust the men they were about to meet.

Parker waved them forward and the man led them to his car without a word. The air was hot and stale inside the vehicle, and not getting any fresher with the windows rolled up and the man appreciating his king-sized cigarette. Ramsay developed a polite cough, but it was lost on the man. He drove erratically and without regard for potholes, and it was remarkable that such a terrible vehicle had lasted so long, but poverty was the mother of innovation and from the sound of it the Lada's engine had given up the ghost years ago, and somewhere, a lawnmower was likely missing its engine for the greater good.

"Nahn huna!" the man said.

"Shkran lak," Ramsay replied.

"You speak Arabic?" Luger said, getting out of the car but not hearing the answer as he stared at the open door to a dilapidated building, with two armed men standing casually on the doorstep, their AK-74 assault rifles pointing at them.

"A translate app," Ramsay replied, following Luger's stare. "Oh, my..."

The driver was already pulling away, leaving them in a cloud of dust. Luger started to raise his hands, but Ramsay pushed past him and said, "We have a business proposition for you. I believe an audience has been arranged with your leader, kindly take us to him immediately..."

Both men looked bedraggled and sported long beards without moustaches. One man wore combat fatigues and a flak jacket, the other wore a T-shirt with an AC/DC tour calendar from the nineties on it. Both wore sandals and their feet looked like they hadn't been washed in months. The man in the combats and flak jacket dropped down the steps, caught hold of Luger and spun him around. He patted him down, seemed disappointed that he found nothing, and spun him back around. He did the same to Ramsay but took his messenger bag and glared at Ramsay when he started to protest, but soon changed his mind.

"Follow my friend," he ordered, and when the two men complied, the man followed with the muzzle of his rifle just inches from their backs. They were led through the ruins and into a large, dusty room with many rugs laid on the floor and piles of cushions arranged in a circle. "Sit!"

Luger sat down and crossed his legs. Ramsay followed suit. "I like what you've done with the place," Luger commented. "Shabby chic, right?"

The men did not rise to it, but they tightened up when another man walked in. He stared at both Luger and Ramsay, then walked around the circle of cushions and sat down heavily. Around his neck hung a compact AKS-74U rifle, so small that to Luger it looked like a toy from a beach shop.

"Give me one reason why I should not have my men cut off your heads and play football with them." To both men's surprise the accent was pure Mancunian. "More than one reason may help you more."

"Apart from breaking their toes on our heads, we have a team of special forces soldiers over the hill," Luger offered.

"Six mercenaries, two vehicles. My men have mortars trained on them, and snipers watching them right now just waiting for my word."

"Well, it'll have to be shed-loads of money, then..." Luger chided.

"Moreover, we have a job that we want done in exchange for a small fortune," Ramsay added.

"Who is we?"

"Use your imagination," Ramsay replied. "We certainly won't admit to anything."

"Want to bet?" the man smirked, confident that he could extract any information he wished.

"Let's cut to the chase," said Luger. "We want a job done, and we don't want anything coming back on us. It calls for a simple kidnapping. There are two caveats. The child is not injured or hurt in any way, and the child's father is left unharmed as well. However, the man's bodyguards are not only fair game, but it is essential that they are eliminated for our operation to succeed."

The man rubbed his wispy beard thoughtfully. "Where?"

"Morocco."

"And what are you offering?"

"It's a job for five or six men. A million pounds." Ramsay paused. "How you divide it as leader is up to you."

The man stood up, shaking his head. "No, no, no..." He stopped and stared at them, his eyes fierce and unyielding. "I want pardons," he said. "I will take your million. And I'll take a million more. But I want pardons, and I want our passports back. Essentially, new ones issued. We are state-less persons."

"Missing Manchester already?" Luger commented flippantly. "Tired of this shithole?"

"Wouldn't you be?" the man glared back at him. "It's not exactly what the brochure said it would be..."

"To be fair, you've more than involved yourself in the itinerary and activities..." Luger replied coldly. "So, have you successfully spread the word of Islam?"

"Perhaps. Or at the very least, our interpretation of it."

"Bullshit." Luger shook his head. "At first, you enjoyed the ideology. It made you feel important, better than your fellow man. Then you enjoyed the power. The feeling of invincibility that indiscriminate killing gave you..."

"And now?" the man smirked. "Tell me what I enjoy now..."

"Money," Luger replied. "You enjoy the reward of killing, the money and trinkets that being here gives you."

The man unslung the tiny assault rifle and aimed it at Luger, watching Luger's uncertainty and enjoying the power he held over him. "I've always enjoyed killing non-believers..."

"A million and a half," said Ramsay.

The man looked at him and asked, "Cash?"

"No. Better than that."

"What, then?"

"Are you familiar with gold bullion websites?"

The man frowned, lowering his weapon. Luger looked to relax, if only a little. The man still took pleasure from the other man's uncertainty. "I suppose..."

"We have set up accounts across various sites and have pre-paid credit." Ramsay paused, rather pleased with his scheme. "You basically order what you want, and you can sell your stock anytime you wish. You have options to have your cold coins or bars sent to you or held in Hatton Garden vaults. These same gold sites buy back gold. You'll lose a few hundred pounds, perhaps a few thousand, but the money is legitimised and paid to whatever bank account you supply. Or you hang on and cash in when the prices have risen. There's the odd dip, naturally. But gold has only gone one way for the past decade." Ramsay pointed to his messenger bag resting in front of the man. "I can put the accounts in your name and give you access to the passwords right now. Which, of course, you can change. You will, however, only receive the full funds once the job has been completed."

"How much?"

"Twenty-five percent in advance."

"Fifty."

Luger shook his head and said, "Let's just get this done. Fifty percent. Half the accounts will have access to them immediately, the passwords for the other accounts will only be handed over upon completion." He paused, looking at both Ramsay and the terrorist leader. "Sound fair?"

"I have no objection," said Ramsay, looking at the man opposite him. "But know that if we are double-crossed, then you will find yourself at the top of a very long list, that is being worked through as we speak."

The man stared at them both. After a somewhat uncomfortable silence, he said, "Why should I trust you?"

"I can't answer that," said Luger. "Because why should we trust you to allow us to leave here alive? Trust goes both ways."

"It does," the man replied, his accent at odds with his appearance. But that was the uncomfortable truth. Many of Britain's enemies came from within.

"But even if you wipe out our security parked over the hill, there are Predator drones up there armed with Hellfire missiles, circling twenty-five-thousand feet above your head that can really ruin your day. We found you once, you can be found again..." He paused. "But friendships of convenience can be forged in the unlikeliest of places. You get money, passports and effectively, a clean sheet. We get our target's bodyguards taken out, and we get the leverage we need for our endeavours, without having any comeback. It's a win-win for all involved."

# Chapter Forty-One

The driver drove them back with as much disregard for the potholes and rutted road surface as before. For Jack Luger, the feeling of trepidation he had experienced on the drive in was nothing to the feeling of relief he now felt on the drive back out. His hands tremored slightly, and his mouth and throat were dry. He wondered whether he had made the right career move when MI5 had come knocking on his door. He turned to Ramsay – in his opinion, a highly unlikely field agent, or indeed, a man who would cope with what had just transpired – but he now seemed so relaxed that it was difficult to imagine that it had even happened.

"How do you do it?" he asked.

"Do what?"

"Experience what went on back there and seem so unfazed."

Ramsay looked up from his laptop and stared at the arid landscape passing by them in a blur. "The others don't think I know they talk about me," he said. "But I know that I'm different. They say I'm autistic, and I suppose I meet some of the criteria, but I don't ever see it as a problem. I can work out things more quickly than the people I meet, remember things in minute detail and draw conclusions quicker than most. But I also don't worry like many people or accept things differently."

"That man might have killed us."

"No, he was already sold on the idea. He just wanted to assert dominance. That's what people armed with guns do when others are not." Ramsay paused and looked back at him. "I'm unbeatable at chess. Or at least, have been until now. Certainly, I lost games to my father as a young boy, but once I hit my stride at about twelve or so, I never lost a game. I see seven or eight moves ahead, when others barely know their next, or only have a few ideas for a couple of moves. That's the secret in the espionage game. You need to calculate the odds, the risks, and the outcome. The fact that those clowns even agreed to meet us was enough to tell me that we had beaten the odds. Yes, they rob and pillage, but let's face it, this is rural Syria after a decade or more of civil war, there is little left to steal. A million pounds, even at its current weakness against the euro and the dollar, is unimaginable for this lot. I knew that they would bargain for pardons and papers, and a million and a half was to be expected."

"But you weren't scared for your life?" Luger asked incredulously.

"No." Ramsay paused. "It did not factor in my calculations."

Luger shook his head and looked back out of the window. He could not see the sniper or the machine gunner, but he imagined they were there somewhere. Hidden by scrub or boulders, or lying inside a camel's rotting carcass, or whatever bullshit the SAS would have people believe. He thought back to his days in Naval Intelligence and wondered whether he was right for this line of work. Suddenly, sifting through satellite images or stolen files or photographs of unknown developmental Russian fighter jets in his comfortable Portsmouth office seemed more appealing than playing the role of a pawn in an autistic analyst's immensely consequential game of real-life chess. "I'm not sure I'm cut out for this work," he said, but Ramsay did not look up from his laptop, apparently not hearing him, or waiting for him to elaborate. Or maybe it was the autism in him. Maybe he simply heard the statement but did not feel compelled to answer a questionless statement. He wasn't *ghosting* him; he just didn't need to answer.

The Lada slowed and Parker walked towards them, his folding-stock AK-74 hanging loosely from an elaborate shoulder harness. He was drinking water from a US issue military canteen and looking rather pleased with himself. "Did they do the deal?" he asked.

"None of your business," Ramsay replied as he got out of the Lada and headed for the Mercedes.

"We've just got a good bounty come in on those guys, so we're going to need compensating if you want a lift home and whatever deal you've just done to hold."

"You are working for British Intelligence today," Luger chided as he reached into the vehicle for his belongings, fastening his wristwatch and tucking the Glock into his pocket. "You can't ignore that fact..."

"Yeah, but the Americans pay more," Parker shrugged.

"You'll be blacklisted!" snapped Ramsay.

"What can I say?" Parker replied without any apparent concern. "It's like the Goldrush in the Wild West out here..."

Ramsay shook his head. "Firstly, we're in the East, not the West..." He paused. "And secondly, the Goldrush was a completely different period in history..." he was cut short as Parker's face disappeared in a puff of pink mist to the sound of breaking bone and released blood and brain matter cascading onto the dusty ground. The gunshot rang out a full second later. "Luger get down!" Ramsay shouted, but as he ducked for cover, he could already see the young man rolling across the dirt and fumbling to release Parker's weapon from its harness.

There was a fizzing, whistling sound in the air, and as both Ramsay and Luger looked up, mortars rained down and blew up flame and dust, sucking the air and driving them into the ground with their concussive blasts. Somewhere, a machinegun was rattling away. Luger's ears were ringing, and he looked up for the sound, in time to see a mortar land on the ridge and cut the machinegun's chatter short. Two of their protection team ran to them through the smoke as multiple weapons opened fire on their position, but both men bypassed them and got into the Mercedes. The engine wailed, the gearbox whined, and the rear wheels tore deep into the gravel as they fled. Luger pulled at Ramsay's shoulder, and he ran them both to a rocky outcrop as bullets rained down around them. He saw another of the ex-SAS men fall, and then the Mercedes was blown into the air as an RPG screamed like a giant firework and exploded in flame and smoke and debris. The vehicle rolled onto its roof and for several seconds, Luger stared transfixed until one of the men crawled out but was immediately cut down by gunfire. Luger unfolded the Kalashnikov's stock, shouldered the weapon, and fired a series of short bursts at three men in Russian military uniforms who were working their way down a rocky slope. Two men fell, and after a few more bursts, the third man stumbled forwards and rested still.

Luger pulled at Ramsay's jacket again and together they ducked and weaved for the Toyota Land Cruiser. The ex-SAS man with the sniper rifle was sliding down the slope and when he landed at the bottom, he ran towards them and shouted, "Russian soldiers! Either that, or Wagner forces! Either way, we're fucked if we don't get out of here!"

"Where is the rest of your team?" Ramsay asked as he got into the rear of the vehicle.

"Fuck'em!" the man replied as he got behind the wheel and jammed his rifle into the passenger footwell. "They know the fucking score!"

"We can't just leave them!" Luger protested, but the vehicle was already moving.

Bullets impacted against the vehicle and the windscreen spiderwebbed and was covered in blood as the sniper slumped in his seat and the Land Cruiser slowed to a crawl.

"Shit!" Luger shouted. He leaned across the body, opened the driver's door, and tipped the man out onto the ground. He slid in behind the wheel and used the back of his hand to smear the blood away, but it streaked and if anything, made it worse. When he glanced to his side, he saw a Russian solider aiming his rifle at them. Luger snatched at his Glock and fired through the glass. The fifth or sixth bullet found the man, and a few more put him on the ground. Luger rammed the pistol under his left thigh, sandwiching it to the seat, and hammered his right foot on the accelerator and the V8 engine leapt into life, sending great rooster tails of dirt and stones into the air. Luger swung the wheel and they powered around in a donut shape, the dust cloud hiding them from view, bullets slamming into the ground all around them. When he levelled out the steering, they were heading back towards town leaving the Russian army in their wake.

"There's one of Parker's team!" Ramsay shouted, pointing at a figure running towards the road. He had clearly been injured in the left arm and was cradling it in his right, his weapon apparently abandoned. "Stop and get him!"

Luger was already slowing the big SUV and when he was clear of a gulley beside the road, he swerved over and bounced across the meagre farmland scrub towards the running man. A track of bullets ploughed the field up behind him and the sight made Luger feel helpless. And yet he was drawn to the sight, like a moth to the flame. The heavy-calibre bullets from a vehicle-mounted machinegun thundered across the valley, getting ever-closer to the fleeing man.

"Forget it, he's done..." Ramsay said fatalistically. "Get back on the road while we still can!"

They were getting closer to the man, and he looked at him pleadingly through the shattered window. Behind him, the track of bullets was gaining on him. Something inside him, a voice, or perhaps maybe just instinct told him that Ramsay was right. The chess genius, unbeaten and unquestioning in his ability. Luger rolled the steering wheel to the left and hammered down on the accelerator, the automatic gearbox changing up with the increase in revs, taking them close to seventy-miles-per hour – a tremendous speed on the rough ground – and in his rear view mirror, Luger watched the man torn to shreds and the same track of bullets follow them all the way to the road, gaining all the time until they hit the asphalt and thundered out of range of the heavy-machinegun altogether.

# Chapter Forty-Two

**M**orocco

King allowed the water to wash over his body as he slowed in momentum and was finally suspended. He opened his eyes, the salt stinging briefly. The seabed was rocky with pockets of sand here and there. A shoal of silver fish darted near him, exploring the bubbles he had made on his dive, then swimming away when they realised there was no food to be found. King swam to the surface, taking a mighty gulp of air as he bobbed in the light swell. Above him, Caroline watched from the ledge. Her arm was out of the sling, but still bandaged. She did not wave as she stared at the horizon, her oversized Gucci sunglasses hiding her expression like a mask. No doubt, thoughts of the yacht and the life they briefly had concentrated her thoughts. Hoping what was, would once be again.

King swam to the rocks and climbed up the natural

steps to the ledge. He dripped water playfully on her as he reached for the towel.

"How's the water?"

"Refreshing."

"Lucky you," she chided, holding up her arm. The wound had started to knit and would leave a prominent scar, although Stella Fox had promised Caroline would see an old friend of hers in Harley Street who would perform plastic surgery at no charge. Caroline sensed the two had been more than merely friends. However, many Middle Eastern sheiks and princes sent their wives there, and it was more likely that the specialist would gain their confidence enough to benefit MI5 with the odd snippet of information.

King held out his right hand and she took it and he pulled her to her feet. He kissed her and she responded tenderly. The weeks had gone by in a whirlwind, and they had snatched what opportunities they could to be together. They stopped kissing when they heard giggles and looked to find a girl and boy of around eight or nine-years-old spying on them from behind the rocks. The pair took off laughing, and Caroline smiled, the moment lost as the fires of passion had been well and truly dowsed. "Come on," said King. "Let's get back for a bite to eat."

They took the path to the villa, which stood alone on the headland. A quarter of a mile to the south a small village sat atop the mighty cliff; fishing boats pulled high on the pebble beach below. King could see the two children running home across scrubland meadows, goats dashing out of their way, bells around their necks chiming hollowly on the air. As King and Caroline drew near, they could smell spices and chargrilled lamb. King held the gate open for Caroline and as they walked the path and climbed the three steps to the pool and patio, they saw Jack Luger sprawled in a chair nursing a bottle of beer in his lap and Rashid turning lamb skewers on a charcoal grill, battling high flames and the hiss of igniting fat. Flymo walked out from the kitchen carrying two bowls. He placed them on the table and fished a beer from a bucket of ice.

"Smells good," Caroline said as she walked to the table and helped herself to a beer.

"Thought you'd want a pinot grigio or a gin and tonic, *Milady*..." Flymo grinned, doffing an imaginary cap.

"Idiot..." Caroline said, then opening the bottle cap with her teeth, said, "I was in the army long enough to get a good grounding, fly-boy..."

King stared at her wide-eyed. "How come I haven't seen *that* party trick before?"

"Because we're old and seldom party..." she chided.

"Nice..." King helped himself to a beer but used the bottle opener beside the bucket.

"I thought this would go well in our surroundings," said Rashid as he placed a plate of sizzling skewered lamb on the table.

"Good call," Caroline agreed.

There were two salads – one of sliced peppers, coriander and cous-cous and another of sliced onions and cucumber with the zest and juice of a whole lemon. A bottle of shop-bought chilli sauce, some flat breads, and a bowl of yogurt with chopped mint complemented the simple food perfectly. Beers were handed round, and nobody stood on ceremony.

"Big Dave usually cooks for us," Caroline explained to Jack Luger.

"Meat served with meat, usually," said King. "Nothing green. He doesn't tend to eat the food that his food eats..." he smiled wryly.

"Your cooking skills were a well-kept secret, Rashid," said Caroline.

"Let's talk about his other skills," King suggested. "Like surveillance..."

Rashid smiled and handed him his mobile phone. The screen showed the footage from four camera angles. "The man definitely has our target marked," he said. "He's good, but not good enough..."

"A sniper?"

"I haven't seen a weapon..." He held out his hand for the phone, then flicked through and enlarged an image. "Recognise anyone?"

"Shit..."

"Who is he?" Luger asked.

"Ex-SAS," King replied, handing Luger the phone. "Scott MacPherson. A good man, fundamentally. But he left Rashid, Flymo and me stranded in Russia during a search and destroy mission."

"Why?"

"Orders," Rashid replied with a shrug. "But he's an *orders* man and doesn't think outside the box. What we were faced against... well, let's just say, the operation needed following through."

Luger nodded. "Is he a problem?" he asked, handing the phone to Caroline.

"We can't underestimate him," Rashid replied. "He was a captain and did a four-year tour with the regiment – that's the norm for officers. But he was invited back permanently and reached major, so he knows what he's doing."

"So, who's he working for?"

King shrugged. "A secret organisation that pre-dates both the Secret Intelligence Service and the Security

Service. Few personnel, an unknown remit, but every Prime Minister is privy to their existence."

"So, how do we know about them?"

"I was recruited by its leader. It didn't work out..."

"The gold thing?"

"Yes."

"Sir Galahad Mereweather..." Luger nodded. "A bit of a legend in certain Royal Navy circles."

"Ever met him?" King asked casually.

"No."

King said nothing. He knew when people were lying to him. He looked at Rashid. "So, what the hell is Sir Galahad's man doing in Casablanca?"

"Well, it has to be Ahmadi," Rashid replied. "It's too big a coincidence, and besides, he's been watching the man's compound for three days."

"I thought Sir Galahad had stood down," Luger said thoughtfully.

"He knew enough people in high places to bury the story," said King. "His son, Simon Mereweather, as you likely know, was our boss. The previous director of the Security Service. He died on our last operation. All the intelligence pointed to another target, but it was all a ruse, a stalking horse to get to Britain's top counterintelligence officer. We were blindsided. Sir Galahad blames us. Well, me, more to the point. He also has an issue with me changing the course of his last operation and feeding him to the press." King paused. "Sir Galahad and I will cross paths again, but with MacPherson here, I suspect that time has already come. MacPherson has beef with me, too. He put a gun in my face, and I rearranged his liver. To the man's credit, I'm surprised he's up and about so soon..."

"He's tough for sure," Rashid agreed. "You got the

better of him, King. But we can't underestimate the man, and nor can we underestimate the unaccountability that Sir Galahad's organisation has operated with, right up until you exposed him." He paused. "If anything, I'd be more wary of you being their target than Ahmadi."

"That's it, isn't it?" Caroline blurted. "They've got wind of our involvement..."

Nobody seemed to be eating, except for Flymo, who had loaded his plate high and was munching away without an apparent care in the world. King looked at him and said, "Are you clear on what you're doing?"

"Easy street, man. Get the chopper to the landing pad and take-off before they can get aboard."

King nodded. The Prophets of Jihad had the timings and the addresses. They also had strict instructions not to harm either Ahmadi or his son. But plans generally went to pieces as soon as the first bullet was fired, and this knowledge was keeping him awake at night. Bullets fly, ricochet, and penetrate the materials you would least expect. Tragically, during home invasions in the US, more family members died in crossfires or at the hand of the homeowner than intruders. King just hoped that the Prophets of Jihad remembered that they were working for money, and no longer motivated by terrorism.

"What about the asset? Is he up to speed on flying the helicopter?"

"Yes. He's the fastest learner I've ever come across."

"So, he'll pass scrutiny if the occasion is called for?"

"He's a natural." Flymo paused. "Any better and he'd give me a run for my money."

"Put it down to an excellent instructor," Caroline smiled. "You could say the same thing about me," she grinned. "He's a quick learner alright. He's now competent in hand-to-hand combat in several disciplines. We've focused on Brazilian Ju Jitsu, kickboxing, and judo. Some basic karate punches, blocks, and kicks. As for small arms familiarity, and range work... Well, anyone he comes across in the guise of Ahmadi will have no doubt that he knows his trade."

Luger raised his bottle of beer. "To success!" he toasted, then looked around the table as nobody seemed to respond. "Jesus, this feels like the last supper, or something..."

King nodded, but he did not reply. He took a mouthful of lamb and onion and chewed thoughtfully, Luger's toast echoing with him as he thought about the amount of luck he would need, and the very slim chance of success.

"Getting into Ahmadi's inner circle is one thing; getting the man out and the asset in place will be quite another," said Rashid. "And we still have to get past MacPherson and whatever agenda he has."

"I'm not even convinced that saving the boy will give you the pass you need," commented Caroline.

"It will," replied King. "He's a devoted father. He'll want to reward me." He paused. "Jack had the best in," he said, looking at him. "Tell us your plan..."

Luger shrugged, taken aback. He had voiced his idea to King and Ramsay, but there were other ideas to consider. He put down his beer and said, "Water and air. We need both to survive. We either tamper with the villa's water supply, or we contaminate the air via the air conditioning ducts."

"Well, I don't see Ahmadi's wife drinking anything out of a tap," Caroline said firmly. "Besides, this isn't Europe. Personally, I don't even have ice in my drinks in places like this."

"She's right," Flymo nodded somewhat reflectively. "I

drank tap water the first night and by the morning the forecast for the rest of the day was brown rain..."

"TMI!" Caroline hooted.

"So, it's air," said King. "Suggestions?"

"I have already procured a oneirogenic general anaesthetic. It's a combination of gases including methyl propyl ether, methoxyflurane and fentanyl." Luger paused. "The anaesthetist in question worked with me on the size of the building and the assumption that at least two air conditioning vents would be flowing."

"It's not going to be another Moscow theatre scenario, is it?" Caroline asked.

The Moscow theatre hostage crisis, also known as the 2002 Nord-Ost siege, was the seizure of the crowded Dubrovka Theatre by Chechen resistance fighters on 23 October 2002, which involved 850 hostages and ended with Russian security services killing or causing the death of at least 170 people. The attackers, led by Movsar Barayev, claimed allegiance to the Islamist separatist movement in Chechnya. They demanded the withdrawal of Russian forces from Chechnya and an end to the Second Chechen War. Russian Spetsnaz soldiers gassed everyone inside and stormed the building, but as the chemical agent was classified, the FSB would not tell medical staff what the chemicals were, and many died because they could not be treated.

"I hope not, but I wouldn't be so arrogant as to assume complete success."

King nodded. "But I will need to know when the attack is happening. What protection can I use?"

"Well, you're not going to be able to take in either a gas mask or your own air supply..." Luger paused. "So, maybe just something as low tech as stepping outside at the opportune moment."

"What about coming around?"

"Just like after a minor op."

"Well, personally, I feel like crap after anaesthetic, and it always seems to take me longer than anyone else to become *compos mentis* ..." Caroline told him. "How long will it work for?"

"Literally fifteen minutes."

King frowned. "And in that fifteen-minute window, I need to switch off the alarm system, get Ahmadi ready for transit and you need to get the asset in place, *and* make your escape?"

"Well, when you say it like that..." Jack Luger shrugged. "Anyway, I thought as random as it was, a few fireworks set off at the edge of the open ground would serve as a decent warning for you, King. Perhaps we could arrange for some kids to do it, or at least have them run around screaming and laughing as a ruse."

"That'll work," said King. "You will need to bring cable ties, duct tape, a hood and some large safety pins, the old-fashioned nappy type, with you."

"What are the safety pins for?" Luger asked, somewhat bemused.

"So that Ahmadi does not choke and suffocate on his own tongue," King replied. "You pull out the man's tongue, stick the pin through his bottom lip, tongue and top lip before fastening it tight. He will breathe normally, no chance of choking."

"Jesus Christ..." Caroline commented flatly. "I never saw that one in the Security Service handbook..."

King said nothing. He had been trained by MI6, and nobody came tougher than his old mentor Peter Stewart. They had once 'lifted' a terrorist kingpin in Beirut and driven him into Israel jammed under a false floor in the back of an ambulance. Stewart had calmly given the man the safety pin treatment commenting flippantly that if eighteen-year-old university freshers got pierced so willingly, then there must be nothing to it. The man hadn't shared Stewart's sentiment when he had woken up from the chloroform used to subdue him.

"That can be quickly arranged," Luger said, apparently unfazed. "All that would remain is for you and the asset to take your cues. Like a director shouting *action!*"

"Sounds too good to be true," Caroline commented dubiously. "That's even assuming that Alex can get in."

"He'll get in," Rashid reassured her. "When King and I first met, I had infiltrated an extreme Islamic terrorist organisation. The golden rule is to make your actions as convincing as you possibly can. From what we have planned, I'd say that he's going to do that with bells on."

Caroline nodded, but she did not seem wholly convinced. "What about the motorcyclist?"

"He's a junior Foreign and Commonwealth Office worker who has been told where and when and will no doubt regale how he was once James Bond, even if just for an afternoon," Luger replied, somewhat tacitly. "He will be keen to have something classified and redacted on his file and will likely get a promotion down the line on the back of just turning up."

"What about positions?" asked King.

"I will be parked at the intersection to the marina and beaches," said Luger. "That's where it could take an unexpected turn if the traffic is bad, or the police get ahead of you. But I'll have the drone above the restaurant watching and recording your every move."

"And I will be at the marina inside the Discovery with comms and video from the drone," Caroline added. "This feed will relay to Rashid in his position high up in the bell tower..."

"Where I will cover you with the rifle. It's a modified Heckler and Koch G3 with a scope and suppressor. Assault rifle meets sniper rifle. It has the calibre and the range to make the four-hundred metre shots, but semi-auto capability and a twenty-round magazine if things get busy." He paused. "Nobody is going to see or hear anything, and I'll have your back, mate."

King nodded, appreciating the sentiment, but said nothing. He knew that every one of the team had his back, but it was still one hell of a risk. He had to make it look convincing, but he had to make Ahmadi *want* to know more about him, *want* to bring a man of his skills into his inner circle.

# Chapter Forty-Three

E xmoor

"You're ready."

"I'm not sure whether any man would truly be ready for such a thing."

"Trust me, you are," David Garfield reiterated.

Stella Fox nodded. "You wouldn't be here if it were not the case."

Ramsay looked up from his laptop. Constantly connected to MI5's mainframe, he seldom logged out, but when he did his passwords were extremely sophisticated. "The team are in place," he said to the MI5 director. "It looks as if tomorrow is a go..."

The asset sighed and sipped his sweet, black tea. "No going back now," he said fatalistically. "When do I travel out?"

"Tomorrow, perhaps the next day," replied Garfield. "There's no immediate rush. If King gets in, then he could do with a few days to find his feet."

"That said..." Ramsay interjected. "If it backfires, King may be able to do something if the asset is close by..."

"I have a name!" the man snapped.

"And you'd do best to forget it, mate," said Big Dave walking into the lounge from the kitchen. He had a sandwich in one hand a giant cup of coffee in the other. "You are Ahmadi. That's all that counts from here on in."

"We understand that emotions can be fraught," Stella Fox said reassuringly. "But your reports show that your field craft is excellent, as too are your unarmed combat skills and small arms knowledge and handling. This will be enough to back up your physical appearance. That, and your newly acquired flying skills. I am told that you are now flying like a pilot with hundreds of hours beneath his belt." She paused, and bolstering the man's ego further, she said, "You are a walking, talking embodiment of the man we wish you to replace."

"But I may fall down at the first hurdle," he replied. "His wife, his son..."

"Without being crude," Stella Fox said quietly. "Keep it out of the bedroom. Be kind, be attentive. Most women enjoy that just as much as the, er... physical part of a relationship."

"As for the boy, well he's due to return to school within a week, so you may not even cross paths," Garfield proffered hopefully. "Ramsay, why don't you contact King and see if it could be a possibility? The boy will likely suspect less if his father is too busy to video call or is on the move when his son tries to contact him."

The man nodded. "OK, it's just last-minute nerves," he said, then added, "I just need some sleep, that's all."

Fox looked at her watch and said, "Very well, it's getting late now. Let's reconvene in the morning before David and I return to London."

# Chapter Forty-Four

C asablanca, Morocco

King sipped the hot and fragrant sweet tea and watched the Mercedes pull to the curb. The Range Rover followed. Ahmadi got out of the rear of the Mercedes, cutting a fine figure in a dark blue Tom Ford suit with a crisp white shirt open at the neck. Two buttons down, but not spread too far. King imagined the shirt cost more than his own entire outfit, but that didn't take much. The bodyguards got out. Three in all. He wondered if they had kissed their loved one's goodbye this morning. He checked his watch. The body-guards only had a few minutes to live. Tough, but those were the breaks. The greater good. The big picture. At least he wouldn't be pulling the trigger. He could have done with more bodyguards joining him, but those were the breaks.

The boy got out of the same door as Ahmadi. Like father like son, the boy too wore an expensive suit. King knew the boy to be eleven years old. What kind of man took his eleven-year-old son to business meetings? But King already knew the answer. The kind of man who trained his kin young, indoctrinated them, even. In twenty years, the boy would be doing his own deals with terrorists and another agent would be standing in King's place. King checked his watch again. It was a cheap, yet durable military style watch. A plain face, a screw-down crown, and a NATO strap. Durable as hell. It went better with his cover than his own vintage Rolex, and it was the watch his 'legend' had worn into prison after sentencing. Details mattered. He carried no phone, no credit cards either. Just a single debit card to access ten-thousand pounds in savings under an assumed name. The only form of ID he carried was a well-thumbed and heavily stamped passport. It looked good. An older photo to go with the assumed name and plenty of visa stamps to match his legend. King sipped some more of his tea and watched as the bodyguards split into different directions. The lead bodyguard led Ahmadi and his son into the restaurant, followed by another. The third waited outside while the Mercedes and Range Rover drove away to find some parking. With that, a second Range Rover thundered past, the bodyguards intending to wait for their charge down the road.

King was seated at a table outside a café across the street. Throngs of people walked past, some tourists but many Moroccans just going about their day. The warm air was heady with the aroma of spices and strong coffee and delicious breads and baclava, but crucially interspersed with the stench of cigarette smoke, drains and vehicle fumes. The sounds of vehicle horns, whining engines and worn exhaust pipes, people bartering and shouting, and construction machinery filled the air, an assault on the senses. He checked his watch again. Less than a minute to go.

King watched the old Volkswagen Transporter drive past and pull into the curb fifty metres further down the road. The vehicle was dented and scuffed and looked fit for the scrapyard, but then again, so did most of the vehicles in Casablanca. Either that, or the extremes of new BMWs, Range Rovers or Mercedes, visual proof if it were ever needed that the divide between rich and poor was never further apart, and truly a global trait. Another old VW Transporter pulled up short of the restaurant. King finished his tea and checked his watch a final time, before removing the Ray Ban Aviators he had bought eight months ago in the duty-free at Gatwick and slipping them into the thigh pocket of his cargoes. He dried the palm of his hands on his knees, then pushed out his chair almost a foot, his eyes on the motorcycle further down the road, its rider stretching his legs and drinking from a bottle of water. The motorcycle was a Suzuki SV-1000. A powerful street bike with a comfortable riding position and savage acceleration. King looked back up the street where a truck piled high with melons had parked behind the first VW Transporter. The bodyguard standing outside the restaurant seemed to have noticed none of these things, and King wondered how alert the man would be and what his reaction would be when the time came. But he did not have to wonder for long. The VW pulled out in front of the truck and accelerated towards the restaurant and the truck loaded with melons followed, before swerving erratically, counter steering with excess and lifting onto two wheels. With a screech of tyres, it carried on lifting and tipped onto its side, its load crashing into the road. The bodyguard watched incredulously as the melons squashed and scattered and children leapt into the pile stealing what they could carry, some already eating what was split and crushed. The VW Transporter stopped outside the restaurant and the bodyguard was cut down with a burst of automatic gunfire. People scattered and screamed, and men piled out of both Transporters, weapons held at the ready as they stepped over the body and filed into the restaurant and opened fire.

King crossed over the street and stood in the cool shadows as he waited. Three men pulled the boy with them to the lead vehicle. He was bundled roughly inside, his suit torn and stained with blood, but from the way he moved King could already tell that the blood belonged to other people. They clambered in after him and closed the door as the vehicle sped away. Three more men walked out confidently, one of the men changing over to a new magazine as he walked. Six men in, six men out. King stepped out and kicked the last man in the back of his knee, snatching the weapon as he fell. He could tell from the weapon's weight that the magazine was at least half full. He fired into the man's face before he hit the ground and followed up with three shots into the closest man's back. The lead man started to turn but was less than halfway around when King emptied the rest of the compact Kalashnikov AKS-74U into him. King tossed the weapon onto the ground and picked up the man's CZ-75 9mm pistol which had clattered into the street. He checked the magazine as he walked and when he got level with the confused driver of the van, he shot him once in the head and made for the motorcycle. The man saw the gun, held up his hands and King swung his leg over the machine and turned the ignition and pressed the starter button. He tucked the pistol into his waistband, selected first gear and pulled out into the road, the rear wheel spinning as he kept all his weight over the fuel tank to stop the motorcycle from lifting its front wheel. He feathered the throttle to control the rise and knocked the gears up from first through neutral, second and third and had a hundred miles per hour on the needle before the first bend and throng of people in the road.

The VW Transporter was driving on its handling limit for the streets, the driver swerving to avoid children and goats, stray dogs and motor scooters as Casablanca put on a show of diversity and blocked its path with a *Youtuber* posing for selfies in front of an orange Lamborghini. The van swerved in time but knocked over a bicycle laden eight feet high with beach toys and souvenirs on a custom-made rack. The man guiding the bicycle fell to the ground and his mobile stall toppled and spread his wares into the road. King, with nowhere left to steer stamped down on the gears twice, then twisted the throttle and squeezed a quarter pull of clutch, launching the front wheel into a wheelie. The *Youtuber* dropped his phone and dived for safety as the front wheel touched the bonnet of the supercar and the bike rode up the wedge-shaped car and launched into the air. King stood on the foot pegs; his knees slightly bent to cushion the landing some ten feet to the rear of the Lamborghini. The motorcycle landed heavily and bounced, King fighting hard to regain control, which he did with a twist of throttle to right the wobble. The VW Transporter was now only sixty metres in front of him, the driver swerving and stamping on the brakes to try and force King back.

King knew that he did not have much time. There were four men in the van ahead of him, and he could hear police sirens somewhere. They were heading downhill now, the port in sight. From there the options only favoured the kidnappers. Vehicle changes, fast speedboats, passenger ferries – all could present a place to hide, a way out of the city. There was even a heliport. With a helicopter waiting, the boy could be lost within minutes. Or at least that was the plan.

The rear doors of the van opened, and King swerved and dropped back to avoid the burst of gunfire from a Kalashnikov. There were screams and King could only imagine where the bullets had ended up with people scattering on all sides. He weaved the motorcycle across the road and bounced up the pavement, people parting ahead of him like water against the prow of a ship. The van had accelerated, and King caught sight of people being thrown into the air as it drove relentlessly through the crowds. King weaved back into the road and gained rapidly on the van. The men inside the van were being thrown about in the cargo bay, and while the man with the rifle was reloading, another was clamped around the boy to restrain him. The third man had made it to the front passenger seat and was leaning out of the window aiming a pistol at King as he swerved and dodged fleeing pedestrians. King wound the throttle on full, the front wheel almost touching the rear bumper, and in one fluid move, he released his grip on the throttle, drew the pistol, and shot the man in the forehead from less than six feet away, the motorcycle dropping back all the time as it underwent engine-braking. He struggled to tuck the weapon back in his waistband, and by the time he got back on the throttle, the van had skidded out onto the main road and left the busy street behind. King accelerated hard, the powerful motorcycle whining as he used all the engine revs and gear changes, threading the machine through traffic north of one-hundred-and-thirty miles per hour. He flashed past the van and around a truck laden with bottled water, then came hard off the throttle, stamped down two gears, and was engulfed in tyre smoke as the motorcycle skidded and decelerated down to fifty miles per hour and the van caught up with the truck giving King all the cover that he needed to draw the pistol and fire. The man in the passenger seat slumped and sprawled across the gearstick and the driver struggled to control the vehicle, swerving both left then right and crashing into the truck beside him. King tried to accelerate out of trouble, but the truck caught his rear wheel, and the motorcycle defied the laws of physics by going in what felt like every direction at once. King held on as the motorcycle was launched in the air, then landed on its rear wheel. He didn't know it at the time, but he twisted the throttle and the machine accelerated and went past the point of no return. King was spat to the rear and the motorcycle twisted and spun and when the tyres caught traction on the tarmac, it twisted and turned and rolled down the road amid sparks and fuel and caught fire. King was sliding on the tarmac, and just as the tyres had done, his boots caught the road, and he was upended and thrown into a series of summersaults and rolls. The van continued down the road in front of him, and as King staggered to his feet, he could hear nothing but vehicles skidding and horns sounding behind him.

King looked around him but could not see the pistol. He watched the van now in the distance, then turned and looked at the traffic now stationary behind the truck and the burning hulk of the motorcycle. Shouts turned to chatter and from what French and Arabic he knew, he realised that he wasn't the most popular person in Casablanca right now.

An open-topped Porsche and a slick-looking man in his thirties wearing a white shirt, wrap-around sunglasses and talking on his phone using EarPods is a universal thing, and King headed towards the estate agent/salesman, reached inside, and unlocked the door. He unfastened the protesting man's seatbelt and pulled him out. The man tried to fend King off, but was no match for King's strength, who twisted away from his blows and shoved him hard to the ground. King was behind the wheel and working his way through the seven speed PDK paddle-shift gearbox. With a break in the traffic flow, he had the Porsche at over a hundred miles per hour in seconds and was still climbing in speed when he caught sight of the van pulling off the road onto the slip road leading directly to the port. He eased off and rode the brakes, keeping the van in sight but maintaining distance. The driver of the van had seen King fall off the motorcycle, likely seen the burning wreckage in his mirrors. He would not have seen King take the Porsche, so there was no sense in giving away his advantage.

The van headed away from the commercial port and to the marina. King held back, but certainly the Porsche fitted in here with newer, expensive vehicles and chic cafés, restaurants, and boutiques. It would have been a different story in the old fishing port. He reached over and checked the glovebox hoping he'd get lucky, but this wasn't America, and he already knew the chances of finding a gun was slim to none. The van slowed ahead of him, and King eased back but he could already hear sirens behind him and knew that it would only be a matter of a minute or two before he would see the flashing lights as the police closed in.

The van screeched to a halt and on a raised platform on the edge of the marina and breakwater separating the calm harbour from the raging surf of the Atlantic Ocean, a helicopter's rotors were spinning. The remaining man in the rear of the van roughly pulled the boy out of the vehicle and pushed him ahead of him. The boy tried to run, but the driver grabbed him as he got out from behind the wheel and the two men sprinted for the waiting heli-copter. King accelerated hard, the Porsche bellowing from its exhaust, its tuned six-cylinder engine whining as the turbo kicked in. One of the men turned and fired and the windscreen and bonnet were peppered with bullets. King raised a hand to protect his eyes from the shattering glass and heaved the vehicle to the left to take cover behind the van. King leaped out over the passenger seat and ran to the open rear doors of the van, where he picked up one of the dead men's' weapons. He checked the magazine of the Browning 9mm pistol, knew he had at least twelve rounds remaining from the inspection holes in the rear of the magazine, and eased the breach open a fraction to see a glint of brass. Ahead of him, the helicopter lifted off, banked an impossibly steep turn, and spun around heading northwards up the coast. It was probably the easiest day's work the pilot had ever had, and from the way the two men sagged as they neared the helipad, the last thing the kidnappers had expected. But forewarned was forearmed, and King stopped running and fired at one of the men, sending three 9mm bullets into the man's back. The second man turned, but he had the boy in front of him and a gun at his head. The boy was sobbing. The man looked confident. In his periphery, King was aware of vehicles pulling up, people getting out. Uniforms, suits. He dared not look, could not take his eyes off the man's in front of him. Twenty metres. It could well have been twenty miles for all the good it would do him. Again, in his periphery, weapons were being aimed and someone seemed to be taking charge, holding people back.

"Give it up," said King. "Put the gun down and let the boy go." His finger tightened on the trigger.

The man smiled. "Shoot me and my muscle reflex will

cause me to fire. I have a great deal of pressure on the trigger. Now, back away and..."

King fired and the boy sagged as his leg gave out. The man's weapon discharged, the bullet passing just inches above the boy's head. King's second shot hit the man in his throat and as he staggered backwards, the third shot hit him dead centre in his forehead.

King dropped the weapon to the ground and raised both of his hands above his head as he turned and faced the police officers now sprinting towards him. There were shouts and weapons aimed at him, but he knew the drill and he got down onto his knees as rough hands pushed him down and handcuffs secured his arms behind his back. He was dragged unceremoniously to his feet and marched towards the waiting police vehicles, while paramedics tended to the boy, who was writhing on the ground behind them.

Ahmadi barged his way to the front of the crowd, his blue Tom Ford suit and white shirt no longer looking so stylish now that it was ruined with someone else's blood, and much of his own. His nose had been clearly broken and his right eye socket was as black as night. He eyed King warily, snapped something at the highest-ranking police officer and ran to his son's side as he was loaded onto a gurney and wheeled without delay to the waiting ambulance. Behind him, two bodyguards looked fraught. They had lost colleagues and would most likely be losing their jobs before long. Ahmadi returned and spoke to the police officer again as the ambulance drove through the parting crowd with blues and twos. King watched Ahmadi dominate the police officer. He was clearly a man of influence, and a man used to getting what he wanted. He pointed at King, spoke sternly with the police officer, and the man dutifully walked over, stood his men down and ordered the handcuffs to be taken off. King rubbed his wrists, looked Ahmadi in the eyes.

"You saved my son..." he said humbly, his accent almost neutral English, the slightest hint of Middle Eastern only detectable on the word saved, which he pronounced as *sav-ed*. "I will be forever grateful," he said, stepping forwards and kissing King on both cheeks. King, familiar with such customs, composed himself in time. "You are my guest," he added. "I will reward you greatly. Please, come with me. I will have my driver take you to my home while I visit my son at the hospital."

"I don't need a reward," King replied.

*Always resist, never suggest...*

Ahmadi shook his head. "Please, indulge me. I must be with my son in hospital, but I wish to talk to you, show you the extent of my gratitude." He spread his hands compassionately, hopefully. "It is in my faith. You have saved my son, and in turn, my life. For if I lost my son, then my life would have been no longer worth living. I must repay the debt you have put me in."

King studied the man before him. He was a man used to his position of power, but King could see a chink in his armour. His vulnerability. "Alright," he replied. "But I have travel plans and won't be able to stay long..."

Ahmadi smiled. "I will be more than willing to have you flown anywhere in the world, if you spare me a little of your time."

King considered this for a moment, glanced back at the black Mercedes and the two bodyguards standing beside it, then looked at the Iranian and nodded. "Let's go, then."

Ahmadi got into the Mercedes, but King was ushered

into a Range Rover by a man-mountain who got in beside King and grunted for him to move over.

"Ahmadi is a perceptive man," said the man-mountain holding up a bandaged left hand. "And quite ruthless. He made me cut off my own finger because of a small mistake. If he feels that you are not telling the truth about what you have just done, then you will lose more than just a finger..."

King looked away as the vehicle sped over the cobbled surface and followed the Mercedes. His only regret was that he had not foreseen the other two men in the Range Rover holding back as their boss had eaten with his son, and that the Prophets of Jihad had not killed his entire protection team.

# Chapter Forty-Five

King had been seated in the open-plan lounge area for three hours. He had worked his way through a pot of sweet tea and a carafe of water, and had naturally paid attention to the air-conditioning, which was humming quietly above him, the room still warm but not as torrid as outside. He had noticed another humming air-con unit in the hall. He just hoped there would be similar units in the bedrooms upstairs but was confident that it was a given. Ahmadi was Iranian, hailing from the north of the country where the mountains were snow-capped, and the winters were notoriously cold. Alya Shareef-Ahmadi (Iranian women rarely changed solely to their husband's name) was born in the south, and while acclimatised to the more arid weather, she had spent much of her early life in Paris and Geneva, and holidayed in Western Europe, so it was likely she enjoyed the villa's amenities, right down to the air conditioning. That was a good thing, but he had no way of letting Luger and the team know. Not until he could gain Ahmadi's trust. The camera and microphone that Luger had bribed the guard to plant had gone offline two days ago. The bodyguard had taken King's wallet and passport when they had arrived and handed them to another guard. King just hoped that he had done enough to put Jon Wood on the map.

The bodyguard stood at the door and King had to acknowledge the man's professionalism and stamina. He was armed with something large under his jacket. From Luger's account, the weapon was likely to be a replacement Uzi machine pistol. Outside the door there were four security personnel – one was the driver of the Range Rover, the other Alya Shareef-Ahmadi's personal bodyguard and the other two men had remained at the villa as static guards. It had certainly been their lucky day. The man-mountain put a finger to his ear and King could tell that something was happening.

The bodyguard grinned at King and said, "Now we shall see..."

King ignored the man. He had counted six weapons he could use. There was a ceremonial knife of some description on the wall beside him, a sword hanging under an Iranian flag on the far wall, a heavy-looking glass paperweight on the writing desk, a bronze bust of the Ayatollah resting on a marble plinth, a fire poker beside a spotlessly clean open fireplace and beside the bodyguard, a walnut half-moon Queen Anne table that sported three curved legs that King reckoned he could break off fairly easily, giving him two handy clubs. He wasn't short on options.

The door opened and Ahmadi stood before him. Behind him, the boy was being pushed in a wheelchair, the slender figure of his wife bent over their son as she fussed with him. The woman looked up and stared at King. She was elegant, demure and he had to admit, stunningly beautiful. A woman in a nurse's uniform pushed the wheelchair and a man wearing a white coat, with stethoscope hanging round his neck needed no introduction as a doctor. The show moved on, but Ahmadi still stood there. King noticed his own wallet and passport in the man's left hand. As he stepped inside, Alya barged passed him, walked up to King, and slapped him hard across the cheek.

"You shot my boy!" she raged.

King, who had recoiled at the blow, rubbed his cheek, and replied, "I saved your boy, ma'am..." he said firmly, pausing to allow the fact to sink in. "Let me guess? Just a minor flesh wound, am I right?" He already knew the answer. The boy had appeared in good spirits and no hospital would have discharged anyone in need of further treatment, especially when a family like Ahmadi's was concerned.

"Luck!" she snapped.

"A calculated risk. If they got to the helicopter, then you may never have seen your son again." King paused, looked at Ahmadi and said, "I'll have my passport and wallet back, and you can show me the quickest way out of here. A lift back into town from one of your apes would be most welcome, considering I stopped your son's abductors and kept him off that chopper..."

Ahmadi nodded. He snapped something to his wife in Arabic and walked over to King and handed him the two items. Alya flounced out of the room and slammed the door closed behind her. "Forgive my wife," he said dismissively once she was out of earshot. "I, however, am pleased you are here."

King thought the comment strange. No thank you for

saving his son. No mention of the incident altogether. He watched as the Iranian walked to a silver cloche and lifted the lid. He offered King some Turkish delight of various colours and a heady scent of rosewater. King supposed it was the North African equivalent of offering a guest a whisky. "I'm sorry that your son was shot," he said, realising that the statement was quite ridiculous really. "It was a gamble, but if the man shot me, then nobody would have stopped him. And if he shot your son, well..."

"You are a strange man, Mister Wood. No, not strange, more of an enigma." Ahmadi paused. "You have been busy these past months..."

King shrugged. "Luck hasn't come my way recently."

"You are a common criminal. In my country, you would have lost a hand, perhaps a foot by now. Who knows? Maybe more."

"And what country is that?"

"What a strange question."

"Well, Morocco has a better human rights record than many Arab countries, and you have an Iranian flag hanging on the wall."

"Most Westerners would not know such things."

"I enjoy pub quizzes," King replied flippantly. "Flags are usually a three pointer."

Ahmadi smiled. He looked over at the man-mountain and spoke quickly in Arabic, dismissing him. When the man had left the room, the Iranian smiled wryly. "Who are you, Mister Wood?"

"I am who I am," King replied. "I just do what I must do to survive."

"Paris, Monaco, Georgia..." Ahmadi nodded sagely. "I have a great many contacts."

"In crime?"

Ahmadi shrugged. "In crime, in law enforcement, in intelligence agencies..."

"And what do they all say about me?"

"Many things," the Iranian replied. "Many, many things..."

# Chapter Forty-Six

L ondon

"He's in."

David Garfield sat back in his leather seat and closed his eyes. "I never thought..."

"I wouldn't let King know how little faith you had in him, if I were you," Ramsay said coldly.

"Oh, Neil! For God's sake man!" Garfield snapped. "This was only ever a bloody hail Mary."

"A what?"

"It's an Americanism. A desperate pass of the ball that will either succeed against all odds or fail dismally."

Ramsay looked at him impassively. "I don't like Americanisms," he said. "They're too... American..." He paused. "In my opinion, after studying the man, after calculating the risks and laying the foundations of a legend, I was confident that Ahmadi would want to thank King but would also be curious of his motivation and want to use such a man in his own agenda."

Garfield scoffed. "Luck, pure and simple." He checked his slim gold watch, then said decisively. "Get yourself back down to Exmoor. We'll reconvene there."

"Surely we need to get the asset in place?" he replied. "It's just a case of Lomu escorting him on the plane and getting him to the safehouse."

"No, Dave Lomu called this morning, the asset wants to meet. A classic case of changing the terms of the deal, I should imagine." He paused. "I can't blame him, but we need to keep him on track, even if he's about to step through the gates of hell..."

# Chapter Forty-Seven

MacPherson looked around the outside seating area of the Casablanca Marriott Hotel. Wicker furniture with glass table tops and piles of cushions placed on Middle Eastern rugs left visitors knowing in no uncertain terms where they were staying. Background music piped a similar theme, and the aroma of sweet tea, rosewater and what MacPherson would have called 'Christmas spices' were heady on the air. Indeed, the cinnamon, nutmeg and ground ginger were from the baklava which the city was famous for. The aroma of pungent spices and searing lamb wafted from the restaurants and there was an enclosing sense of the dramatic surrounding this oasis of calm beside the pool.

He saw Sir Galahad Mereweather relaxing in a wicker chair taking in the views of night-time Casablanca and the brightly lit hotels around him. The old man looked utterly distinguished and physically fit. Wearing a light cream linen suit with a blue silk shirt unbuttoned at the collar, boat shoes without socks and a Panama hat resting on the glass table beside him, he looked the picture of colonial sophistication. MacPherson also knew that the man's attire would cost him more than his own monthly salary. Sir Galahad sipped amber liquid in a tall glass of ice. When he saw MacPherson, he waved him over and caught a waiter's attention with a simple gesture of his fingers from a man used to commanding attention and getting what he wanted.

"Another whisky sour, Mohammed, if you please..." He looked at MacPherson and said, "What are you drinking? Hotels are the last bastion of the alcoholic in Morocco..."

"A beer, please. Something light and cold." He sat down as the waiter bustled away. "Nice place."

"Do you think so?" Sir Galahad frowned. "It's a little touristy for me, a little too Ali Baba and the Forty Thieves. Themed and insincere. I once stayed in this wonderful hotel in Marrakesh that was essentially a large town house. You know the type of place... whitewashed, stone walls, flagstone floors, a wonderful courtyard with a plunge-pool that barely caught the sun and was deliciously refreshing in the heat. Absolutely authentic. The sort of place that would be featured on *Instagram* constantly these days, with unintentionally ironic taglines. Like, *today I found the real Morocco...* but with a hundred other camera holding attention seekers forming a queue behind them for the same moronic poses and ever-reaching hashtags..."

"I think I understand," said MacPherson.

Their drinks arrived, along with a small bowl of olives and an even smaller bowl of pistachios. MacPherson sipped from his frosted glass and approved of both the strength and temperature. It was a perfect moment in the heat, like the scene from *Ice Cold in Alex*. Before he knew it, most of the beer had gone and as if he and the Moroccans had a fluent sign language going on between them, another waiter was dispatched for a beer with a simple half wave from Sir Galahad.

"We need to shut this thing down," Sir Galahad said quietly.

"Understood."

"Like pressing the delete button."

"Consider him gone."

"Such orders are always a last resort. It gives me no pleasure to ask you to do this task."

"I've done worse," MacPherson replied.

Sir Galahad nodded. "That saddens me," he commented genuinely. "And what of the competition?"

"Nothing I can't handle."

"Good. Good," replied Mereweather with a satisfied nod of the head. "And remember we're all on the same side, when all is said and done."

"Of course." MacPherson replied, just as his beer came. He took the glass from the waiter and raised it in a toast, which Sir Galahad seemed reluctant to join, but did so with a slight awkwardness to the way he held his glass. "Here's to success," he toasted.

Sir Galahad did not add to the toast, but instead reflected on the whole affair being anything but a success, and that MacPherson was no more than a janitor, mopping up other people's mess.

# Chapter Forty-Eight

The dawn shone brightly through King's window, the sun somewhere over the Sahara, gilding the day in hues of red and gold. King felt no annoyance at the intrusion; sleep evading him despite his best efforts. He could hear his old mentor Peter Stewart saying, *Eat when you can and sleep when you can, sonny. You never know how long you'll go without either when the shit hits the fan...*

King could confirm that the air-condition was indeed set low throughout the villa. He supposed he would have to wait until he heard the fireworks to know that Jon Luger's plan was going ahead, but his own window was locked, and even though the ensuite bedroom was not locked, when he had tried the door shortly after midnight, he had been met with an armed bodyguard standing on the landing who had worn an expression telling King in no uncertain terms that he would not be allowed to leave.

A flask of tea and a jug of water, together with a bowl of fruit had been waiting for him in the room, so there really was no excuse for him to leave. King slid off the bed and

stretched before pouring some water. He drank down two
glasses, then did a short press-up and sit-up routine lasting
twenty minutes before drinking another two glasses of
water and heading for the shower. He ran the jets cold and
soaped up with the new bottles of assorted toiletries that
had been left on a silver tray complete with a toothbrush,
toothpaste, shaving soap and a safety razor. After ten
minutes of ablutions, he emerged clean shaved, smelling
fresh and feeling thoroughly invigorated. He dressed
quickly, towelling his hair off as he did so, and walked to the
French doors which had been locked, and leaving no sign of
a key.

The distant view of the Atlantic Ocean encapsulated
both old and modern Casablanca, with tall five-star hotels
towards the seafront and low, stone-built dwellings that
could have been built a thousand years previous. Dotted
between roads and areas of desolate scrubland, a myriad of
oases spread glorious colours of greens, yellows, reds, and
browns which played host to olive groves, tomato and
cucumber farms, maize and vines, and a whole host of fruits
and vegetables between. King briefly wondered how the
crops were irrigated, but then remembered reading somewhere that Morocco had seven great rivers, all originating
from the Atlas Mountains. He figured that groundwater
would provide the rest. From what he could see, the vegeta-
tion looked lush, and the ground looked fertile.

King turned as a knock came from the door. "Yes?" he
said clearly.

The bodyguard had been replaced by another man, but
most people would probably not have noticed. "Mister
Ahmadi will see you now." The man paused as King walked
towards him. "We are all armed, Mister Wood. You would
be a fool to try anything."

"Then let me go, dickhead. I'm beginning to wish that I'd let the little shit get kidnapped..." King told him as he followed. There was no harm in protest. He wanted to be here, naturally, but as far as they were concerned, the more he asked to leave the less they'd suspect him of anything untoward. "What time is bacon and eggs served around here, anyway?" he asked, hoping to needle the Muslim guard.

The man ignored him and stood aside at the door to the study-come-lounge where King had been held last night. He opened the door and as King stepped through, said quietly, "We don't fucking eat pork, you treacherous kafir bastard..." then closed the door behind him.

King had been left no time to reply, or even question what the man had meant by the insult. He looked at Ahmadi, or rather the back of the man's head as he stared out onto the grounds of his compound. "How's the boy?" King asked.

"Good, good," Ahmadi replied, although he seemed far from convinced. "Well, apart from having a nine-millimetre bullet punch through his calf..."

King shrugged. "Fleshy, away from bone and arteries. It was a gamble, but judging from how quickly he was discharged, it looks like it paid off."

"We hired a nurse and a doctor from the private hospital," Ahmadi argued. "They have watched him round the clock, administering pain killers and fluids alike."

"Money talks," King replied, apparently uninterested in how the man spent his money.

"Let's take a walk, Mister Wood..." King shrugged and followed him. Ahmadi led the way out through the villa to the front door and dismissed both the man-mountain and the guard who had shown King downstairs. Neither man looked compelled to stand down, but they did so eventually after Ahmadi spat Arabic at them. They crunched across the gravel and onto a slate path which led to a golf-green perfect lawn. King looked at the swimming pool; clear and inviting. Ahmadi seemed to gravitate towards it. Beside it, the sound of the fountains and water features made it seem even more appealing in the dry heat. "We can talk out here," Ahmadi said eventually. "Something has changed. They have started to view me with suspicion..."

"Suspicion?" King frowned and stopped walking.

"No, keep walking," he said quietly. "The running water should deter any use of a parabolic microphone."

"I'm confused..."

"Tell me, what is your real name?"

"My name is Jon Wood," King replied adamantly, although inside his stomach was churning and his heart raced. "You've got my passport..."

"Who were the men who took the boy?"

*The boy? Not, my son...*

"The Prophets of Jihad."

"Did they deserve to die?"

"From one perspective, yes."

"Did the old man send you?"

"You'll have to do better than that."

"Tall, slender, neatly trimmed white beard."

"Better than that."

"London gentlemen's clubs, oozing wealth and class."

King's heart raced more, if indeed that was possible. "No, but I think I know who you mean." He paused beside the loudest and most powerful of the fountains. "Who are you?"

The man stared at him tentatively, but then something seemed to give. King sensed the man's emotions were about to go the way of the fountain in front of them. "My name is Darias Hassan. I came to the UK when I was twelve years old and am now a British citizen. I was recruited from GCHQ last year, where I have worked as an analyst for the past ten years, by the man I have just described to you," he said. "Ahmadi is part of a group..."

"The Iron Fist," said King flatly.

"That's a false flag," the man replied. "Designed to keep the intelligence services busy. What are you? MI6?"

King shrugged. "A new department, but from MI5," he replied. There was no sense in lying to the man.

"It doesn't matter either way." He paused. "The fact is everything has changed recently."

"How so?"

"The big bodyguard is different towards me."

"The man-mountain?"

"Yes."

"I believe you made him cut off his little finger. That would probably do it."

The man cursed. "A moment of madness. His name is Malik Al-Shabnam. He was an enforcer for the secret police in Tehran. He would punish street urchins by cutting off their little fingers on their second offence, then take another finger for every other misdemeanour. We're talking kicking a football at a wall, or simply running through the wrong place at the wrong time. I grew up in Tehran. He cut off my little cousin's finger. He contracted septicaemia and had to have his arm amputated, but it was too late, and he died in agony three weeks later." He paused. "If I didn't blow my cover then, well, yesterday's escapade seems to have done the trick." He shook his head, fear in his eyes. "They know..."

King stared at the fountain, then closed his eyes, his

shoulders sagging. "Where is the real Ahmadi?" he asked quietly, yet somewhat fatalistically.

"The same man who recruited me was working him to discover more about the people behind the Iron Fist, the people pulling Ahmadi's strings. I think the plan was devised to keep his family safe while Ahmadi provided information, to stop his masters suspecting anything."

*That sounded the sort of thing* Sir Galahad *would come up with,* thought King. *Shit, it's what we came up with, but just a few months too late...* "What about Ahmadi's wife and son?" he asked.

"She knows," the man replied. "She's playing along, for now. The boy is a little pain in the ass, though. If his mother continues to spoil him and he gets what he wants, then there is no reason for him to suspect anything. Ahmadi was a pretty strict father, my leaning towards leniency has the boy off balance and grateful that he's not getting a swipe around the ear..."

King looked around him. Malik Al-Shabnam was watching them intently. "I need a phone," he said.

"I expect they're tampering with the lines and mobile accounts as we speak."

"Then I need to get out of here," King replied. "We have a dead ringer for you, and we were going to make a switch..."

"Nothing changes. Intelligence agencies never talk to each other."

"It would appear not."

"I'm not staying here," the man said. "I need out."

"Who is your handler?"

The man shrugged. "Medium height, medium build, short cropped black hair. Military-looking."

"English, no real regional accent?"

"Yes. Do you know him?"

King had a feeling that he did. MacPherson. That was why he had the place under surveillance. But what the hell was he going to do next?

"Do you have access to the car keys?"

"I did up to last night."

"Okay," said King. "What intel can you gather together to bring?"

"USBs, a few paper files, but I suspect most of it has been taken already. Ahmadi would have wanted something to drive up his worth to whoever is working him."

King watched as Malik started towards them. "Alright," he said, turning towards the man-mountain. "Follow my lead but get us a vehicle. Something capable of ramming those front gates..."

# Chapter Forty-Nine

E xmoor

Ahmadi listened to the MI5 director and the man who was heading the so-called elite unit with a clear remit. The irony that he had infiltrated the heart of the British intelligence services, with the unwitting help of Sir Galahad Mereweather was not lost on him. He had played the man and his machine. He had played Scott MacPherson, too. The ex-soldier who had acted as go-between for both the intelligence he fed them, and the rewards in doing so. And that intelligence had been carefully collated, correlated and selected as nothing more than a direct feed for disinformation. Not only had his masters had a clear and concise line into deceiving British intelligence, but the foundations they had laid could not be verified once he broke cover. Any operation they mounted for the next decade would always have that sense of doubt, the chance that they were being played rather than pulling the strings.

"You *are* ready for this," Stella Fox reassured him. Ahmadi must have looked glazed over as she spoke, if only she knew what he was thinking. "Are you alright?"

"Yes," Ahmadi replied, suddenly snapping to. "Where is Neil Ramsay?"

"Why do you ask?" Garfield queried.

Ahmadi shrugged. "I just thought that if I'm going, then I'd say goodbye..."

"He's on the way."

"And Big Dave?"

"He's fetching Ramsay from the train station." Garfield paused. "You know, you're well versed in every aspect of this. You can do this, and what you do will make a difference."

Ahmadi nodded and smiled. "You're so right," he replied. "It will make *all* the difference..."

# Chapter Fifty

C asablanca

King reached the man-mountain as the man went for his weapon. King sprinted the last few paces, leapt and drove his knee deep into the man's ample stomach. The man staggered backwards, and King had both hands gripped tightly on the man's right wrist, the weapon pointed at the ground. Malik started to resist, but King kept his grip and dived past the man's right side, curled, and rolled onto the ground. His fourteen stone and vice-like grip tore the man's arm backwards. It would either go two ways - the man would flip, or his arm would dislocate. It was the latter. The man hollered and King snatched the weapon from his grip and clubbed him across the back of the head with the metal butt of the Uzi. He dropped to his knees and King hammered the weapon down again on the top of the man's head, and he fell forwards onto his face and stomach, his legs behind him curling like some huge scorpion's tail, before they dropped the other way and impacted on the grass, the toes of his shoes creating two large divots in the golf-green surface.

"Is he dead?"

King said nothing. All he knew was the man wasn't going anywhere in a hurry. He picked up the pace and Darias ran beside him. They rounded the corner of the house, where one of the guards was standing, holding his earpiece, and talking into a microphone attached to his wrist. King fired a short burst from the Uzi and the man slumped and twitched on the ground. Darias stared at the dying man as they rushed past, and King dragged him past and pushed him ahead of him up the stairs. Inside the hall another guard fired his pistol and King shoved Darias force-fully enough to send him sprawling on the marble floor. King fired a sustained burst and the man caught four rounds in his chest and stomach. He staggered a few paces, then slid down the wall, streaking the whitewash with blood as he rested still. King tossed the Uzi aside and picked up the man's Sig Sauer P225. He checked the magazine, but there were only a few rounds remaining. King checked the body for a spare and switched over. Darias was dragging himself to his feet and fumbling for a set of keys in the dresser.

"Got them!" he said excitedly. "The black Range Rover!"

King nodded and together they headed for the door. "Can you release the gate from here?"

"Inside the car. There's a button on the dashboard." Darias stepped out onto the steps and turned to King. "Thank you for getting me out..."

King blinked, the sting of blood and brain matter in his eyes, bone fragment's peppering his face like shrapnel. Darias Hassan's faceless body was lying prone at his feet, blood pooling at the top of the steps and cascading down the short flight to the bottom. Snapping back to his senses, King dodged behind the edge of the door and swept up the bunch of keys. No follow-up shot came. He had not heard the gunshot, but he knew a high-power weapon when he saw the signs, and it had clearly been a sniper shot. The height of the gate negated a short-range shot, and from what he recalled of the terrain and view, the marksman had to be at least twelve-hundred metres out, somewhere in the row of distant buildings. King ducked back inside the villa. Alya and her son stood at the top of the stairs trembling at the sight of his bloody face, and King shouted for them to get into the bathroom and take cover in the bath. It was all he could think of, and the budget of the interior design did not point to plastic bathroom fixtures. A cast-iron tub could provide them with some protection if the sniper started punching out the windows.

King knew that there was at least one more guard, but he could not chance going out the front door, and with another armed hostile inside, he had little option but to find another exit. He had barely taken four steps when he paused beside the window to his right and fired four rounds, forming a square. One more shot in the centre, then he kicked out the toughened glass and leapt out onto the hard standing. He checked the gate to his right, but no land or building was visible. And if he did not have line of sight, then nor did the sniper. The sniper had utilised the top step to the villa. King thought about the distance, the accuracy and speed the sniper would have had to identify and kill his target. It was too much of a coincidence that MacPherson was watching the building and hadn't made the shot.

King reached the Range Rover and got inside. The engine fired into life, and he could tell at once that it was a powerful version, the slight rumble of the exhaust and the way the engine hummed as the revs dropped upon starting. He selected drive and floored the accelerator. The V8 leviathan thundered through the gates and the moment he had cleared the obstruction, he steered to the left and after a hundred metres he veered left again and was not only covered from the sniper by the perimeter wall but was putting in a huge distance between them. The vehicle bounced and shuddered over the rough ground, and King did not slow as he scythed through a field of maize and bounced over an irrigation channel, sending the Range Rover a metre into the air before it came crashing down at speed on a narrow track. King slowed and settled behind the wheel. He was out of range, out of sight and out of danger, but as the vehicle brushed the olive trees on either side, scattering the olives like falling hailstones, he could not help thinking that the worst was yet to come.

# Chapter Fifty-One

Rashid saw the Range Rover crash through the gates and head around the side of the compound. He still had eyes-on MacPherson, but the man hadn't moved from his position in the lee of a low wall, three-hundred metres from the villa.

"Jack! Did you see that?" he shouted into his mic.

*"Yes! What the hell is going on?"*

"No idea! I have you covered, go and check on MacPherson." He paused. "And have your weapon ready!"

*"Okay..."* Luger replied, although a little hesitant. *"And what am I checking for?"*

"I think he's given me the slip..."

Rashid watched through the rifle scope as the white Jeep bounced over the rough ground and came to a halt behind the low wall. Luger approached, his pistol in his right hand. He barely hesitated, then returned to the vehicle.

*"Yeah, he's gone,"* Luger told him. *"Just some clothes stuffed with cloth and paper to form a body. Looks like he set this up a while ago, the clothes are covered with dust."*

Rashid could see part of the form. It had been a convincing ploy. He trailed the rifle scope further out and focused on a two-storey building a full thousand metres or more from the compound. He increased the magnification and could see movement inside one of the buildings. He increased it again and caught the flash of someone darting from the open window. He remained focused for a full two minutes but saw no more movement. He could hear sirens and see blue strobe lights in the distance. "Jack, get back to the villa," he said. "It's about to get busy here..."

# Chapter Fifty-Two

E xmoor

Neil Ramsay placed his laptop on the table and opened the lid. Beside it, he placed his mobile phone, a Moleskine notepad, and his Montblanc pen. He then spent a good minute lining them up so that the leading edge of each item was around an inch from the edge of the table, and two inches distant from its counterpart.

Stella Fox had stopped talking as she observed. "Am I boring you, Neil?"

"Yes. But I have heard and understand everything you've said so far," he replied without looking up.

Ahmadi watched as Ramsay switched on the laptop and checked his phone for a text message. The Iranian was perspiring, but it had gone unnoticed by Garfield and Fox, and Ramsay, so it would seem, was in his own little world.

Ramsay frowned at the text, typed lightly across the keyboard. When he clicked on the mousepad, Ahmadi stretched and stood up. When Ramsay looked up at him, his expression racing from one of puzzlement, to realisation and through to terror in a mere second. Ahmadi had the derringer in his hand in an instant and shot Ramsay in the chest. The noise of the .38 special in the confines of the house was deafening, and the smoke from the nitro powder was thick and pungent. Ramsay had fallen backwards and was shaking on the ground, his eyes wide and a rose of crimson spreading across his chest. Stella Fox gasped, and Garfield froze. Ahmadi aimed the tiny weapon and put a bullet in Garfield's right eye. The man rocked in his chair, blood pumping from the empty black eye socket in time with his slowing heartbeat. Ahmadi quickly fiddled with the weapon, tilted the double barrels upwards and ejected the two spent cases on the ground. He loaded another two bullets and had the weapon closed again before Stella Fox had realised that her only chance of escape had just vanished.

"What do you want?" she managed, choking back tears.

Ahmadi nodded to the laptop. "That. Up and running and connected to MI5's mainframe..." He kept the pistol aimed at her as he backed away to the table and slid the laptop around to look at the screen. He could not hide his satisfaction. Deftly, he typed in a new password, then closed the lid and tucked it under his arm. "That was part one..." he said.

"And part two?" she asked fatalistically, already knowing the answer.

"That would be you..." Ahmadi replied, then pulled the trigger.

The MI5 director slumped forwards in her chair, blood dripping from the hole in her forehead and into her lap. Ahmadi did not give the bodies a second glance as he walked out through the hall and picked up a set of car keys off the dresser.

# Chapter Fifty-Three

C asablanca

"What the hell happened?"

King slammed the door of the Range Rover and kicked the dusty ground aggressively. "It turned into a huge fucking mess, that's what happened." He paused, shaking his head as Caroline waited impatiently. "Ahmadi was shot and killed..."

"Oh my God!" she exclaimed.

"Only, he *wasn't* Ahmadi. He was a double. He looked exactly like the same as the guy we trained for the job. His doppelgänger. But of course, that would be too big a coincidence, so..."

"Ahmadi is really in England, having infiltrated the Security Service?" she asked, catching on typically quickly.

"Exactly." King climbed the steps to the villa. "We'll need to dump that car, if there's a tracker on it, and expensive cars like that generally always do, then they'll already know where we are. I've texted Neil and told him what's happened. No reply yet. I didn't want to call in case it compromised him and tipped off Ahmadi."

"We'll be out of here in minutes," Caroline told him. She put an arm around his shoulder and said, "We need to let them know. If the man in the farmhouse is really Ahmadi, then everybody is in danger."

"My fears exactly," King replied.

"Are you sure he hasn't replied yet?"

King checked his phone, then looked at her ever more earnestly. "No, he hasn't."

# Chapter Fifty-Four

E xmoor

Big Dave had heard the gunshots from where he was clearing out the office across the courtyard – sorting the files to be destroyed and the others that would be locked away until they could be released into the public domain decades from now, when it probably wouldn't even matter. Some details would be redacted, but it wasn't for him to decide which.

Big Dave cursed not having his weapon with him, King's words about that to Stella Fox echoing uselessly in the back of his mind as he ran down the stairs and paused to listen at the doorway, hearing another gunshot. The silence which followed was ominous. He ducked outside, saw the asset heading for a vehicle, but the man turned and saw him, too. Big Dave ran across the courtyard as the man aimed. He had not seen the tiny gun in the man's hand, but

he knew the gesture all too well. The gunshot rang-out but
went wide. Big Dave heard a window smash behind him,
but he kept running and thundered his shoulder against the
door, and it gave in under his weight and momentum. He
sprawled on the kitchen floor, still nowhere near his pistol,
but thankfully surrounded by weapons. He snatched a large
cook's knife from a wooden knife block and turned towards
the door, hearing the man's footsteps crunching on the
gravel. He snatched a large frying pan off the wall and as he
met the man head on, threw the pan at him and stabbed the
man in his gut as he flinched under the impact of the pan.
The man fell backwards, but he managed to keep his aim
and fired. Big Dave grimaced as the bullet hit him in his left
shoulder. He darted backwards, slammed the door shut and
jammed the knife deep into the doorjamb, pinning it shut.
A second gunshot thundered from the other side of the door
and a small hole appeared in front of him, and in the
cupboard behind him. He checked that he hadn't been hit
as he ran into the hallway. He knew what he would find in
the lounge, so pounded the stairs and charged through the
door to his bedroom and heaved the bed aside. Panting for
breath and his shoulder now burning and sending jolts of
pain around his body, he got the gun box open and pulled
out the Glock 19 and a loaded magazine. He loaded the
weapon and made it ready as he took the stairs. He could
hear a vehicle engine starting and he charged for the door.
The BMW X5 slewed on the gravel surface and into his
sights. He fired a sustained burst, holding back after ten
shots as the vehicle disappeared behind the first bend.

Big Dave stepped back inside and made his way to the
lounge. He could see that both Stella Fox and David
Garfield were dead. No movement, no bleeding. They were
gone. Big Dave pulled the table aside and looked down at

Neil Ramsay on the floor. There was a flicker in his eyes. The big Fijian crouched down and found a pulse. It was weak. "Neil..." Big Dave said quietly.

"Get..." he panted. "Get... the... laptop... back..." he sucked air through his teeth. "Open... mainframe..." He managed, then gasped. "I'm done, Davinder... don't waste... time... here..."

Big Dave held his colleague's hand. He had been here once before with Sally-Anne Thorpe. Ramsay must have known he was going to die. He had never used Lomu's first name before. As he watched Ramsay's ashen face, he could never remember the man ever having called him Big Dave like the rest of the team, and certainly not his given first name, which hardly anybody knew, much least used. He released his grip and pulled away. As he passed the landline phone, he dialled 999 and left the receiver on the dresser.

Lomu took the Jaguar XJ. It was a gamble, but he took the right at the end of the lane and floored the accelerator taking the coast road towards Minehead. The big saloon handled the corners well with plenty of power on the straights and sharp brakes and firm suspension to make it swiftly through the bends, the traction control keeping everything in check. He overtook two cars, dodged a van on the crown of the road, and kept up his rapid pace. With the moors on his right, and the rough, green sea with white horses spraying in the wind on his left, the drive would have been scenic, but both views rushed past, Big Dave staring straight ahead with tunnel vision as he waited to see the black SUV. He just prayed that the man had turned right, and not taken the winding road down to Lynmouth. If he had any idea of the geography around him, then Minehead would offer the best chance of escape.

After another two bends and a long straight, Big Dave

finally saw the BMW ahead of him and kept up his epic pace. The big SUV, although more of a road car than an off roader, didn't quite have the edge over the Jaguar when it came to the corners, and the Jaguar could hit 60 mph a full second quicker, which meant everything on a road such as this. Then Big Dave saw the sign: Porlock Hill. It was all to play for here because nerve would be everything now. Porlock Hill is Britain's steepest A-road and is two and a half miles long with an elevation gain of twelve-hundred feet, with an average gradient of 9.3%. However, near the bottom the gradient is a rollercoaster-like 23.5%. Big Dave barely lifted off the accelerator for the first section of road, then hammered on the brakes, the traction control cutting in constantly, as he negotiated the bends and caught up with the BMW so rapidly, that for an instant he thought he was about to collide. Throughout all of this, he felt his arm going more and more numb and he was aware that he was losing a lot of blood, but he couldn't give up. Not for Stella Fox or David Garfield, and especially not for Ramsay. As the road dipped down for the final drop and sweep of the sharp turn, Big Dave slammed his foot down hard and the Jaguar lurched forwards and smashed into the rear quarter of the BMW. The sound of crunching and scraping metal as the BMW rolled over sounded like gunfire. It tumbled and rolled and spun in the road, sparks flaring like a dying Catherine wheel. Big Dave watched the SUV slow but was aware of movement ahead and swung hard to avoid four cyclists riding in twos and about to start their hill challenge. The big Jaguar caught a wheel on the grass verge, and he was aware only of a sensation of weightlessness, then everything blurred as he spun end over end, slammed against a great oak tree growing perilously close to the road and rested still. Fuel and other fluids dripped onto the road and the axel whirred, driving the wheels impotently in the air. He realised that he was upside down, but he could not reach his seatbelt button with his right hand, and his left arm was hanging limply and uselessly beside him.

Big Dave blinked, trying to focus on the road outside. He was aware of a pair of feet, and then a pair of knees as the man bent down. And then he saw the tiny silver pistol, as small as a child's toy. He saw the muzzle flash and heard the deafening gunshot, felt the hot, burning powder residue on his face. He was aware that he was bleeding and that his chest felt both numb yet burned like fire simultaneously. Suddenly there were more feet, lightweight trainers and pairs of bare legs and he knew a scuffle when he heard it and another gunshot rang out and a man fell to the ground and stared lifelessly at Lomu, a bullet hole just below the rim of his cycle helmet. There were shouts and screams and the sound of an engine revving and tyres squealing, and as Big Dave blinked in and out of focus, everything started to fade to black, and silence...

# Chapter Fifty-Five

Jack Luger was on his own. He had received a curt message from Caroline and had been told to head for the airport after he had 'cleaned' the villa. It was vital that they did not leave DNA or fingerprints behind, and then there was the problem with the stolen Range Rover. Luger had dealt with the Range Rover by taking it to the cliff and sending it over the edge. He watched it plummet the three-hundred feet or so into the Atlantic, then waited just a few minutes for it to sink in a hundred feet of water. He had contemplated the time it would take to sanitise the building; over the time it would take for either the police or hostile forces to turn up and had decided that a couple of cans of petrol would save a whole lot of time. He doused the bedrooms and soft furnishings and turned on the gas stove and flame-effect fire, then trailed the fuel outside and let it pool on the steps. A handful of matches burning as one did the trick after he put them back inside the matchbox where the rest of the matches caught and threw the burning box into the fumes and ran like hell. It wasn't the safest, nor the most complicated plan, but it worked. After the initial thump and whoosh of ignition, the villa burned fiercely, and Luger paused by the Jeep as he saw Rashid driving erratically up the driveway leaving huge rooster tails of dust in his wake. He slid to a halt and got out so swiftly that the car had barely stopped moving.

"Original," he said, looking at Luger's handiwork.

"Where are the others?"

"Flymo is taking them to Malaga. He reckons that he can do it in three hours and that will allow them to get on a flight to Newquay airport in Cornwall. A helicopter will be waiting there to get them on Exmoor inside forty minutes."

"So, what happened?"

"Ahmadi wasn't Ahmadi. He was a plant. Somebody else had already done what we were trying to do. Only we think the real Ahmadi was *our* asset. The man we thought was Ahmadi was shot by a sniper. King was lucky to get away. We've been played, and worse than that, Exmoor has gone dark. We can't get hold of anyone..."

Luger frowned. "Anyone?"

"Not a soul."

The colour in the young man's face drained as he contemplated both the reality and significance of this. "And this guy, MacPherson, you think he killed Ahmadi, or at least the man we thought was Ahmadi?"

"Absolutely."

"Then we need to find him."

"That's easier said than done."

Luger looked thoughtful for a moment, then said, "What would you do in that situation?"

"I'd bug out. Literally the next plane anywhere."

"You wouldn't hole up somewhere and wait for it to blow over?"

Rashid shook his head. "If I were in a country with other countries nearby, then I'd shoot for the border. But Casablanca isn't close to anywhere. He's also white, so leaving a tourist area for the interior of the country, either the Sahara or the Atlas Mountains, will draw attention. Right now, he'll want to blend in and get the hell out while the police are tied up elsewhere."

"Airport then?"

"Absolutely."

# Chapter Fifty-Six

E xmoor

"Commander Barclay, Special Branch. Bit of a mess you've got here..."

King watched the private ambulances being loaded with the bodies on folding gurneys, the black Mercedes ambulances as ominously black as the body bags. In the background the helicopter was still powering down and police forensics vehicles were parked in a line, doors open and technicians in white all-in-one suits were getting the equipment they would need. He turned to Barclay and said, "I hope your talent is more than just stating the fucking obvious..." He gave the police commander no more of his time, instead walking to the house and singling out a young detective who was talking to Caroline and simultaneously directing her investigation team. This woman would certainly know more than the politician in uniform who was delighting in picking through MI5's mess.

"This is DI Bishop, lead investigator," Caroline introduced them.

"King," he said, shaking her hand. "What can you tell us?"

"Two dead, one critical."

"Who?"

"The deceased are Stella Fox and David Garfield," she said with just the right amount of sympathy. "The other victim is Neil Ramsay, who I believe is in a critical condition." She paused respectfully. "You should know, the paramedics don't think he'll pull through..."

Caroline sighed, then asked, "We have a missing colleague, Davinder Lomu..."

DI Bishop nodded. "We have another serious incident six miles away at the village of Porlock. Two dead. I don't have the details, but shootings are so uncommon in the southwest, that we are treating the two incidents as related."

Caroline raised a hand to her mouth, clearly upset. King squeezed her shoulder gently. He knew the two were close, had a great rapport and had worked together numerous times. Big Dave always seemed to treat her like a younger sister. "Tell me, have your team recovered a laptop?" he asked. "It would have been near Neil Ramsay. It's a bulky thing, he built it himself using an older military style shockproof casing."

"He built it himself?"

"It has power and memory that NASA would be jealous of," Caroline quipped, but King could see from her expression that she was running on adrenalin and was clearly shocked by what they had walked into.

"Would you like some tea?" DI Bishop asked. "We have

flasks in the van. And no, there was no laptop in the farm-house, just an array of computer equipment and files in the converted barn."

"You can't take that," said King.

"We can and we will," DI Bishop replied. "We have orders from Special Branch, and until a higher authority tells me otherwise, the files are being boxed and entered as evidence. Now, how about that tea?"

# Chapter Fifty-Seven

C asablanca Airport

Luger and Rashid had bought tickets to Paris and Dublin respectfully. Not for the ride home, but because these two flights would not be boarding for two hours and would allow them enough time in the duty free and departure lounge. Rashid had described former SAS officer Scott MacPherson in the minutest detail, as well as sending him a screenshot of the image he had earlier taken, and they had separated after the security checks, carrying just their passports, and leaving everything else behind.

Luger stood in front of a screen, checking the flights. There were three to the UK leaving within two hours. He wondered whether MacPherson would head straight to London, or whether he would be canny and fly into Manchester or Glasgow. There was every chance that the man would fly to Paris and take the Eurostar to

London. He walked another circuitous route, pausing at the coffee shops and cafés along the way. His phone vibrated in his pocket, and he took it out and checked the text.

*Got him. Drinking coffee near the watch store.*

Luger had to force himself not to hurry, and as he drew near, he could see Rashid reading a magazine, with MacPherson drinking a coffee several rows over in the middle of an empty line of five chairs. Beside him, his travel bag rested on a chair on one side and a duty-free carrier bag was on the other. A clear indication that he wanted to be alone. Luger sat down beside Rashid.

"What's the plan?"

Rashid shrugged. "Just go with me..." He got up and walked over, pushed MacPherson's bag on the floor and sat down beside him. Luger followed suit, but a heavy bottle inside the carrier bag broke and whisky pooled on the floor. People looked up at the noise, but soon lost interest. "Hello Scott..."

MacPherson smiled. "Well, if it isn't the second-best sniper in Morocco..."

"Not denying it, then?"

He shrugged. "Seems little point." He looked at Luger and scowled. "That's a bottle of twenty-year old Macallan you owe me, sonny..."

He went to stand, but Rashid pushed him back in his seat. "Best not make a scene..." He paused. "What's the deal with Ahmadi?"

"If you think I'm talking to you..." Luger picked up the carrier bag and took out a handkerchief to mop up the whisky. Rashid frowned at him, and MacPherson smiled. "That's right, sonny. Clean up your own mess..." He paused, sneering arrogantly. "If I shout for help, airport security and police will come. None of us will be getting out of here in a hurry."

"Ahmadi has successfully infiltrated the Security Service," Rashid said. "Our command has gone dark."

"Oh dear..." His smile waned when he glanced down and saw that Luger had wrapped a particularly large and sharp-tipped shard of glass in the handkerchief, and that the tip of the shard was pressing into his thigh, perilously close to his femoral artery. "Steady..." he said, nervously eyeing the glass.

"If I drive this shard home, we'll just walk away while you bleed out in less than a couple of minutes," said Luger. "So, I suggest you start talking..."

"Did Sir Galahad mount a hostile operation against MI5?" Rashid asked, buoyed in confidence now that Jack Luger had turned the tables.

Reluctantly, MacPherson said, "No. That part was never intended."

"So, why did you kill the man you put in as Ahmadi?"

"He was in a tight spot. He agreed to weapons deals simply to retain his cover. We had a feeling he was making deals without informing us. In Turkey I observed him dealing with a Russian GRU officer working with Wagner. He agreed to supply Chinese biological weapons to use in Ukraine. He agreed to a tremendous deal. Whether the asset could cream some of the money off for himself, I don't know. But he allowed a deal to go through, and he did not report it. I get that he wanted to keep his cover, and I get that he was scared, but it unravelled too far."

"And he had to die?" Luger asked dubiously.

"We needed to completely sever our involvement," MacPherson replied somewhat reluctantly. "We lost Ahmadi, but then realised that he had used the opportunity to infiltrate Five. How he did this, we aren't sure, but it has something to do with the AI capabilities his masters are peddling. The program fed GCHQ with all the attributes of Ahmadi, but under the legend of one pre-determined by his own masters back in Tehran. Once MI5, MI6 and GCHQ decided that Ahmadi was a link to the Iron Fist, their own AI data streaming found the legend and shoe-horned him into the role of playing himself." MacPherson shrugged. "It's a brave new world, and I guess we're all behind the curve..."

Rashid shook his head despairingly. "Have a nice flight," he said, standing up.

MacPherson waited for Luger to stand, then said, "That's a bottle of Macallan you owe me..."

"Don't hold your breath waiting," Luger replied, tossing the shard of glass onto the carrier bag.

"So that's it?" Luger asked as they found a table outside a popular coffee house. "He gets away Scott free?"

"Would you have rather cut his femoral artery?"

"Not really..."

"That was a nice touch, by the way," Rashid said approvingly. He placed his phone on the table and switched off the record function. "It's all on there. Sir Galahad Mereweather's involvement, the Iron Fist's agenda, and MacPherson's confession in the murder of their agent."

"Bang to rights..."

"I doubt it," Rashid replied. "That's not how intelligence work tends to pan out. But it will be a tremendous amount of leverage, probably *cart blanche* for future bumps in the road."

Luger nodded, as Rashid checked a text message. When he had finished reading, he sighed and shook his head despairingly. "That was from Caroline. Stella Fox and

David Garfield have been murdered. Ramsay is in a critical condition and the man we now suspect as being Ahmadi has disappeared. The only good news is that Big Dave is in a stable condition." He paused, frowning at Luger's expression. "Tough, I know..."

"Stella Fox was my aunt," Luger said, looking as though he was struggling to hold back tears. "My mother's sister. She encouraged me to leave the Royal Navy and come and work for MI5."

"Oh, shit..." Rashid said quietly. He realised how dumb his comment must have sounded. "I'm so sorry."

"She kept it quiet," he said. "As did I." He stood up, nodding at the screen. "My flight's boarding. I'll see you on the other side."

"We'll get this guy," Rashid assured him. "And when we do..."

"You'll have to get in line, my friend," Luger said coldly. "Because when I find him, he's a dead man..."

# Chapter Fifty-Eight

**G**eneva, Switzerland

He sipped his coffee and watched the sailboats vying for wind and position further out on the lake. Along the marina the moored boats bobbed up and down on the swell, masts and rigging ringing like bells on a distant wind. The rich and the beautiful strolled the promenade, walking adverts for Gucci, Armani, and Dolce & Gabbana. Ferraris and Lamborghinis revved their engines as they crawled through the sharp left-hand turn onto the lakefront and cruised the length of the strip, exhausts burbling like an alpha's mating call to the female of the species.

The man stood up when he saw Ahmadi approaching. He blended in with the crowd, fashionable and confident in an expensive-looking tan suit, collarless open blue shirt, and polished tan leather brogues. The man beckoned Ahmadi to a chair and clicked his fingers at the nearby waitress. He ordered them espressos and *langues de chat* biscuits.

The man noticed Ahmadi wince as he sat down somewhat tentatively. He knew that he had been injured during the operation, but he could not have been more pleased with the outcome. "Our technicians have breached MI5's firewalls," he announced proudly. "They have installed spyware and downloaded crucial files for our cause." He paused. "This could not have been done without you. We are eternally grateful for your service."

"Thank you, General," Ahmadi replied. "If I may be so bold as to ask a favour?"

"We are friends, Ahmadi. What is it you wish to ask?"

Ahmadi waited for the waitress to put down the two espressos and cat's tongue biscuits. This café was regarded to have the best and most buttery biscuits, a renowned Swiss delicacy. When she had left them, he said, "My family, General. I wish you to fly them out to me..."

"Of course, of course," the General replied. "Consider it done. I will make the arrangements personally. We have a lodge for you in the Alps. It is in the snow for five months of the year, and in glorious meadows for the other seven. There are lakes nearby, villages and schools. You will perform many missions for us, but your family can live here in safety. When you return, your life will be idyllic."

"Thank you, General."

The two men sat and sipped their coffee and watched the boats and people walking the promenade. Eventually, the General said, "We must strike again while the iron is still hot..."

"Of course."

The General reached beside him and retrieved a file

from a leather messenger bag. "Your next assignment," he said coldly. "Read, digest and destroy."

"Yes, General."

The older man looked at his slim Patek Phillipe watch and said, "I will keep you no further. But first, I have a gift..." He reached into the messenger bag and pulled out a small cloth-wrapped bundle and placed it before Ahmadi. "I understand you had to discard the last one..." Ahmadi lifted a corner of cloth to reveal a tiny silver derringer pistol. It had become something of a rite of passage for agents of the organisation. The General had awarded his best officers with one of the pistols when he had headed the Republican Guard, and he continued to do so now that he worked for a private entity and recruited agents from his former command. "For last resorts," he said. "Never allow yourself to be captured..."

"I will not," Ahmadi replied dutifully. He stood up and nodded at the General, tucking the file under his arm as he crossed the road and blended in with the great and the good.

The General smiled and took out his phone, dialled the number from memory and when it answered after five rings, said, "Ahmadi's family... have them killed with extreme prejudice." He paused. "And make sure it looks like the British did it..."

# Chapter Fifty-Nine

**H**arley Street, London

"No change, eh?"

"No." King paused. "He's in an induced coma in the Royal Exeter and Devon Hospital. The service will eventually send him someplace like this, but he can't be moved at present."

"That bastard," Big Dave said and meant it. "Ahmadi is a dead man when I get out of here..."

"There's a line forming," said Caroline.

Big Dave had been moved to the service's preferred private hospital. He wasn't new to the place. He would be kept in for a week, until the swelling went down around his heart. He had been lucky, the first .38 bullet had struck his shoulder and embedded itself in his clavicle. The second bullet had missed both his heart and aorta, slowed dramatically by his huge left pec, helped insurmountably by the tiny derringer's short barrel, barely half an inch longer than the tip of the bullet. The bullet's drop in both muzzle energy and velocity, and Lomu's physical stature had hedged the odds in his favour. Neil Ramsay, by contrast, had not been so lucky. With gunshots, just like in matters of physical beauty, millimetres counted for everything. The bullet had missed vital organs but had damaged the man's spine. He was unlikely to walk again, and only time would tell as to the extent of his paralysis or physical and mental limitations.

"There may be a line forming, but Ahmadi has gone, and we've met a dead end," said Rashid. He glanced at Jack Luger, who was sitting a few paces away eating grapes that had been intended for Big Dave. He had not told anybody of Luger's relationship with Stella Fox, he figured that the man would do so if he wished people to know the truth.

"The police report says that Ahmadi killed a cyclist at the scene. There were three of them who tried to stop him from shooting Big Dave," said Caroline. She had read the report so many times that she felt that she could recount it word for word. "He killed another man at the crash site and stole his car. The vehicle was later found in Taunton. A stolen vehicle there ended up in Reading, and another disappeared and turned up in Crawley. From there, Ahmadi simply disappeared. But the best assumption would be he flew out of Gatwick on a false passport. He must have disguised himself because from Crawley, the trail goes cold."

"I feel for those poor souls. Feel for their families. It's a hell of a thing knowing somebody died trying to help you," said Big Dave heavily. He looked back at Caroline and asked, "What about the new director?"

"Martin Forbes is interim director until a permanent director can be found," Caroline replied.

"Don't know him," said King. "Don't know anyone there anymore."

"He's communications director."

King pulled a face like he couldn't care less.

"I'm not sure who'd want the job," Caroline commented. "First poor Simon, and now Stella Fox…"

"Do we even have jobs now?" Rashid asked. "We had already been distanced with David Garfield heading the new department, now we won't even have a paper trail when the new director of the service is appointed."

"I'll probably meet back up with Jenny," said Big Dave. "She's taking a yacht down to the Cape Verde Islands next month, I figure I could do with getting lost for a while."

Caroline stood up, bent down, and kissed him on the forehead. "Don't go without saying goodbye," she said sincerely. "I'm going down to Devon to visit Neil, see if there's any improvement. His wife and children are down there, I'll see if I can be some support, take the children out for something to eat, whatever I can do."

"I've got some errands to run first," said King. "I'll head down tomorrow." He kissed her and they hugged briefly, then headed outside. He had parked his motorcycle right outside the door and by the time Caroline, Rashid and Luger reached the pavement, King had the Triumph Scrambler 900 at the end of the road, the throaty exhaust note echoing of the multi-million-pound buildings. Caroline got into her mini and waved goodbye.

"Are you tracking him?" asked Luger.

Rashid took out his phone and swiped the screen. "Yes."

"And his phone?"

Rashid nodded. "He's going to be madder than hell..."

"How do you know he's really going after Ahmadi?"

Rashid grinned. "Because it's as given as night follows day..."

# Author's Note

To order Alex King's next adventure click below:
The Enemy

Hi - thanks for reading and I hope you enjoyed my story. I'm hard at work on another story, but couldn't do it without you. It means a great deal write, and even more that people actually enjoy my reading my books! If you did, then a quick review or rating on Amazon would be great.

I can't wait to entertain you soon...

A P Bateman

Printed in Great Britain
by Amazon

26084722R00179